BREEZING

BREEZING

a novel

MICHAEL FERRARA

Distributed by Bublish, Inc.

ISBN: 978-1-64704-092-5 (paperback)
ISBN: 978-1-64704-093-2 (eBook)

CHAPTER ONE

Ritchie Gallo sat on his track pony and watched the sun slowly rise. The mist and fog shrouding the Saratoga racetrack filtered the sun's light and allowed him to look at the glowing orange ball without shading his eyes. This was his favorite time of day. The morning was still cool, so he could fully enjoy the muffled drumbeat of horses' hooves hitting the dirt. Other trainers sat at the rail in front of the empty grandstands to watch their horses run. They measured speeds with stopwatches and made notes in their journals, detailing the progress their thoroughbreds were making in their exercise regime.

Gallo preferred to be mounted on a horse when his colts and fillies went through their paces. He was a horseman, and a horseman should be astride a horse.

As he stared down the backstretch, a colt burst from the mist like an apparition charging down an apocalyptic battlefield. Backlit by the rising sun, the horse shot bolts of breath through its nostrils, creating contrails of vapor that streamed down its body. When the racer and its rider drew closer, the ghostly appearance faded, and the animal was once again a brilliant athlete sculpted for speed and endurance.

Gallo's track pony, General Custer, stood perfectly still, even when the thoroughbred thundered by just a few feet away. The General was a gelding. The removal of his family jewels had done wonders for his personality, making him calm and docile around people and other animals. However, his bulk and strength prevented him from the speed desired in thoroughbred champions, so Gallo had purchased him eight years ago to be his mobile work platform. Together, they had spent countless hours observing some of the most expensive creatures in the world—thoroughbreds preparing themselves for the glory and riches that come with racing success.

Although Gallo now lived in Kentucky, he looked forward to these late summer races in his hometown of Saratoga. His family bred horses on a farm just a few miles from the track, so he'd been around thoroughbreds all his life, even dreamed of being a jockey as a child. His quest to develop the skills necessary to guide a twelve-hundred-pound animal around a one-mile oval at more than forty miles per hour began with a summer job working as an exercise rider. But those dreams were dashed when a growth spurt at age eighteen made a racing career impractical.

With no prospects of earning a living in the saddle, Gallo decided to become a trainer. After graduating from college with a major in animal science, his father connected him with one of the nation's top trainers at a farm in Kentucky. There, Gallo learned the art and science of developing racehorses.

He endured long hours, hard work, and low pay for thirteen racing seasons before he was asked to join the team at a small breeding and training farm near Lexington. They were looking for a young man with a great eye for horses and a willingness to use technology and science to create the ultimate methodology for turning a talented horse into a winning racehorse.

For four tough seasons, Gallo and his staff of grooms and horse attendants travelled across the country, winning races at regional tracks and then major venues like Belmont, Santa Anita, Saratoga, and Churchill Downs. He earned a reputation as a trainer who could design the right regimen for select thoroughbreds and ethically prepare them to compete and win. Gallo took on several horses that other trainers and breeding farms passed over and trained them to run in the money at good quality races. Over time, his compensation grew to six-figures—excellent pay in an industry notorious for its demanding schedules and low wages. Despite his success, Gallo knew he still hadn't been lucky enough to train a world-class racehorse, one that could compete and win at the highest level.

At least, not until now.

Gallo pulled the reins to the right and walked General Custer down to the finish line. An exercise rider approached on a black colt that was covered in sweat and breathing heavily after a one-and-a-half-mile gallop. "How did he feel today, Hector?"

"Ah, he's okay, Mister Gallo. He is a big, strong, fast horse, but *el es un niño obstinado*. He don't want to do what he don't want to do."

"Yeah, I know. He's giving me some sleepless nights. Okay, take him back to the stable and let the boys cool him down, give him a shower, and feed him breakfast."

The rider guided the colt to the northeast corner of the track, where security guards waited to halt Union Avenue traffic at the crossing to the stabling area. The drivers didn't seem to mind the wait, and never honked. Why would they? It was a chance to see these magnificent athletes at close range. Some horses were moving from the stables to the track, fidgeting in anticipation of the activity for which they are bred. Others walked from the track to the stables, drenched in sweat, muscles quivering, and blood vessels popping through their skin. It seemed to Gallo that people were always a little overwhelmed by this sight. When did you ever see humans give 110 percent effort in their daily lives? These horses didn't know any other way to live.

Five of the six thoroughbreds Gallo had brought to Saratoga had now completed their daily workout. The black colt that had just left the track was Tackle Tim Tom. He held tremendous potential but was difficult to train. Only two years old, the horse had already run impressive split times in his last four races. Gallo didn't want to geld the colt because he still felt he could train him to compete effectively. He hoped he could find a jockey that could connect with the horse and ride him to victory. If Tackle Tim Tom found success on the track, he would be worth a lot of money as a breeding stallion. Gallo also had a hunch that this thoroughbred was that one-in-a-million colt who could compete and win in the highest stakes races. To win a Derby, Preakness, Belmont, Travers, or Breeders' Cup Classic was only a dream for most trainers. More than twenty thousand foals were born every year, but only a handful could win the biggest races.

As Tackle Tim Tom disappeared across Union Avenue and headed for the stable, Gallo's other great hope moved across the street and stepped onto the track. Hit the Bid was one of the most beautiful horses Gallo had ever seen: a dark bay with white sox below her knees. Physically, she was the perfect horse—superb conformation from her head to her tail. She was big for a filly at 17.2 hands, and now that she was a three-year-old, she tipped the scales at 1,215 pounds. When she ran, she was what trainers referred to as an "A" mover: a low, smooth stride with no wasted energy. Her limbs moved forward and back on a straight line, and when she navigated the turns on a course, there was no lateral movement in her body. She carried herself with a sense of majesty and had a great personality—often playfully nudging the grooms that worked in the stable and entertaining the patrons at the racetrack with the prancing dance moves she made on her way to the starting gate. The only problem with this horse was that she loved to run too much. Unlike Tackle Tim Tom, who had to be in the right mood to run his fastest, Hit the Bid never wanted to do anything except breeze at top speed.

As soon as she stepped on the racetrack, she began to dance, moving her hindquarters left and then right. Her head bobbed up and down, and her ears stood upright as though searching for the roar of an adoring crowd in the gallery. In the saddle was Jacinto Robles, a jockey that had never ridden the filly before and was scheduled to be in the stirrups for her first race at Saratoga just eight days away. Gallo wanted Robles to put her through an exercise run to see how she handled and to get a feel for her ability.

Hit the Bid had already achieved substantial success as a race-horse, having won several Grade Two and Grade One races. She was on the industry's radar as an up-and-coming star, and Gallo's goal was to prepare her to race on the biggest stages against not only other fillies and mares, but colts as well.

"Are you ready to go, Jacinto?"

"Sure, Mister Gallo. Boy, she is really a rambunctious filly. Is she always this excited when she gets to the track?"

"Yeah, but it's excited in a good way. Here's what I want you to do: let her canter for a quarter-mile and then bring her up to a gallop. Don't go faster than eighteen seconds per furlong. She doesn't like to gallop—she wants to run, so she'll fight it all the way. We have a heart monitor on her, and I don't want her heart rate to get too high during the gallop. Once you've covered a quarter-mile at a gallop, back her up just before the three-eighth pole and let her breeze to the finish line. Make sure you get a running start at the three-eighth pole, because I want to see what her top speed is for the final three furlongs."

"No problem, *jefe*. I got it!"

The jockey guided the horse away at a canter, moving in a clock-wise direction around the outer periphery of the track where horses could walk, canter, or gallop. Once he had covered a quarter-mile at a canter, he eased up a little on the reins and stood in the stirrups, raising his butt off the saddle.

Just as Gallo had predicted, Hit the Bid wanted to run, and Robles had to use his hands, arms, and knees to hold her back. When the filly passed the finish line—where Ritchie Gallo and General Custer were standing—Robles let her gallop for another minute before turning her around and moving her down along the inside rail. He asked her to run just before the three-eighth pole. He didn't have to ask twice; in a matter of five strides, Hit the Bid was at top speed, hurtling around the far turn and approaching the top of the stretch.

Gallo clicked his stopwatch when she was at the pole, watching her make the turn through his binoculars. Every time he watched her run, he was astounded by the athletic grace of this beautiful lady. As thoroughbreds run through a turn, they generate a force on their legs more than eight times their body weight. Despite this physical pressure, Hit the Bid maintained her line as she ran through the turn and kept a constant distance from the inside rail on her left. Her strides were straight, smooth, and powerful, and her head was in perfect alignment with her body.

As she transitioned from the turn to the straightaway, she made a lead change to her right front foot and accelerated toward the finish line. When the filly crossed the line, Ritchie hit the stopwatch and immediately looked at the time. He shook his head and shared the good news with General Custer. "We got us one hell of a horse here, big guy. Three furlongs in thirty-four seconds after a mile-and-a-quarter gallop. Damn, she's good!"

It took a concerted effort by Robles to bring the filly to a trot after her breeze, but he finally got her to slow down and turn around, moving to the outside of the track. When he met up with Gallo, Ritchie bent over and hooked a rein to the filly's bridal so he and General Custer could walk her slowly back to the stables, allowing the jockey to relax in the saddle.

Once they got back to her stall, Gallo checked her nose for any traces of blood and then took the wraps off her lower legs to examine her knees, cannon bones, ankles, and feet. Everything looked good, so he had his grooms unsaddle the horse and walk her around a paddock ring to slow down her heart rate. After that, she would be thoroughly washed down, brushed, and given a breakfast of oats, hay, and a small amount of other grains.

"So, what do you think, Jacinto?" asked the trainer.

"At first, I think she got a problem because she dances so much, but once you ask her to run, she does everything right. She's got heart—*un gran corazón*. I think she can win against the boys."

"Yeah, me too. Okay, she's entered in the American Oaks on July 22. It's a Grade One race for three-year-olds and up. As far as I'm concerned, you're my rider. That work for you?"

"Yes sir, Mister Gallo. Just close the loop with my agent and we're good to go. If we win that one, it's a big payday for both of us!"

"Thanks, Jacinto."

Satisfied that all six of his horses were being serviced by his grooms, Gallo made his way to a trailer that served as a temporary office for himself and several other trainers. Inside the trailer were a cluster of desks equally spaced throughout the interior with a couple of chairs at each station. It wasn't an elegant workplace, but rather a functional one, where trainers could make phone calls to agents, racetrack officials, owners, and the farms where they each trained horses.

Now that the athletic activities for the day were done, Gallo spent the rest of the workday completing race entry paperwork, lining up jockeys, and giving upbeat progress reports to the owners of the horses he trained and to his partners at Stone Fence Farms in Kentucky. He enjoyed the business side of his job, but sometimes he felt it took too much time away from the horses, forcing him to rely on his chief groom to be sure the horses were safe, healthy, comfortable, and properly fed. As he had become more successful, the commercial aspects of being a winning trainer became more demanding. Keeping up with the increasing value of the horses, as well as the size of the purses in the major stakes races, was a lot of work—but his love for the horses and the competition made it all worthwhile.

At 4:30 p.m., he decided to call it quits. Since his workday began at five o'clock in the morning, he needed to be in bed early, which only left a couple of hours every evening to do something other than be a horse trainer. He liked to hit the gym several times each week, but tonight, he just didn't have the energy for it and decided to enjoy a quiet dinner at one of his favorite restaurants in Saratoga Springs. After one last check on the horses, he got in his truck and began to drive towards the section of town where the eateries and nightclubs were located. Whether by accident or just drawn by nostalgia, he reached the street he considered to be his favorite in this small upstate New York town. Even though it was where he suffered the worst heartbreak of his life, he couldn't resist its charm, so he made the left turn he had made so many times as a young man.

Both sides of the street boasted large, older homes that screamed "old Saratoga money" to anyone that knew the grand history of this neighborhood. His pickup truck was the only vehicle on the street, so he slowed down to give himself time to admire the handsome and exquisitely maintained houses. Halfway down the block, he pulled over to look at a home he remembered all too well from his days as an exercise rider—over twenty years ago, now. He turned off the ignition and found himself just sitting there, looking at the soaring grey-shingled house with green trim around the windows and thick columns framing a porch that wrapped around the width of the dwelling.

The porch swing he'd enjoyed on cool summer evenings was still there, right in the same place—just to the left of the large mahogany front door. In his mind's eye, he could see himself laughing with Channing Mellon. They used to tease one another and kiss when they thought nobody was looking. Dark eyes, olive skin, and long black hair framed an amazing smile that wouldn't let him forget he was with the sweetest girl in the world. Gallo was only five feet seven inches in height, but he would still think about how tall he felt when he placed his arms around her petite frame and held her close. He still thought about her a lot, actually, if he were being honest with himself.

Gallo had taken the time to stop in front of this house many times over the last two decades, whenever he returned to Saratoga for the racing season. And somehow, whenever he did, he always thought about the lyrics of a song entitled Summer of '69:

"Standing on your momma's porch,
You told me that you'd wait forever,
Oh the way you held my hand,
I knew that it was now or never,
Those were the best days of my life."

He'd had some great moments since the days of holding Channing Mellon's hand on that porch swing—but he always wondered how his life might've looked if she'd been his partner through the years, rather than a memory. Life imitated art as the story of his love for this young woman unfolded. He was the farm boy and exercise rider who thought the greatest place in the world was on the backstretch of a racetrack among the horses, stables, and horsemen. She was the daughter of a Wall Street scion who truly believed that horse racing was the sport of kings, and he wasn't about to let his princess commingle with the help.

Gallo kept his eyes on that porch swing. It swayed in the breeze, as though still pushed by the ghosts of his memories. He fought off a frown, thinking about how Channing's father had felt he'd made a mistake allowing her to pursue her love for horses by working at the racetrack—even though it was only during the summertime, when they resided at their Saratoga home. Perhaps it had been a mistake, but not for Gallo. That's when he'd met her.

She was mucking stalls, helping the grooms with the thoroughbreds, and walking the horses in the cooldown ring. It didn't take long for him to find out she'd considered him handsome, funny, and a person whose work ethic and love for the racetrack had earned him the respect of everyone working behind the scenes. He'd introduced her to several trainers who paid her to exercise the horses. Her father was appalled when he'd found out about that. He didn't mind her wearing riding britches, a black jacket, and a helmet with a visor if she was jumping over fences that were only three feet high and competing in equestrian dressage. Breezing racehorses, to him, just seemed so blue-collar. It was a job carried out by small men with foreign accents or white trash who couldn't do anything else for a living.

This time, Gallo couldn't fight off his frown. Channing's father had eventually insisted she bring her relationship with him to an end and shipped her back to Manhattan as quickly as he could.

That was another thing he'd never forget: Channing tearfully telling him goodbye in their final moments together. She'd promised she would be back after graduation from Wellesley, as an independent woman who would take control of her life. He'd waited hopefully for that event, but over time it became clear that she wasn't going to keep that promise. Whenever he drove by this house, he wondered if her family still owned it and if she continued to summer in Saratoga. He had never seen her or her father again. He guessed that she'd chosen to put a love affair that lasted two summers in her past, moving on toward a very different future—one without him.

Gallo started up his pickup truck and pulled away from the curb. As he drove to the downtown section of Saratoga Springs, he knew that in his future, he would always compare every horse he trained to Hit the Bid and, hopefully, Tackle Tim Tom. Trainers measured potential by comparing a colt or filly to a benchmark. He also knew that he had never married because when it came to women, Channing Mellon had always been his benchmark.

CHAPTER TWO

G allo dumped a large splash of cream into his insulated mug—an effort to mollify the strength of the over-brewed coffee in the trainer's trailer. The coffee was never very good, but it gave him the boost he needed at 5:00 a.m. to get the workday started.

Stepping out of the trailer into the darkness, he could see a slight glow coming up on the horizon. Despite the early hour, the long barns filled with horses were staffed with attendants preparing the thoroughbreds for their morning workouts. Hay was being delivered on flatbeds pulled by all-terrain vehicles. Gallo paused to inhale deeply, enjoying the way the smell of hay tempered the odor emanating from the stalls that had yet to be mucked out. The commingling of scents infused the air, welcoming the horsemen to the start of their day.

Gallo made his way to the section of the backstretch where his horses were stabled, but as soon as he got there, he was confronted by his chief groom, Jimmy Crowder.

"What's up, Jimmy? You got that constipated look on your face again."

"We got a problem, boss. We got nobody to ride T-three this morning."

"Where's Hector Sanchez? He's been the exercise rider on Tackle Tim Tom for the last week."

"Ah, I guess there was a card game in the Hispanic section of the dormitory last night. It didn't end well."

"So, what happened? Sanchez got arrested?"

"He's in the hospital; somebody pulled a knife."

"Oh, for crying out loud—there's too much nonsense going on in these dormitories at night. I guess I'm surprised more of these guys don't end up in the hospital or jail."

Gallo walked over to a chalkboard where the names of his six horses were listed, along with the name of the exercise riders scheduled that day. Jimmy had erased Sanchez's name, so they were short one rider.

"We're in the 6:30 time slot on the Oklahoma training track," said Jimmy. "We only have the slot for forty-five minutes before the next crew of horses takes over the track. I'll have to run around the barns and see if there's a rider that doesn't have a mount yet this morning."

"No, you keep getting our horses ready. I'll check around and see if I can get a loaner from one of the other trainers. I don't want to put just anybody on T-three. He's a tough horse to ride, and we need someone good."

As Gallo and Jimmy stood there discussing the situation, they were approached by a woman. "I can ride him for you. I'm looking for exercise rides this morning."

When they turned around, the two men found themselves confronted by a young lady wearing a down vest over a polo shirt, a riding helmet, jeans, and riding boots.

"Are you an exercise rider?" asked Gallo.

"I'm a jockey—an *apprentice* jockey. I need to do some exercise riding so trainers will get to know me and be willing to hire me for races." When the girl spoke, she looked down at the ground and didn't make eye contact with the men.

"Where did you get your apprentice license?"

"Santa Anita; I live in California."

"Who's your agent?" asked Gallo.

"John McCann."

"John McCann? He's the agent for the best jocks in the country. Why would he be handling an apprentice?"

The young woman just shrugged and continued to look at the ground.

"You know, young lady, in the racing business it's all about relationships. A big part of building a relationship is looking someone in the eye when you're speaking to them. Looking someone in the eye gives you a sense that you're getting the straight skinny from somebody, or maybe they're just bullshitting you. So . . . this little impromptu job interview we are having right now isn't going so well for you because I can't see the color of your eyes. Do you want to ride for me or not?"

The woman took a breath, placed her hands in the back pockets of her jeans, and turned to look squarely at Gallo. "I heard you were a really good trainer and you had a couple of good mounts. I would like to ride for you."

Now that Gallo could see the young lady's face, he was struck by her good looks. She had dark eyes and jet-black hair, which she'd pulled back into a long braid and fastened with a colorful artificial flower. She certainly fit the profile of a jockey, being around five feet tall with an athletic build. He was also surprised by the clothing she was wearing. Everything she wore looked brand new and sparkling clean, especially her polished riding boots.

"Well, you're certainly the best-dressed exercise rider I've ever met. What's your name?"

"My name is Cicely Jamieson, but everybody calls me CJ."

"How old are you?"

"I'm twenty."

"Shouldn't you be in college or something like that, rather than riding around on horses?"

"I'm a student for part of the year. I go to Pomona College full-time in the spring, but I take my courses online the rest of the year so I can train to be a jockey."

"How many mounts did you have at Santa Anita, CJ?"

"During the six weeks of the meet, I had seventy-two rides. I won five races, ran second place nine times, and had ten show finishes."

"Jeez, that's pretty good for an apprentice. I'm guessing you weren't riding the classiest horses at the meet."

"No, sir."

"Why are you at Saratoga?"

"This is where the best horses and trainers are at this time of year. I just want to prove I can ride to the people that count." As she spoke, she refocused her gaze to her boots.

"Hey, you really gotta stop looking for the place your snot hit the floor and look at me when I'm talking to you."

Reluctantly, she turned back toward the men. "Mister Gallo, I watched your black colt work the other day. I think he's spectacular, but you have to know how to ride him. If you get the right jock on his back, he could be something special."

"Oh, and *you* think you're the right jock?"

"I would just like a chance to prove it."

Gallo looked over at Jimmy and gave him a quizzical look.

"We need a rider boss, and we need 'em soon," offered Jimmy.

The trainer gave it a thought for a second or two, and then let his intuition overrule rational thought. "Okay, put her on Tackle Tim Tom. If she can ride T-three, she can ride anything."

"If you put a jockey saddle on him, rather than an exercise saddle, I think I can give you a better idea as to how well I can ride him. You can put some weights in the saddle if you want."

Gallo again looked at Jimmy, who shrugged and rolled his eyes. "Okay, Jimmy, put ten pounds in a racing saddle and get her on board."

Gallo walked into the stall where General Custer was stationed and saddled the gelding himself—the grooms being busy with other horses. He always talked to the General when he saddled him, and today, he spoke about the strange young woman he had just met. General Custer never said anything in return, but he was a great listener.

As Gallo prepared to lead the General out of the enclosure, he happened to glance down the concourse and saw Jimmy staring into another stall with his arms folded. Leaving the General alone for a moment, he walked down to see what the groom was looking at.

"Boss, look at this. You won't believe it."

Gallo stood next to Jimmy, looking into Tackle Tim Tom's stall. The large black colt was standing perfectly still with his head bowed, forehead pressed against CJ's as she gently stroked the side of his neck.

"They been standing like that for thirty seconds," said Jimmy. "You ever see that colt stand still for thirty seconds?"

"What the hell is going on?" muttered Gallo under his breath.

The small woman and the big animal continued like this for a few moments until CJ whispered something in the horse's ear. He came back to life at her words, raising his head, and CJ turned to face Jimmy. "Okay, you can saddle him up now. We're ready to go!"

Jimmy looked at Gallo, shaking his head. "Man, this is getting weirder and weirder. I sure hope this little girl can make the young stallion run."

Gallo smiled. "Yeah, you and me both."

Once all six horses were saddled and the riders were up, Ritchie took the lead on General Custer and walked the thoroughbreds single-file out of the stable area. They entered the Oklahoma training track that was adjacent to the barns, and Gallo briefed the riders on the exercise routine he wanted each horse to complete. He'd designed a specific training regimen for his horses—tailored to their strengths, their ages, and the distance they were being trained to run. With the Saratoga meet about to commence in a few days, he wanted his charges prepared physically and mentally for the competition they would face.

As the other horses dispersed one by one in a clockwise direction around the outer periphery of the track, Gallo guided General Custer up next to Tackle Tim Tom and held the rein that allowed him to control the colt.

"You can take him around the track on the outside, and see how he responds to your hands on the reins and your verbal commands," he instructed CJ. "You can walk, trot, or gallop. It's up to you as long as you're confident he is doing what you want him to do. If you gallop, don't go more than one mile at that pace. When you think you're ready to let him run, back him up before the half-mile pole and get a good start. I want to see how fast he can cover the four furlongs to the finish line. I believe he's in good shape, but if you think something isn't right with him physically, bring him to a halt and get him back to me. I don't want any injuries at this point."

For the first time since they had met, Cicely Jamieson looked Ritchie Gallo directly in the eyes with a broad smile. "Don't worry, Mister Gallo. He's gonna do great!"

The trainer unhooked the rein from the horse's bridle, and with a verbal click of her tongue and a tap on the shoulder, CJ walked the colt off to begin the workout. She let him walk for about one furlong, and it looked to Gallo as though she was talking constantly to the horse. She then let him trot, and it was obvious that he was complying with her verbal and physical commands. CJ gracefully absorbed the up and down motion of T-three's stride, holding the reins softly in her hands. It was surprising how easily she directed the movements of a colt with a reputation for doing his own thing; that was the sort of handling Gallo only witnessed in experienced riders.

After an eighth of a mile canter, CJ changed position in the saddle and moved Tackle Tim Tom up to a gallop. The horse didn't fight the move, nor did he try to run away with the jockey. His stride was effortless, and CJ's smooth motion on his back enabled the horse to run easily and unencumbered. Once she passed the half-mile marker, she slowed the colt down and turned him around so he could move to the inside rail and breeze in a counterclockwise direction. By the half-mile pole, he was flat-out running.

Gallo watched from his position near the finish line. "General Custer, I like the way this woman looks in the saddle. She's really making things work." He had his stopwatch running and was observing the body motion of T-three as he ran the far turn and came to the top of the stretch. As he transitioned out of the turn, CJ tapped his right shoulder with her whip, and he changed from a left lead to a right lead without missing a beat. T-three had the strength to overpower racetracks. He didn't have the athletic grace of Hit the Bid, but his muscled chest and powerful hindquarters allowed him to accelerate through turns and step it up a notch when he was already cruising at top speed.

As he thundered past the one-eighth pole—where most riders would strike their horse on the rump with a whip—CJ lowered her body without touching the saddle or T-three's back, and with her whip stowed, gave him a hand ride through the finish. Once she passed Gallo's position at the finish line, she stood up in the stirrups and softly pulled on the reins while imploring the colt to slow down. He gradually decelerated to a walk, and she turned him around so they could return on the outside section of the track.

Gallo looked down at his stopwatch. "Damn! He ran that half-mile in forty-five and a fifth. General Custer, this colt just might be the fastest two-year-old in the country. That's Secretariat-kinda speed." He bent over and patted his closest confidante on the neck. "This is good, big guy. We may be drinking mint juleps next May at Churchill Downs!"

CJ walked the colt up to Gallo and General Custer. She had some dirt on her face but still looked cleaner and better kept than most exercise riders. She was smiling broadly. In the light of the sunrise, it was evident to Gallo that she was quite a beautiful young lady. "He's amazing. I've never ridden a horse with his power. He accelerates like he's been shot out of a cannon; I almost got tossed off when I asked him to run."

"You never touched him with the whip."

"I didn't need to. He just listens to me."

"Do you connect with every horse this well?"

"No, not every horse—but I really love them, and sometimes they respond." She stopped smiling and cast her gaze towards the dirt track.

"Hey, what did I tell you about the eyeballs?"

She looked up. "Sorry, I forget sometimes. You're going to yell at me a lot, aren't you?"

"Yeah, probably. Okay, walk him back to the stable so Jimmy can cool him down and get him fed. Why don't you meet me in the trainer's trailer in about thirty minutes?"

When all six horses had completed their workouts and returned to the stable area, Gallo dismounted the General and walked back to the trailer. He picked up his cell phone and hit the contact number for John McCann—the agent that represented CJ.

McCann answered on the second ring. "Hey, Ritchie, it's only 7:45 in the morning. I know you're halfway through your workday, but I still haven't left my hotel room."

"Where are you, John?"

"I'm in New York. I just wrapped up some business at Belmont, and I should be in Saratoga this evening. What's up with you? How's that filly running? I may be able to put a really experienced jock on her back for The American Oaks."

"Well, right now, I have Robles scheduled to ride her. I'll keep you posted. I do have a question about another one of your people: What's the story on this young apprentice, Cicely Jamieson?"

"Ah, I see she was able to hunt you down. The story on her is that she's the daughter of an influential guy out in California. He's the president of a bank and a general partner in a syndication group that sells partnerships in thoroughbreds. There's a lot of money behind this guy, and his group can market shares of horses to some of the wealthiest people in the business. He asked me to help get her a license and take her under my wing. She had an exceptional rookie season at Santa Anita, and she's determined to win at Saratoga."

"Right. I let her exercise one of my colts, and I was very impressed. She seems a little strange but she can really ride."

"The kid is a bit off center, but when she's on the back of a horse, she's a different person. The last time I spoke with her, she knew about you and said she wanted to ride for you. I was going to call you today to pitch her services, but I see she beat me to the punch."

"Hmmm, well, I might just give her a shot. I have this colt, Tackle Tim Tom, entered in the Sanford Stakes on July 21. It's a Grade Three race for two-year-olds, six furlongs on the dirt. If she's not already scheduled, I'd like her to be the jock."

"Okay, she's available. That colt's kind of an enigma, isn't he? He's won two of his four races but put out a really strange performance in his other two outings."

"I just think he needs the right rider, and she may be it. I assume I'm getting the discounted rate since I'm hiring an apprentice?"

The agent laughed. "Yeah, you get the discounted rate—but if she keeps winning and improving, she may be able to drop the bug before the end of the fall season at Churchill Downs. Right now, her weight allowance has been lowered from ten pounds to seven because she's ridden five winners. With her skills and a seven-pound allowance, I think you're getting a pretty good deal."

"Well, I appreciate that, John. You're a real humanitarian. Let's play golf when you get to Saratoga."

Gallo finished his call with McCann and made entries in his journal detailing the results of the workouts completed by his horses that morning. He could hear someone knocking on the door of the trailer, but none of the three trainers working at their desks got up to see who was seeking entry. When the knocking continued, Gallo stood up, mildly exasperated, and opened the door to find CJ standing there. "You don't have to knock, kid. You just come in. We don't have a lot of protocols here. This isn't the United Nations."

"I know it's not the United Nations, Mister Gallo. It's Saratoga Racetrack."

She made the statement in such a flat and emotion-free tone of voice, Gallo couldn't figure out if she was being sarcastic or just repeating the obvious. "Come on in and sit down, I want to talk to you."

CJ sat in the chair next to the desk. Gallo informed her that he'd spoken with her agent, and she was scheduled to ride Tackle Tim Tom in his first race at Saratoga. He expected her to be happy and excited at that news, but she just sat there with a blank look on her face and stared at her knees.

"You know, this race has a purse of $150,000, with $90,000 going to the winner. If you ride T-three to a win, you'll make $9,000. Isn't that something to get excited about?"

She glanced at his face for a second before responding. "That's nice, but I just want to get the colt to do his best. He was born to run and win."

"You're a very strange girl. You know that, don't you?"

"Yes, I know that," she said softly.

Gallo put his head in his hands and rubbed his forehead. He wasn't really sure if he was getting through to this young woman, but he knew he saw an unusual talent when she was in the saddle with the colt. He needed to see if she was the rider that could enable the horse to reach his potential.

"The race is only a week away, and I need you to build a rapport with the colt. I want you to exercise the horse for me. We'll work him five more times on the track. We'll only breeze him for a couple of furlongs in the first two workouts, but we'll let him gallop for endurance in the last three. Check in with Jimmy and schedule yourself for those rides. We're paying thirty-five dollars a ride—that good for you?"

She nodded her head in agreement.

"I've got another horse I want you to work for me. She's a filly named Hit the Bid."

The hint of a smile came to CJ's face. "I love Hit the Bid. I saw her win the Kentucky Oaks."

"You were in Louisville during Derby week?"

"Yes, with my mom and dad. Watching Hit the Bid on Friday was better than watching the Derby on Saturday. I would love to ride her."

"Okay, you'll get your chance the day after tomorrow. We'll see you then."

CJ stood up and walked toward the trailer door. As she placed her hand on the doorknob, she hesitated and turned her head slightly in Ritchie's direction. "Thanks, Mister Gallo."

CHAPTER THREE

With the racetrack opening in just a few days, the traffic on Broadway in Saratoga Springs continued to increase in volume. Visitors in town for the thoroughbred meet clogged the streets and sidewalks as they visited the restaurants, art galleries, and quaint but elegant hotels situated on this main street.

Gallo hustled into an eatery where he was set to dine with three clients, all of whom held ownership stakes in several horses he was training. Once the lunch was completed and the clients were satisfied that their horses were ready to run, Gallo excused himself and moved to the bar at Morrissey's for a quick drink with John McCann. Gallo engaged several more of McCann's jockeys to ride his race entries over the first few weeks of the meet. McCann again pressed Gallo on a rider for Hit the Bid, but he wasn't ready to yank Jacinto Robles off the mount.

"I'm not sure Robles is the right jock for the filly, but I haven't found anyone else that could ride her better. I'll give him this race to see what he can do."

"What's the issue, Ritchie? She's blown away every field she's run against so far. Hell, even I could ride her to a victory."

"Look, she's established herself as the best three-year-old filly in the country, but she's only raced against other fillies and mares. We've never gone more than a mile and an eighth. She comes out so hot and fast that I'm not sure she'll have the extra punch you need over the last furlong to beat the colts in a longer race."

"You mean a race like the Travers?"

"Right, the Travers, or. . . the Breeder's Cup Classic four months down the road."

"Whew, those are big-time races with big-time horses. The field will include plenty of colts that performed well in the Triple Crown races or other Grade One contests. Winning those will be tough, especially since you didn't run her in the Derby."

"Yeah, I didn't think she was ready then, which is why I put her in the Kentucky Oaks. She was born in May, so she's young for her year group, but I gotta tell you, John—every workout or race she completes, she gets bigger, stronger, and faster. I just have to find someone who can get her to run off the pace, so she's got the strength to kick it home in the stretch."

"You know, Ruffian was one of the greatest fillies ever, and she ran from wire to wire at the head of the pack in every race she ran."

"Yeah, every race she ran until she broke down. That's exactly what I don't want to happen with this horse. Both her sire and her dam had racing careers cut short because they had front leg issues. If Hit the Bid is really destined for greatness, I need to be extra careful with her training and how I race her."

McCann laughed. "You're a good guy, Ritchie. You really care about these horses. I'm a believer when it comes to Hit the Bid. I'll get you the best jock in the country, if you want."

After agreeing to meet the next day for eighteen holes of golf at Saratoga National, Gallo returned to the track, going straight to the trainer's trailer. He was in the middle of a phone call when Jimmy stopped by his desk and tried to get his attention.

"Hey, boss? There's a lady outside that wants to talk to you. She's dressed really classy, like she's got some bucks. Maybe she's an owner and needs a trainer."

Gallo didn't look up, and was trying to ignore Jimmy since he was engaged in a business discussion with his partners at Stone Fence Farms. He gave the groom a flip answer to get him out of his hair.

"Sure, sure—send her in."

He was so engrossed in the phone call, he wasn't aware of the woman who seated herself in the chair next to his desk. As he continued his animated discussion, flipping through some papers on his desk, he briefly glanced to his left. When he saw her, his train of thought came to a screeching halt.

"Uh, hey guys, let me call you back in a minute, okay? Yeah, yeah, I'll call you right back."

He hung up the phone and stared at the lady with a look of bewilderment.

The woman smiled. "Hello, Ritchie. It's been a long time. How are you doing?"

"Wow, I—I can't believe it's you." Gallo tried to sort out his thoughts. "Well . . . Uh, you look the same."

She laughed. "I don't know about that. I'm twenty-one years older."

"Did you just graduate from Wellesley?"

They both began to laugh at that statement, and for an instant, it seemed like they were on that porch swing at her mother's house.

"No, I never did graduate from Wellesley. Just a few months after I left Saratoga that summer, I met someone. We fell in love, and we were married." Channing paused, and though her smile never left her face, he could see her fingers twisting in her lap. She always did that—*fidget*—when she was nervous. Some things never change. "To be honest, this is the first time I've been back to Saratoga since we last saw each other. I've been very busy for the last twenty-plus years."

"Jeez, well, I guess that's great." Gallo had to practically hold his tongue at gunpoint. So many questions flooded into his mind, he didn't know where to begin. "I'm glad it worked out for you. You look successful and happy."

24

They traded uncomfortable smiles. Gallo wondered if she was trying to assess him the way he was her, taking stock of the things that had changed and things that hadn't. When they were dating, Gallo was very thin, since he was trying to make it as a jockey. Even though he weighed forty pounds more at age forty-two, he worked hard to remain trim and athletic. He hoped the touch of grey in his hair gave him a distinguished look, rather than the look of a trainer who spent too much time worrying about horses.

"You should be a male model, Ritchie. Father Time has been very kind to you. He seems to treat men better than women."

"Yeah, I don't think the model thing would work for me. Every time I showed up at a studio smelling like horse poop, they would probably throw me out."

Channing laughed at his joke. Gallo remembered how her eyes sparkled and danced when she was happy.

"I guess you don't really need a job as a model—you're doing fine as a trainer. I've been following your career over the last few years. You've done so well since you hooked up with Stone Fence Farms, and it looks like you are on the cusp of something big with this filly."

"You're still into horse racing?"

"Very much so. My husband is involved with the industry, so we keep tabs on the top thoroughbreds each year, which is why I know about Hit the Bid. What can you tell me about this terrific horse?"

Gallo smiled, filling with the sort of pride he imagined a father might have for a child. "Well, I got a little lucky three years ago. Right about the time she was foaled, the couple that owned the mare was getting a divorce and they wanted to raise money quickly. The farm bought the mare, and I bought the foal for twenty thousand dollars. It's rare to be an owner and the trainer of the same horse, especially a horse with this much talent. The only problem with her is she loves to run so much, it's hard to hold her back. In her maiden race, she was so anxious to get out of the starting gate, she tripped when the doors opened and almost did a face plant. The jockey got her upright and took her down on the rail, but she was already ten lengths behind the leader. From that point, she powered herself through the pack and lost by a nose. It was only a four-and-a-half-furlong race. If it had been five furlongs, she would have won easily. After that disaster, she shot out of the gate to the lead in every race and just blew away the competition. We won the Pocahontas Stakes at Churchill Downs last year and that qualified her for the Breeders' Cup Juvenile Fillies race, but she had some swelling in her knees above the cannon bones, so I cut her training back for a few months and skipped it."

"Passing up the Breeders' Cup means you passed up on a lot of money."

"Yeah, it did," said Gallo. "I don't want to sound like an idealist, but the money isn't as important to me as the chance to race a filly that can achieve some great things. Do you know how many women come out to the tracks just to see her race?"

"Actually, I do. I saw her win the Kentucky Oaks in front of a big crowd."

"You were in Louisville during Derby week?"

"Yes, with my husband and daughter. Watching Hit the Bid on Friday was better than watching the Derby on Saturday."

Gallo remembered hearing that same statement just a day earlier. He began to connect the dots and a smile came to his face. "I should have known the moment I saw her face clearly in the sunlight. She's got your eyes, olive skin, and long black hair. She looks like you, Mrs. Jamieson."

"So, you figured it out. CJ is my daughter, and I really wanted to come here today to thank you for giving her the opportunity to ride for you. It means more to me than you can imagine."

Gallo shrugged. "She's a really nice young lady, and from what I've seen so far, quite a good rider."

"She is a wonderful rider, but have you—" She paused a moment, her demeanor shifting. "Have you noticed anything . . . different about her?"

"Not at all, she seems like a delightful young person."

He saw a patronizing look on her face. "Please, Ritchie, be honest with me."

Gallo slowly conjured up the words he was looking for. "She seems really, really shy, and she has a very monotone, unemotional way of talking to people. The thing that's strange is that when she's in the saddle, she smiles and speaks with enthusiasm. As soon as she jumps off the horse, she goes back to being . . . well, herself."

Channing nodded and gave Gallo a reluctant smile. "In addition to thanking you for offering her a chance to ride, I wanted to explain some things about CJ."

"What kind of things?"

"Things associated with a terrible accident she had as a five-year-old." The woman composed herself, knowing that she was about to tell a very emotional story. "As the parent of a young child, you want to do everything you can to protect them, but at the same time, you want to let a kid be a kid. We were at a park with several other moms and their children. The boys and girls were running around playing tag or some such game. I took my eyes off CJ for just a moment as I spoke to another mom and then I heard screaming. CJ was chasing another girl who stepped out of the way and her momentum took her over the edge of a wall near the sidewalk. She fell six feet head-first onto a concrete walkway. She fractured her skull and suffered a traumatic brain injury."

Gallo could see tears welling up in Channing's eyes. He didn't know what to say or how to console her, but it was clear she was still the sweet and gentle girl he fell in love with so many years before. He began to feel a lump in his throat but said nothing and waited for her to compose herself and continue. "She was in a coma for a week, and when she came out of it, we were faced with a real challenge. Over the next year, she had to learn to speak and walk all over again. We had her in a rehab facility five days a week and it was just heartbreaking to see this beautiful child, who had been so full of life, struggle just to speak and move. It was a long and painful twelve or thirteen months, but finally we reached a point where her speech and physical movements were almost normal. I spent every minute of every day during that time focusing on CJ and feeling tremendous guilt for allowing this accident to happen. My friends and the pastor at our church assured me that it was just bad luck, and I had nothing to do with it, but as a mother . . . you can't explain something like that away so easily."

Gallo had a box of tissues in his drawer, which he strategically placed in front of Channing. She blew her nose, wiping a tear from her cheek. "At that time, we hoped she could return to school and continue on with life as a regular kid. Unfortunately, traumatic brain injuries often have long-term consequences for how someone thinks or reacts to the world around them. In CJ's case, she developed a personality disorder that left her withdrawn, uncommunicative, and unwilling to go out and do the things that once made her happy in life. She was moody, didn't talk clearly or consistently with us, and she didn't show affection, just impatience or anger if she didn't like what was going on around her. Her speech skills continued to develop, but very slowly. We continued taking her for psychological treatment at a center that specialized in brain-damaged children, but we didn't see much improvement. Then, a strange thing happened. My husband and I took her to the yearling auction at Santa Anita. She was only six years old. When she first saw a horse, her eyes got wide and she became very animated. We carried her up near one of the colts and when she placed her hand on the animal's face, it was like someone flipped a switch in her brain. For the next ten minutes, she seemed like a normal kid. Unfortunately, when we tried to leave, she threw a temper tantrum like you wouldn't believe. She was inconsolable and wouldn't calm down until we brought her back the next day to see the horses again."

"I saw her with one of my colts yesterday. It was obvious she had some kind of spiritual or emotional connection with him. There appears to be something we don't understand between her and these horses."

"That's right," said Channing. "After the incident with the horse, we consulted with a psychiatrist who specialized in something called acquired savant syndrome. It's kind of rare but there are documented cases of brain-injured people who suddenly develop a skill or ability that they didn't have prior to trauma. Usually, this acquired skill involves artistic abilities, enhanced memory, or a tremendous ability to deal with numbers or mathematical equations. In CJ's case, her acquired skill is even more unusual and is referred to as a 'soft savant' trait."

"So, what is this soft savant trait?" asked Gallo.

"We don't know how she does it, but she has the ability to communicate with horses."

"I've met a lot of people in my career who can communicate with horses."

"Not like CJ. When her psychiatrist accompanied her to a stable or a farm, he was shocked at her ability to relate to the horses and to understand what was going on in the horse's head. She could spend a few minutes with a mare and predict that she was pregnant. She told a vet that a horse was in pain because of a problem with his rear left foot. When the vet checked it out, he confirmed an infection in the soft tissue under the hoof. One of her more memorable feats was taking an incorrigible pony that couldn't be trained or ridden, and in less than six days, riding him to a blue ribbon in an equestrian event. She would pull off stunts like that on a weekly basis."

"Wow, that's crazy. Did this work with horses have a positive effect on her?"

"Absolutely. It was just incredible how she changed and grew as a person. She began to speak normally, she was much calmer and easier to deal with, and when we hired a tutor for home schooling, she responded well to the educational process. She evolved from being a textbook case of avoidant personality disorder to someone who could function productively in daily life. The key to her continued growth was the interaction with horses. I'll never forget when she was eight years old, she was all dressed up in her black jacket, riding britches, boots, and pot helmet. She was on her way to jump fences with a show horse. Before she got into the car, she ran back to me and gave me a hug, telling me she loved me. It was the first time since the accident she expressed an emotion like that. I cried for two days!"

"Gosh, I can see how that could be really emotional. It seems like a miracle that she could change so much."

"Well, she's obviously not perfect. She still has trouble relating to people and initiating friendships. We thought it was important to send her to high school, and it worked out okay. She didn't have a ton of friends, and she never had a boyfriend who could take her to the senior prom, but if she got time with her horses, it didn't seem to bother her. She has difficulty understanding jokes, figures of speech or sarcasm, and doesn't like to look people in the eye."

"Yeah, I noticed that," he said, feeling a rush of guilt for giving her grief about it. *If only he'd known.* "What about the squeaky clean and neat appearance?"

"That's another obsession; she has a little bit of OCD. She's very neat. I was just at the apartment we rented for her in Saratoga Springs. The bedroom looks exactly like her bedroom at our home in California—all of her furniture is in the same place, her clothes are arranged the same way, and her bookshelves, too. She just has this *thing* about being neat, clean, and orderly."

"Yet she doesn't mind walking through horse droppings piled up to her ankles?"

Channing laughed and shrugged. "What can I tell you? We don't understand it either, she just is who she is."

"So, is there anything I should be aware of to ensure the safety of everybody involved?"

"Nope, she really knows her way around a racetrack. We were so proud of her performances at Santa Anita. It really gives her a great sense of accomplishment when her mounts perform well. You just have to be patient when you're communicating with her one-on-one."

"I kinda feel bad about how I spoke to her yesterday," he confessed, speaking his concerns out loud this time. "Maybe I shouldn't give her such a hard time."

"Ritchie, please don't change how you interact with her. She doesn't warm up easily to people, but she likes you. You and a groom named Jimmy. That's unusual with her. Whatever you guys are doing, just keep it up."

"How about your husband? How does he get along with her?"

Channing sighed and shot Gallo a hesitant look. "When CJ turned eighteen, she decided she wanted to transition from equestrian riding to riding thoroughbreds. She and her father, Crawford, had several big arguments over this, but eventually he relented and allowed her to exercise racehorses at Santa Anita. After a year and a half, my husband reached out to John McCann and asked him to help CJ get licensed in California. I think he was secretly hoping that McCann would be unsuccessful at getting CJ a license but John came through and she started racing last spring." Channing paused for a moment, as though drawn into the memory. "Crawford has always been supportive and would do anything for me or for our daughter. He's been there every step of the way with CJ and suffered through the same anguish and heartbreak I have. Crawford is not a guy who wears his heart on his sleeve—he's very reserved when it comes to showing emotion, but I know how deeply he cares for me and CJ. For some reason, the close attachment I've established with my daughter

31

since her accident hasn't taken place with Crawford. I know it hurts him, but he remains supportive, patient, and loyal to our family. He tries to be a good father and husband, Ritchie."

"It sounds like it. I know it's got to be tough for the guy. What does he do for a living?"

"He's the president and principal shareholder of a bank founded by his grandfather in California. The Jamieson family has had ties to horse racing for almost one hundred years, and because of that, he formed a partnership that syndicates thoroughbreds. It's been a profitable side business that keeps us involved in the sport."

"Well, he sounds exactly like the kind of blue-blood your dad wanted you to marry." Gallo wished he hadn't said it as soon as the words left his lips. "Ah, shoot, I'm sorry. I shouldn't have said that. Crawford sounds like a stand-up guy, and I'm really happy for you, I really am."

"Thanks, I believe you. I know the way we parted was an awful situation for you, but I am so proud of you, Ritchie. You're really doing well in a business you love. That's a great thing."

Gallo wasn't sure how to respond—his thoughts kept stalling on the way she'd said, "it was an awful situation *for you*." As a result, their conversation slipped into an awkward silence. Eventually, Channing changed the subject.

"CJ tells me you're going to let her work Hit the Bid tomorrow. She's really excited. She's had a love affair with that horse ever since we saw her run."

"Well, I was so impressed with her handling of T-three that I thought I'd give her a shot on the filly. I've learned a lot about the business end of the racing industry. Can you imagine a female superhorse with a lady jockey? They could be on the cover of *Time* magazine six months from now."

"Or a Wheaties box! Now that's *really* big."

They laughed together—a little too easily, perhaps—and for a single heartbeat, it felt like no time had passed at all. But as reality settled back in, so did Gallo's twenty-year-long disappointment. He could've sworn, as silence funneled into their porous conversation, that he'd seen that same disappointment in Channing's eyes, too—even if only for a brief moment.

Gallo figured it was probably a good time to bring the reunion to an end. Their eyes met for an instant, and they each immediately averted their gaze.

"Hey, look—I appreciate you stopping by, and I will do my best to take care of CJ. I'm glad you told me about her. C'mon, I'll walk you out to your car."

After they stepped out of the trailer, Channing approached a recent model Mercedes convertible.

"You must be influential around here if you can get parking privileges on this side of Union Avenue," Gallo said with a chuckle. "I have to jog a full block to get to my truck."

"Just lucky, I guess. It was great to see you," she offered, and Gallo truly hoped she meant it. "Thanks again for helping CJ."

"Who knows—if she turns out to be the jockey I think she could be, *she* may be the one helping *me*."

Channing smiled, but there it was—that sense of sadness he'd seen earlier, a sliver of disappointment, buried deep under the mask.

Maybe it was just his imagination or wishful thinking, but it seemed like a happy face was covering a troubled heart.

Channing got into her car, drove down the dirt road to the entrance gate for the stables, and took a right turn onto East Avenue.

Ritchie watched the Mercedes until it disappeared from view.

CHAPTER FOUR

Jimmy Crowder left the dormitory building and walked toward the stables, followed by the five grooms he supervised. Two of the men were full-time employees of Stone Fence Farms, just like he was. The others were local workers who were hired for the duration of the Saratoga meet. They walked in single file, saying nothing as they tried to come alive at five o'clock in the morning. When they reached the barn where Gallo's horses were stabled, each moved to a different stall. They opened the top half of the stall door and turned on a light, signaling to the horses inside that their training routine was about to begin.

As Jimmy approached the last stall where Hit the Bid was located, he could see that the door was already opened, and the light was on. When he stuck his head into the enclosure, he saw the filly standing in the middle of the space—calmly nuzzling the shoulder of CJ Jamieson.

"Girl, what the heck you doin' here so early? You don't have to ride this horse for another hour. I was about scared to death that someone came in here and took this lady away when I saw the door open! You shouldn't be here at this time."

CJ smiled as she stroked the side of the thoroughbred's neck. "I just wanted to come in and get to know her before I ride her this morning. She's an amazing horse. She'll be a champion, just like Tackle Tim Tom."

"Well, we're all hoping that's the case. They run different, and they got different personalities, that's for sure." Jimmy entered the stall and began to organize the tack that would be needed for Hit the Bid's run that morning. "Girl, you go on outside, I got work to do."

"Do you want me to help you?"

Jimmy put his hands on his hips and gave CJ a stern look. "Little lady, my job is to take care of this horse, and your job is to ride her. I do my job well, and you got to do your job well. I don't ride, and you don't groom. Do you understand that? Now get on out of this stall. You can watch it from outside if you want. Just be quiet; I got to sing to her a little bit. She likes that in the morning."

CJ stood up and moved outside the door, so Jimmy would have room to prepare the horse. As the groom began to brush the filly's back, he started to sing:

> "I find me a place in a boxcar
> So I take out my guitar to pass some time
> Late at night when it's hard to rest
> I hold your picture to my chest
> And I'm alright
> A rainy night in Georgia
> A rainy night in Georgia
> I believe it's raining all over the world."

"That sounds like a sad song, Mister Jimmy."

"It is sad, but it calms the horse, and it reminds me of when I left Georgia forty years ago."

"Is that when you started working with horses?"

"Yup, I went to Arkansas and started working as a groom at Oaklawn Park. I was there for quite a while until a trainer I knew asked me to come and work at a farm in Kentucky. That's where I met Ritchie Gallo—about ten years ago. When Ritchie ended up with the trainer job at Stone Fence Farms, he offered me the position of head groom. That's been a good move for me. I like working for Ritchie,

35

and the owners of the farm treat me real nice. Hell, I got a *four-oh-one-kay* and full health benefits. And, I got this nice little apartment right there on the farm near the horses. Yeah, it's a pretty sweet life. I like travelling, but I'm always happy to get back to Kentucky."

"If you're so happy, why do you sing a sad song?"

"Well, sometimes you gotta remind yourself of the bad and lonely days in order to appreciate the good days. I guess if you're a rich little white girl, you don't have any bad days to remember, but most people got 'em."

CJ leaned against the door jam and put her hands in her pockets. "I've had bad days too, Mister Jimmy, but thanks to my mom and horses, my days are getting better and better."

Jimmy reached into his pocket and pulled out three dollars. "You know what would make my day even better? If you go down to the break truck next to the barn and get me a coffee! Get a cup for yourself, too. I like mine black with three sugars."

CJ took the cash and began walking down the concourse. "Was that two sugars, Mister Jimmy?"

"Three, girl, *three*," shouted Jimmy. "Dang-it-all, this strange little white girl just don't listen!"

———————— • ————————

Ritchie Gallo was on his way to the stalls when suddenly CJ cruised by, head down and blinders on, a woman on a mission. When she'd passed by without saying a word to him, he shouted, "Hey, don't you say good morning to people when you first see them?"

"Oh, I'm sorry, Mister Gallo. I didn't see you."

"I know you didn't see me; you're too busy searching for your snot again."

"I don't think so, Mister Gallo. I'm not ill, and my nose isn't running."

Gallo hung his head in exasperation. After speaking with her mother, he knew he should be patient when communicating with CJ, but patience was a commodity in short supply so early in the morning. "I know you're not ill. It's just a figure of speech. Look, you gotta fix this whole *not-looking-people-in-the-eye* thing, you know what I'm saying? Where are you going?"

"I'm going to the snack truck to get coffee for me and Mister Jimmy."

"Okay, I'll go with you. The coffee there is better than the stuff in the trainer's trailer."

As they walked toward the truck, they discussed the objectives for CJ's exercise ride that morning. Ritchie explained his training philosophy regarding Hit the Bid and some of his concerns about the filly's welfare.

"The problem with this horse is her penchant for running at top speed. It's been difficult to train her to run off the pace until the point in the race where she needs to sprint for the finish line. If we're going to be successful in the most prestigious races, she'll need to run farther than in previous contests, and she will run against colts that have the physical strength to maintain their speed over the final furlong. In addition, because she runs so damned hard, I'm afraid she may become a bleeder. Thoroughbreds often suffer from exercise-induced pulmonary hemorrhage, a condition that results from the extraordinary level of pressure their heart places on the lungs when running at top speed. Hit the Bid doesn't seem to know how to operate at any level of performance other than top speed. I'm concerned that this constant elevation of heart pressure could cause her to bleed internally and affect her performance and her health."

Gallo was also well aware that Hit the Bid's father and mother were both racehorses that showed great promise as two-year-olds, but were retired early because of injuries.

"Bid's sire had bucked shins that never completely recovered. He had micro-fractures in his cannon bones that never healed. In addition, the mare that gave birth to Hit the Bid was retired because she had bowed tendons in her forelimbs due to chronic tendinitis. I'm always worried that Hit the Bid might have a genetic predisposition to these injuries, so I try to regulate her training to avoid too much stress on her legs, and we're extremely vigilant when examining her forelegs after a workout."

When CJ was to ride Hit the Bid later that morning, he wanted her to gallop the horse at a consistent rate of about eighteen seconds per furlong, and then accelerate to a speed of roughly twelve seconds per furlong.

"We know she can run consistently at eleven seconds per furlong, but no horse can do that for an entire race. I need a jockey that can get the horse to vary her speed on command, and to maintain her place in the pack until she's asked to run," instructed Gallo, pouring himself a black coffee and securing the lid.

CJ cocked a brow, dumping two sugars into a cup of black coffee for Jimmy. Hers sat beside it—no sugar, multiple creams. "So, you want her to run like Zenyatta, not like Ruffian?"

"That's exactly right," he replied, taking a sip. This coffee *was* so much better than the coffee offered at the trainer's trailer. "Those were two of the greatest fillies to ever race, but Zenyatta came from behind to win and went on to a nice retirement on a horse farm. Ruffian blew the doors off everybody right out of the gate but broke down in her eleventh race and was euthanized. I don't want that to happen to Hit the Bid."

Carrying their coffees, they returned to the stalls. Jimmy seemed relieved that CJ *almost* got the sugar dosage right and sipped his coffee as he led Hit the Bid around the walking ring.

When five of the six horses were saddled and the exercise riders showed up, the grooms gave each rider a boost, lifting them into their saddles. Tackle Tim Tom remained in his stall so he could be worked out later in the day, after CJ exercised Hit the Bid.

Gallo and General Custer led the procession across Union Avenue to the main track. The sun was rising at last—it was a *beautiful* morning—and the track was tranquil as horses and their minders gradually sauntered into the dirt oval. The riders gathered around Gallo, awaiting another briefing on the level and type of exercise he wanted for each horse.

Once he was finished, Gallo watched the riders disperse. In just a few days, the grandstands would be filled with 30,000 patrons cheering on the thoroughbreds as they raced for the finish line. But right now—in this moment, with the sun slowly rising—he could sit astride the General and absorb the spirit and tradition of this unique stadium. The main track surrounded two verdant turf tracks, which in turn encompassed a beautiful infield ordained with flowers, manicured hedgerows, and a pond.

In the pond, a canoe floated along, moved about by the gentle forces of the wind. The canoe was painted with the colors of the owner whose horse had won the most recent Travers Stakes. Gallo looked at the canoe and dreamed that soon, with the help of Hit the Bid or Tackle Tim Tom, the colors would represent Stone Fence Farms.

He had the horses to win that race. Now, he just needed to find the right rider.

Gallo's thoughts were interrupted by CJ. "Hey, Mister Gallo? We're ready to go. I'm going to get her to run at a gentle gallop and be sure she maintains that speed for a mile or so. Then I'll let her breeze on the inside but try to hold her speed to twelve seconds per furlong."

Gallo refocused on his all-female team and had another idea. "CJ, when you're ready to let her breeze, turn her around after another horse passes you. Bring her up on the right hind of the other horse and see if you can keep her there for two furlongs. I don't know . . . maybe she just doesn't like having dirt kicked in her face, or maybe it's just some inbred sense of competition, but we must see if we can pace her off another horse. When you get to the one-eighth pole, ask her to kick it in and see what happens. Slow her down after you pass the finish line and get back to me."

"I got it, Mister Gallo. I'll be careful."

With a click and a tap, CJ started Hit the Bid off around the periphery of the track. The filly immediately began to dance and move her head up and down as if bowing to an imaginary audience. CJ turned around in the saddle and flashed Gallo a huge smile. Gallo smiled back and gave her a thumbs up. He then guided the General over to his viewing position near the finish line.

As CJ walked the filly in a clockwise direction, Gallo once again noticed she was talking to the horse and patting her on the neck. Hit the Bid remained calm and obedient, even as her gait moved up to a trot—which was a pleasant surprise. When CJ asked her to gallop, Hit the Bid predictably started to run. It took about a quarter of a mile, but CJ gradually took control and backed her down into a more relaxed pace, maintaining that pace for about four furlongs.

Throughout it all, CJ consistently talked to Hit the Bid until she was able to decrease her pressure on the reins entirely. Gallo held his breath, certain the horse would bolt—but she kept calm and appeared to *listen* to CJ's whispering.

He was genuinely impressed when they galloped past his position. CJ's movement on the back of Hit the Bid complemented the athletic movement of the filly.

"It looks good, General Custer," he said, and the horse snickered, as though in agreement. "Smooth and relaxed . . . smooth and relaxed."

When CJ reached the backstretch, she brought Hit the Bid to a walk, waiting for a colt that was breezing on the inside rail to approach the three-eighth pole. As the colt was drawing nearer, CJ turned the filly around, edging her down towards the rail. When the colt raced by, she smacked Hit the Bid on the butt, asking her to run.

Initially, Hit the Bid's clear intention was to blow past the other horse, but CJ was able to calm her down and get her to run at 95 percent of top speed. She positioned her mount just to the right and behind the colt, both horses running along at the same pace.

On the far turn, the colt drifted a bit to his right, so CJ took Hit the Bid down to the rail on the left but stayed behind the colt. The dirt splashing into the filly's face didn't make her waver or hesitate, and she seemed to easily maintain her position behind her competitor.

When they reached the one-eighth pole, CJ just touched her rump with the whip and hollered, "Go, girl, go!"

The filly immediately accelerated past the colt. The other exercise rider snapped his whip several times on the colt's butt, urging him to run. The colt stepped it up, but Hit the Bid had already blown past and was breezing to the finish line, easily winning this impromptu race.

CJ stood up in the stirrups and gently pulled the reins to slow her horse down. As Hit the Bid decelerated, the colt passed by, and the exercise rider shouted at CJ, "What you trying to do there, lady? You trying to show off?"

CJ shot back, "I hope that colt's good in the breeding barn, because he's *never* going to beat my filly!"

CJ brought Hit the Bid to a walk and turned her around to meet up with Gallo and General Custer. When she approached the trainer and his horse, she smiled and asked, "What do you think?"

Gallo responded, "I think Jacinto Robles just lost a job."

CHAPTER FIVE

Ritchie Gallo had participated in Opening Day at Saratoga as a child, a young track worker, and as a trainer. Today's opening, like so many in prior years, was filled with sunshine, warm weather, and a large crowd anxious to watch and bet on the thoroughbreds.

Gallo's opening day began like any other: arriving at the stables in the dark to exercise and groom his horses.

Only one of the horses he trained was entered in a race on the first day of competition. The owner of that horse was willing to sell the animal if he could get twenty-five thousand dollars for the colt, so Gallo registered the horse in a claiming race. As it turned out, no one bid on the horse before the race began, but the horse won the event, leaving the owner with a money-maker instead of a money-burner.

Gallo joined the reluctant owner in the winner's circle for the obligatory photo-op and then left the section of the clubhouse reserved for trainers and owners in order to make his way back to the stables. Just before leaving the track area, he noticed a television monitor in the security guard shack. The next race was about to start, so he stepped into the shack to watch it with the guards. CJ had her first mount of the meet in the race and he wanted to see how she performed. She would be riding a colt on the turf—the grass oval set inside the larger dirt oval where most of the races are run. It was a short race, only six furlongs, so it was important for a jockey to get the horse in the right position soon after leaving the starting gate in order to minimize the distance to the finish line.

When the bell rang and eight horses sprinted from the gate, CJ quickly maneuvered around several other thoroughbreds and positioned her mount on the rail three or four lengths behind the leader. She held that position for most of the race and asked the colt to run with one furlong to go. She didn't have quite enough horse to catch the leader, but managed to finish second by half a length.

"Not a bad ride for a rookie," said Gallo.

"That lady jockey going to ride for you, Mister Gallo?" asked one of the guards.

"She is. Keep an eye on her."

The guards thanked him and wrote down CJ's name. They loved getting tips from the trainers.

Gallo crossed Union Avenue and made his way to the trainer's trailer, where he returned a call to Jacinto Robles's agent, who wasn't very happy about having his client replaced in the saddle by an apprentice. Hit the Bid's first race at Saratoga was a stakes race with a big payoff to the winner. The filly was an odds-on favorite, so this change could cost the agent and his rider money. Gallo explained his reasons for the change and promised Robles several mounts later in the meet that could generate a decent payday for the jock.

After concluding the call, Gallo began to map out a strategy for his two best horses as he looked into the future. He felt confident that Tackle Tim Tom would win The Sanford, which would take place the next day. Two days later, Hit the Bid would run in the American Oaks. If both horses won, he and his partners at Stone Fence Farms would earn nearly three hundred thousand dollars. More importantly, the wins would qualify Hit the Bid to run in the Travers Stakes, and T-three to compete in the Hopeful Stakes—two of the biggest races at the Saratoga meet. Should the horses win those races, they would automatically qualify for Breeders' Cup races in November at Churchill

Downs, where the purses ran to seven figures. The spacing of these races over the next four months would give him time to train the colt and the filly to compete against the best horses in the world. If CJ really had the magic touch he believed she had, winning the Breeders' Cup races was achievable.

Gallo sat back in his chair and tapped a pencil on the desk. He didn't want to get carried away with lofty expectations, but when he thought about the racing season next spring, he knew that Tackle Tim Tom would then be a three-year-old and could qualify for the Triple Crown races. No trainer, he knew, should *ever* plan on winning the Triple Crown. The odds were overwhelmingly against you, but he just couldn't help himself as he envisioned T-three crossing the finish line first at The Belmont. As for Hit the Bid, she would be retired if she won the Breeders' Cup and spend the next few years mating with the best stallions in the business. Her foals would bring six-figure price tags at the yearling sales and she could enjoy the balance of her life jogging about in a field of green grass and entertaining tourists that would stop by Stone Fence Farms just to see her up close.

Gallo's daydream of racing glory was interrupted by the entrance into the trailer of a tall man dressed in a blue blazer, a white shirt, and British tan slacks. The man walked toward Gallo's desk and extended his hand. "Mister Gallo, my name is Crawford Jamieson. I'm CJ's father."

Gallo rose from his chair and shook the man's hand. A Rolex glistened on his wrist. Crawford had the look and demeanor of a wealthy patrician. His full head of hair was combed straight back, and his tanned face enhanced the brightness of his smile.

"It's a pleasure to meet you, Mister Jamieson. I assume you just watched your daughter ride her first race here at Saratoga. A second-place ride isn't too bad for her initial outing."

"Channing and I have a box in the clubhouse, so we were delighted to see her perform so well. Obviously, we are very excited about the next couple of days. She gets to ride two spectacular horses that you train, and I think everyone's expectations are very high."

"Well, I keep my expectations low-key," said Gallo, contradicting his actual thoughts over the previous ten minutes. "I just try to take it one race at a time."

"Of course, of course," said Jamieson with a smile. "It's a risky business—you can't get too overconfident, can you? Do you mind if I sit down, Mister Gallo?"

Gallo offered the man a chair, and Crawford Jamieson began to explain the reason for his visit. "I believe my wife told you that I formed a limited partnership many years ago that invests in race-horses. I'm the general partner, but I have investors from all over the world who enjoy owning a piece of a thoroughbred. It obviously spreads the risk, just like a stock mutual fund, and it gives horsing enthusiasts a way to participate in the industry without having to put all your eggs in one basket, so to speak. I'm sure you understand the concept."

"Sure, I train several horses that are owned by a syndicate."

"Right, well, we've had a few situations lately where horses have been big winners or have become successful stallions that fathered offspring whose success has been demonstrated on the track. As a result, we have some free cash and we want to make a few purchases. I'm aware of the fact that Tackle Tim Tom is 100 percent owned by your partners at Stone Fence Farms and that you are the sole owner of Hit the Bid. I'd like to talk to you and your partners about buying the horses."

Gallo had never considered selling Hit the Bid, and he was sure the owners of Stone Fence Farms weren't ready to sell a colt with the potential of Tackle Tim Tom. He wasn't prepared to address this sur-prising question, so he just stammered out a thoughtless answer: "Hit the Bid's been my baby since she popped out of the womb. I could never consider selling her. As for Tackle Tim Tom, he's unproven. Why would you want to buy him?"

"I'm sure you appreciate the talent that the filly has, Mister Gallo. She can win several bigger races this year. And next year, as a four-year-old, she could make a fortune running in stakes races all over the country. If she ran every two months, she could potentially earn over two million dollars—*twice* that amount if she could win a Breeders' Cup race this year and next. After that, the foals she delivers would sell for big numbers at the yearling sales. Regarding your unproven colt, I was sitting in the empty grandstand the other morning when CJ worked him for you." Jamieson sat forward, smiling slyly. "I know how to work a stopwatch, Mister Gallo. You've got an exceptional colt on your hands if you have the right rider."

Gallo took the time to think about his next statement before responding to the businessman seated next to him. "I will certainly mention your interest in T-three to the owners at Stone Fence. My sense is that they have confidence in my ability to turn the colt into a winner and they would very much like to manage his future career as a sire, seeing as we are one of the smaller breeding farms in Kentucky and a great stallion could really contribute to the financial security of the operation. I'll let you know if they have an interest in pursuing negotiations. As far as Hit the Bid is concerned, my training and racing plans for her are very different from your objectives. I'm not planning to race her as a four-year-old; I'll retire her after she competes in the Breeders' Cup."

Jamieson shrugged, shaking his head in disbelief. "She just might be the best filly in the business right now. You're passing up on a ton of money if you don't race her next year."

Gallo smiled. "Yeah, several people have already questioned my judgment on how I make money with the filly, but I think I know what she can achieve. I love this sport and its great traditions, so I'm more concerned about her legacy than the money. I'm not going to over-train her to run in too many races and risk an injury. Young women who know next to nothing about horse racing come out to watch her race. I'm more concerned about the payoff they get from watching a magnificent female athlete than I am about winning a purse. That's just my view. I may be a fool, but that's the way I'm going to do it."

Jamieson appeared to size up Gallo, clearly shocked by the fact that he'd just been effectively turned down. But, apparently, he wasn't ready to give up. "You understand the risks in this business better than anyone, Mister Gallo. If we put a ton of money in your pocket now, all the risks get transferred to my partnership. Horses go lame, stallions can be impotent, and mares have miscarriages. We accept the losses—and *you* get to look at a big bank statement."

"You're right, Mister Jamieson. I do understand the disasters that can take place in our industry. But that's what makes taking on the risk so worthwhile. These horses imperil themselves every time they set a hoof on a track. Many people say that what we're doing here is immoral and cruel to these animals. In some cases, they may be right. But how many of God's creatures on this earth get to do exactly what they were bred to do? They run because it's who they are, it's *what* they are. There's such a beauty in watching that spirit drive their physical skills. It's hard for me to put the appreciation of that beauty into dollars and cents."

Gallo stood up, indicating that the meeting was over. "As I said, I'll run this by the guys back at the farm to see if they would consider selling Tackle Tim Tom, but I wouldn't get my hopes up if I were you. With regard to Hit the Bid, she's definitely not for sale."

The men shook hands, and a visibly disappointed Crawford Jamieson made his way to the door of the trailer. "Good luck to you, Mister Gallo. You've got two big races coming up."

Gallo smiled. "Hey, a great jockey and two great horses. My life doesn't get any better than this."

CHAPTER SIX

D ave and Becky, the hosts for the cable television show *Saratoga Live,* waited for the director to signal that the commercial break was over, and then immediately began giving racing fans around the country an update on the results of the afternoon.

"Welcome back, everyone, to our anchor desk right here in front of the paddock at the beautiful Saratoga Racetrack. Today marks the third day of the meet, and everybody is talking about the apprentice jockey riding a rising star in the world of thoroughbred racing."

"Right you are, Dave—it was rookie rider CJ Jamieson bringing the talented filly Hit the Bid to the finish line in an impressive performance that has established this horse as one of the top in the country. This was Jamieson's second win in two days. She won the Sanford Stakes yesterday riding a two-year-old named Tackle Tim Tom and then captured the final race run today by winning the American Oaks on Hit the Bid. Let's review the recording of the race and see how this dynamic female duo electrified the crowd of nearly thirty thousand patrons."

The TV changed to a replay of The American Oaks. Becky concentrated her commentary on Jamieson and Hit the Bid. "This is the first time Hit the Bid raced against male competitors, but she demonstrated her ability to win regardless of the gender of the horses in the field. For the first half of the race, CJ did a great job of pacing the filly, running back in the pack, five or six lengths from the leader.

In virtually all of Hit the Bid's previous races, she took the lead right out of the gate and challenged the other mares and fillies to catch her. This race was much more tactical than previous races, wasn't it Dave?"

"Yes, it was, Becky! It seems the jockey kept the horse in contact with the leaders but saved up the energy her mount would need to finish the race. I was really impressed by the way CJ Jamieson took the lead over the last quarter mile. You can see here," he went on, gesturing to the recording, "as the horses are entering the far turn, that Hit the Bid is boxed in with colts in front, behind, and on either side of her. Jamieson patiently waited for a crease to open between the horse in front and the horse to her right."

"Exactly, Dave," Becky interjected excitedly. "When the opportunity came, Hit the Bid accelerated through *this* small opening, and Jamieson took her to the outside. At the top of the stretch, she was four horses wide of the rail with a clear path to the finish line. CJ applied one slight tap on the rump with her whip and then gave the filly a hand ride down the stretch, distancing herself from the pack by four lengths. Hit the Bid ran the race in a blazing speed of one-forty-six and two-fifths. Quite a performance! This filly is sending a message to the racing industry that she isn't just a pretty face—this lady can run with any colt in the country!"

"You're right, Becky, that was an amazing performance. Now, let's send it down to Mary Tierney, who is standing by in the winner's circle with the winning jockey and the horse's trainer, Ritchie Gallo. Take it away, Mary!"

"Thank you, Dave. I'm standing here with CJ Jamieson, who just won the American Oaks aboard Hit the Bid. CJ, you ran a very tactical race. Was that the plan you and Ritchie Gallo had for the horse?"

"Yes."

The interviewer continued to the next question. "This horse has a reputation for being a speedster—was it difficult to get her to run off the pace?"

"No."

Again, there was an awkward pause, so Mary Tierney kept it rolling. "I understand that you have also been helping Gallo train the horse by working as the exercise rider. Do you think that helps you to ride her more successfully in a race?"

"Yes."

Tierney appeared determined to get some useful information from the jockey. "Will you be aboard Hit the Bid in her next race?"

CJ said nothing and looked over at Gallo, who was clearly enjoying the fact that someone other than him could be perplexed by Jamieson's lack of communication skills. "Mary, I can tell you for sure that CJ is my jockey on Hit the Bid as long as she wants to ride her. She's done a great job helping me train the horse, and I think they make a great team."

Mary Tierney was delighted that Gallo's personable response had bailed her out of a lackluster interview. "Well, Ritchie, you've got a female jockey on top of a great female thoroughbred. You guys are really going to get a lot of attention in the world of sports. Back to you, Dave and Becky!"

When the camera operator indicated that they had switched back to the broadcast anchors, Mary turned to Gallo and lowered her voice. "You're going to get a lot of press interest, Mister Gallo. You'd better get her a speech coach."

"Yeah, tell me about it."

CHAPTER SEVEN

allo accompanied CJ back to the jockey room after the interview in the winner's circle. When she entered the white picket fence enclosure reserved for jockeys, she stepped on a scale, still holding the saddle and tack used in the race so the stewards could verify the horse carried the correct weight. As she was about to enter the section of the locker room reserved for the three female jockeys working the meet, Gallo leaned over the fence and called her over.

"Listen, CJ, we just won two big races and made some decent bucks for ourselves and our owners. Let's go out tonight and celebrate. I'll take you to the Brook Tavern for a first-class meal; what do you say?"

CJ merely shrugged and answered in her trademark monotone voice, "That sounds okay, I guess."

"Terrific. I'm delighted to see how enthused you are for a night on the town. You're still in that apartment on Ludlow Street, right? I'll pick you up at seven, and then we can shoot by the track to get Jimmy. I need at least one person at dinner who will talk to me."

About an hour-and-a-half later, Gallo pulled up to a house where CJ's parents had rented an apartment for their daughter. The young woman was waiting at the curb when Gallo arrived. She was impeccably dressed in white pants with a perfect crease down the front and back of her legs. She wore high heels and a navy blue vest over a light blue, short-sleeve blouse. Her thick black hair was pulled straight back, a strategically placed barrette allowing it to flow down her back. To Gallo's surprise, she was wearing a touch of makeup.

"Hey, CJ, you look great. You really are a very beautiful girl. You know that, don't you?"

"Yes."

"Yes? I give you a compliment and that's all you can say?"

"Yes, I know I'm beautiful."

"Well, I guess that clears it up. Get in the truck!"

Gallo drove several blocks to the backstretch area of the track and got his second surprise of the night. Jimmy Crowder was waiting for him on East Avenue dressed in a black three-piece suit with white pinstripes. His shirt was purple, and his tie was a bright yellow. On his head was a dark-colored fedora with a white band around the crown. The hat was tipped down over his left eye.

"Hey, Jimmy," Gallo shouted from his window. "We're just going out for dinner—not to Ebony Magazine's awards night!"

"Now look, boss—the three of us just completed the two most successful days of our careers. We're not a couple of railbirds that just lost a few bucks at the track. We're talented entrepreneurs that should get a lot of respect from the rich white folks hobnobbing around this town tonight. We gotta show some class, you know what I'm saying? How do you think I look, Miss CJ?"

The young woman smiled at the groom fondly. "I think you look *wonderful*, Mister Jimmy."

"Oh, that's great," declared Gallo. "I'm going to dinner with Miss Beautiful and Mister Wonderful. Get in the damn truck—let's go!"

Gallo drove the three blocks to the Brook Tavern on the corner of Union and Nelson Avenues. When they entered the restaurant, he saw that both the bar area and the main dining room were crowded. The clientele were obviously people who had attended the track earlier in the day, and based on the number of sport coats and ties worn by the men, it was primarily patrons who frequented the clubhouse.

Gallo was pleased to see that the bartender was a former classmate from Saratoga High School who worked at the Brook Tavern for the six weeks the track was open. He reached between two people sitting at the bar to shake his old friend's hand and asked if he could get a table for three. "Yeah, no sweat, Ritchie. I'll tell the owner you're here, and I'm sure she'll fit you in. Nice work the last two days, buddy! I had money on both your horses; I owe you a few drinks."

"Great, I'll have a Budweiser, the lady will have a ginger ale, and my well-dressed friend wants a Singapore Sling. We'll just sit at that little table by the fireplace until you can get us into the dining room."

Ritchie, CJ, and Jimmy adjourned to the only open space left in the bar: a small round table wedged between the corner of the fireplace and a large window looking out on Nelson Avenue. They sat around the table, with CJ sitting between the two men. Once the bartender delivered the drinks and told Gallo the owner would have a table ready in the dining room within fifteen minutes, Jimmy proposed a toast, and they raised their glasses. "Here's to the two fastest horses in the country and the fine team of people that train and ride them."

"Hear, hear!" said Gallo and CJ, who both smiled as they sipped their drinks.

Gallo began to brief his key jockey and his head groom on his plans for the remainder of the Saratoga meet: "We've got four weeks until Hit the Bid will run in the Travers Stakes and five weeks until T-three runs in the Hopeful Stakes. In addition, we've got the other four horses from Stone Fence scheduled to run in lower-level races during that time period."

The pair looked on, barely touching their drinks as Gallo continued: "With the success that CJ has had over the last two days, I know John McCann will be getting a lot of calls from other trainers who will want her to ride for them, and I don't have a problem with that. CJ needs to continue to build a career as a jockey, and racing for other farms and owners is part of the deal. What I would like from you, CJ, is your commitment that you'll continue to work with Jimmy and me several mornings each week to develop and train Hit the Bid and Tackle Tim Tom."

"I would love that, Mister Gallo. You gave me the chance to ride these great thoroughbreds, and I kind of feel like they are my best friends now. I want them to succeed and be happy."

"Fabulous. Jimmy and I have to put in the time necessary to try and win with the other horses from Stone Fence, but I want the colt and the filly to get some special attention—and that means I need *you*."

CJ looked at Ritchie and smiled. "Thanks, Mister Gallo. It's nice to be needed."

"Hey, you looked me in the eye and smiled when you said that! I must be some kind of psychiatric savant for people with traumatic brain injuries."

"Hm . . . I don't think so, Mister Gallo. You're a horse trainer, and I actually looked at your nose."

"I knew it was too good to be true. How about another round of drinks?"

As the threesome continued to talk and enjoy their second round, Gallo noticed that a young man at the bar was glancing over at them from time to time. He looked to be in his early twenties and was one of the men in the restaurant still dressed in a sport coat and tie. After several minutes and several looks, the fellow stood and began to walk toward the table. He had a round baby face, a hefty build, and wore glasses. He looked like a college kid who spent more time in the computer lab than the gym, and he was looking straight at CJ.

"Excuse me, miss, but are you CJ Jamieson, the jockey?"

CJ appeared to be caught by surprise, only looking at the man for a second before lowering her eyes to the drink in her hand. Gallo nudged her with his left elbow. "The guy asked you a question. You know who you are. Answer him."

Without looking up, she responded, "Yes, I'm CJ Jamieson, and I am a jockey."

"Wow, that's so cool. I watched you win the Sanford yesterday, and today I was in the paddock when you climbed aboard Hit the Bid. I bet fifty dollars on you, so I guess I owe you a drink or something like that." He reached into the inside breast pocket of his jacket and pulled out the printed program for the day's races at Saratoga. "Would you mind autographing my program, Miss Jamieson? You can sign it right here where the entry for your horse is listed in the tenth race." The man put the program down in front of CJ with a pen.

CJ slowly took the pen and signed her name over the block on the page that displayed Hit the Bid's name, her name as the jockey, and Gallo's name as the trainer from Stone Fence Farms. She said nothing and handed the program back to the young man. The interesting thing? This guy was blushing more than CJ was! Damn if he didn't seem really smitten by the beautiful jockey before him, and now it looked like he didn't know what to say or how to extricate himself from the awkward situation.

Luckily, Jimmy Crowder came to the rescue. "Hey, man—how much did you make on that fifty-dollar bet?"

"She went off at even money, so I won fifty bucks."

"No kidding? Well, that's enough to buy *several* more rounds of drinks. Why don't you set yourself down here while I signal the bartender?"

"Oh, gosh, thanks so much! I'd love to join you." The fellow grabbed a chair nearby that had just been abandoned and dragged it over to the table. As he was about to sit down, he froze and looked at CJ, "Is this okay with you, ma'am? I don't want to impose on your party in any way."

Gallo smiled at Jimmy, and they both looked at CJ as she said,

"Uh, well . . . Yes, it's okay for you to join us, as long as Mister Gallo doesn't mind."

"Oh, hell, I don't mind. This is getting really intriguing."

Jimmy rose and walked to the bar to order another round, and Gallo introduced himself to the young gentleman who couldn't take his eyes off Cicely. The fellow's name was Elliot Monkmeyer. A recent graduate of Rensselaer Polytechnic Institute, he worked as an engineer for his father's software development company. He was an avid horse racing fan because his family owned a vacation home on Saratoga Lake, and he spent summers in the area since he was a child.

"Yeah, I've always been interested in math and science and computers, but I really love coming to the track every summer. My parents and I get all dressed up and go to the clubhouse to watch the races. We don't own any horses, but we pretend like we do. Those are my parents right over there at the bar."

Gallo looked over at a man and woman beaming from ear to ear and waving in his direction. "They know who you are, Mister Gallo, and like to bet on your horses. Maybe you could say hello to them a little later?"

"Sure, I'd be happy to," he said as he smiled and waved back to the happy couple. "So, CJ, why don't you tell our boy Elliot something about yourself?"

Slowly and with great reticence, CJ began to describe her life to her new acquaintance: "I grew up in Southern California near Santa Anita racetrack and I began to ride horses when I was only six years old. I've loved horses since I was little and I really connect with them." She toyed with the glass of ginger ale in her hand. "My dad is the president of a bank, but he also owns a thoroughbred investment business and that's how I became interested in becoming a jockey." She squirmed a bit in her chair, but when she thought about what to say next, a brief smile came to her face. "I have a wonderful mom. I love her very much. She's always worried about me because of the dangers associated with racing. I think my mom would rather have me go to college full time, but she understands I have to be around horses, so she gives me the freedom I need."

As CJ spoke, she looked down at the table, with an occasional glance up at the gentlemen sitting across from her. Whenever she did look at him, he offered a warm and friendly smile, as though he was concentrating on every word that came out of her mouth. Gradually, Gallo noticed she began looking at him more and more until she said something that surprised everyone seated around her. "Elliot, you have a kind face. You must be a very nice man. I like your face."

Jimmy and Gallo exchanged startled looks while Elliot appeared to be at a complete loss for words. Finally, he began to stammer, "When I was watching you in the paddock today getting in the saddle, I just thought, *wow—she is so beautiful.*"

"Were you talking about CJ or Hit the Bid?" joked Jimmy.

"Uh, well, both—but mostly CJ."

"Nice recovery, Elliot," said Gallo.

Elliot's face went from flushed to bright red, now that he had been embarrassed by his lack of social grace. CJ didn't seem to follow the body language and sarcastic conversation going on between the three men that surrounded her at the table. Somehow, she sensed that Elliot liked her, and she was surprised to find that she liked him. Not in the way she liked horses, but in a way she had never experienced before. She stole a glance at Elliot at the same moment he was focusing on her, and his smile gave her a feeling of happiness. Happiness was something she struggled with all her life. She knew she was happy when she was on a horse and she had learned to be happy when her mother held her in her arms. Recently, she experienced happiness and a sense of camaraderie when Ritchie and Jimmy were giving her a bad time. But happiness generated by attraction or proximity to a male was something she only knew from movies or television shows. She had never actually felt that way before and this emotion caught her by surprise.

The bartender waved at Gallo, pointing toward the dining room, indicating that the restaurant owner had set aside a coveted table on a busy night. Gallo apologized to Elliot for cutting their discussion short, but they had to sit down for dinner. "Will you be around for more races this summer?"

"Yes, sir, I'll be here every weekend. Our offices are just down the Northway near Albany, so I stay at the lake house on Saturday and Sunday."

"That's great. Just come by the backstretch area and ask for me; I'll give you a tour of the Oklahoma track area, and if it works out, you can sit with one of my owners in a box at the finish line. Who knows, maybe CJ will be a winner that day and you can come down to the winner's circle," he added with a wink.

"Oh, wow, that would be so cool. Thanks very much, Mister Gallo. I would love to have that opportunity." Elliot stood there uncomfortably for a second and then turned to CJ. "Miss Jamieson, would you mind saying hello to my parents? They were *really* impressed by your performances. I know they would love to meet you."

Meeting new people was something CJ generally avoided, but the level of unease that normally accompanied introductions just wasn't there tonight. "Yes, Mister Monkmeyer. I'd like to meet them."

Elliot led the way to the bar where his parents were seated, followed by CJ, Gallo, and Jimmy. As they walked, Jimmy put his arm around Gallo and whispered, "I used to think she was weird, but now I get it. It's just like training a horse."

Gallo laughed. "Jimmy, you're a genius."

CHAPTER EIGHT

When Gallo, Jimmy, and CJ finished dinner, they thanked the owner of the Brook Tavern for accommodating them and then said goodbye to the bartender and the Monkmeyer family, who were still seated at the bar enjoying the evening. Gallo noticed that the lady jockey and the computer engineer made eye contact several times on their way out, and it was obvious to everyone present that something romantic was taking place. He also sensed that she wanted to speak to Elliot but didn't have the courage or confidence to say anything. As Gallo followed CJ and Jimmy out the front door, he looked back towards the bar and observed a smile on the face of the young man that rivaled the breadth of the first turn at Churchill Downs.

Gallo drove Jimmy back to the dormitory at the stables and then headed for Ludlow Street, where CJ was staying. The dinner conversation had been much livelier than Gallo had anticipated, primarily because CJ was more talkative than she had ever been before. It seemed that an encounter with a smitten young man her age had generated an uptick in her attitude about things that didn't involve horses. Now that they were alone in his truck, she had become quiet once again, and Gallo felt compelled to apologize about something he'd said back in the bar.

"You know, CJ, I joked earlier tonight about being an expert at helping people who had suffered from traumatic brain damage. It was a joke that you didn't seem to understand. I hope I didn't offend you. You give me plenty of opportunities to needle you based on your many strange behaviors, but it's not right for me to specifically mention your injury. You've been dealt a tough hand in life, and it isn't because of anything you did to deserve it. I'm sorry if I made you feel bad or if you felt I was making fun of you. As we've gotten to know each other and share our love for horses, I feel like we've really become friends."

It was so dark, Gallo couldn't see her face, but from the melancholy in her voice, he could tell she was sad. "I really don't remember anything in my life prior to my accident. But after I got out of the hospital, I always knew I was different from other kids—I just didn't understand *why*. I didn't understand why I wasn't accepted by other children if I got dragged off to a birthday party or something like that. I could see these kids having fun with one another and being loved by their parents. It seemed so normal to them. I used to think they were way up there in the clouds, and I was down here in the *dirt*." She said it with a partial laugh, something that was almost normal—but Gallo could hear, woven into the timbre of her voice, that she still suffered daily from this tragedy. "I just couldn't make sense of anything. I felt ashamed because my brain didn't seem to work the way everyone else's did. I couldn't concentrate very well or enjoy anything I was doing. Then, one day, I discovered horses." A sense of happiness re-emerged as she spoke. "My mom would do anything to get me around a pony or a horse, and I gradually understood that this was her way of showing me she loved me. I didn't seem to understand the direct bond of love between a mom and a child that other kids experienced. But when I was able to understand love, I was able to love my mom back. Somehow, when it came to my mother, I got it. I'm so lucky to have her. I want to make her proud of me."

"I'm sure she's proud of you, CJ. Your mom is a very special woman."

"How do you know that? You just met her a little over a week ago."

"Well, I'm very perceptive with women, kind of like you are with horses." Gallo thought it best to leave his history with CJ's mother out of the conversation; he just didn't know how to explain it. "How about your dad? He seems like a really nice guy and someone who has your best interests at heart."

CJ waited a few seconds, considering her answer. "My dad is a good guy. He's been so supportive—you know, paying for my treatments, education, and horse riding. I'm very grateful, but I don't have a close relationship with my dad like I have with my mom. The thing that's weird is . . . I've been able to bring you and Jimmy into my life easier than my own father. Isn't that strange? Isn't that a bad thing?"

"Look, CJ . . . You're a really bright young lady, and you've got a great heart, just like Hit the Bid. You'll figure this out because you're smart and because you're a good person. You're still preparing for the Kentucky Derby of life. Right now, you're training for endurance and you're not ready to breeze near the rail to improve your speed. You just have to work yourself through this in a logical fashion. You'll get there at your own pace; don't exhaust yourself before you get to the finish line."

Gallo pulled over in front of CJ's apartment. As she was about to get out of the truck, she hesitated. "Can I ask you a question, Mister Gallo?"

"Sure, what is it?"

"When Elliot came over to the table tonight to get my autograph, would it have been different if I was a normal girl? I mean, would a regular girl immediately like this guy and want to go out with him? Would there have been an instant romantic connection? I'm not really sure how I feel."

Gallo laughed. "That's a tough question to answer, CJ. It's impossible to say what makes a man and a woman connect, what makes them fall in love. Sometimes people that seem to be perfect for one another just can't make it work, while another couple with plenty of differences may be able to develop a love and friendship that lasts a lifetime. Sometimes—" He found himself pausing to think about that porch swing…the sound of summer crickets laced with Channing's laughter. "Sometimes," he went on, "you can fall in love with someone as a teenager and not see them again for twenty years, and then, if your paths happen to cross again, you find that love is still there. It just doesn't go away."

Gallo took a moment to think about what he had just said and then refocused on his young friend. "I wouldn't ponder this issue too much if I were you, and I certainly wouldn't characterize yourself as not being *normal*. Hit the Bid and T-three think you're better than normal. They think you're spectacular when you're in the saddle. I don't think you're normal; I think you're *extraordinary*. Don't put yourself down. There's something special about you, and you just have to learn how to harness the superpowers that you have."

CJ smiled. "So, you think I'm Superwoman?"

"Yeah, I think you're Superwoman."

"Does Mister Jimmy think I'm Superwoman?"

"No, not until you can consistently bring him a coffee with the right amount of sugar, and you learn not to annoy him around the horses."

"Thanks, Mister Gallo. See you tomorrow."

"You got it, kid."

CHAPTER NINE

The third Saturday of the Saratoga meet was a busy day for Gallo and the employees of Stone Fence Farms. While the next races for Hit the Bid and Tackle Tim Tom were still weeks away, three of the other horses Gallo trained were entered in races to be run that day. For each race, the grooms would coordinate the preparation of the thoroughbreds and the task of parading them from the stables over to the paddock.

Gallo's focus was on consulting with each owner and jockey before the race to lay out a strategy for the competition. One horse was running in a claiming race, another was scheduled for an allowance race, and a four-year-old mare that he'd been training for the last two years was in a Grade Three stakes race.

Two of the horses were being ridden by jockeys that were represented by John McCann, but the mare in the stakes race would be guided by Jacinto Robles. Gallo had agreed to let Robles ride the mare as payback for replacing him on Hit the Bid with CJ.

Ten races would be run at the track that day, and the second race was the claiming race. In accordance with the rules on claiming races, a licensed owner at Saratoga agreed to pay twenty-five thousand dollars for the horse prior to the start of the race. When the race was over, the title to the animal would be transferred to the new owner, and a new trainer would replace him and Stone Fence Farms. Gallo was sorry to see the horse go, especially since he ran well and finished third. However, he understood the importance of claiming races. This type of race provided financial liquidity in the racehorse market for thoroughbreds with average talent and owners who didn't have the deep pockets of large corporate farms or syndicates.

The fifth race on the card that day was the allowance race. Ritchie entered a two-year-old gelding that had won in the past but hadn't registered a win in his last five starts. Based on that criteria, five pounds were removed from the saddle, and the lighter weight theoretically would give him an advantage against the other horses in the race. The theory *almost* worked as the horse got a great ride from the jockey and managed to finish in second place. The owners were happy with the performance, even though they didn't get to visit the winner's circle. Gallo was pleased with the result and assured the horse's owners that the gelding had a decent shot at more wins in the future if he continued to train as well as he had at Saratoga.

The most important race of the day for Stone Fence Farms, however, was the stakes race. This race was designated as a Grade Three race due to the size of the purse and the successful records of the entries. The mare would start from the number four slot in the starting gate, and the race was to be run on the grass turf track. All the contestants would be mares or fillies that were at least three years old. At one-and-a-half miles, this was a long race, and Gallo had been training the mare to run longer distances. She had been a good performer in shorter races but just didn't have the athletic speed of Hit the Bid or the powerful burst of speed that Tackle Tim Tom possessed. However, he'd determined that she had excellent endurance and started to train her with more long gallops and fewer breezes. Today, he would find out if his strategy would work.

In the paddock, he met with a married couple that owned the mare, as well as their jockey, Robles. They watched as Jimmy walked the horse around the walking ring and then brought her to the saddling area to be prepared for the race. Gallo helped Jimmy secure the saddle, place the bit in the mare's mouth, and adjust the reins. The horse seemed calm but was also alert. She knew what was about to happen and appeared ready to go.

Gallo gave Robles his instructions. "Just let her run at a pace where she seems relaxed. I don't want you to lose touch with the leaders, but you don't have to push her over the first eight furlongs. When you've got a half-mile to go, you can gradually move her up near the front. I think she's got the gas in the tank to get there. At that point, let the other mares try to beat her. She should be able to maintain her speed right to the finish."

"Okay, Mister Gallo, I'll give her a smart ride."

Robles shook hands with the owners, and Jimmy gave him a boost onto the saddle. Lined up numerically by saddle number, the horses followed the outrider down a wide dirt lane toward the track. As they moved out of the paddock area, the iconic "Call to the Post" was blown by a trumpeter in a red jacket, white riding pants, and black riding boots.

Hundreds of patrons lined both sides of the lane and shouted out encouragement to the jockeys as the thoroughbreds walked on to the track. Gallo ushered the two owners back to the clubhouse and joined them in a reserved box near the finish line. He could tell that the owners were nervous, but he assured them that their horse was well prepared and had a good shot at winning the race. He overheard them talking about the financial implications of a win, which may have also contributed to their nervous state. The purse was $200,000, with $120,000 going to the winner. Ten percent of that amount would be paid to Stone Fence Farms and another ten percent was due to the jockey. That would leave $96,000 for the owners. Plenty of money to be used for future training, feeding, and stabling costs. If they won this race, they would be one of the few owners in the business to actually make a profit on a horse.

Once all the horses were in the starting gate, the crowd of nearly thirty thousand began to focus on the race that was about to commence. The steward charged with starting the race hit a switch that released the electromagnetic gates on each stall and nine thoroughbreds sprinted from their enclosures. Gallo had witnessed thousands of races over his lifetime, but he never got tired of the excitement and symphony of noise generated by the bettors and railbirds who cheered on their favorites.

The horses began the race by running the long straightaway in front of the grandstands and the clubhouse. The crowd was vocal at this point, but still at the lowest volume level for the contest. After the thoroughbreds ran around the clubhouse turn, the pack began to stretch out, and the people in the stands tried to focus on the horse they were rooting for. As the contenders moved down the back stretch, the voices got louder as it became clear that victory was in doubt for the horses trailing the pack, but the speedsters at the front were still in the hunt for a win. The cheering increased even further as this group of talented mares ran through the far turn. The step-up in noise confirmed to Gallo that his horse was approaching the point where the final half-mile of the race would begin. Gallo watched as Robles used the turn section of the track to squeeze the mare between a horse on the rail and another horse that was drifting to the right. At the top of the stretch, when they turned for home, Robles found himself in the middle of two other racers who were all running neck-and-neck to the finish line.

With just one furlong to go, Gallo focused on the thoroughbreds running on either side of his horse. A trained eye, developed from years of watching thoroughbreds run, told him that the competitors were gasping for air. But Gallo's training method with Jacinto's horse seemed to be paying off; she was still running with powerful strides. Gallo stood a little straighter when he saw the jockeys to Robles's right and left going for their whips—but it was clear, very quickly, that their horses were unable to accelerate.

The noise generated by the thousands of excited fans was

deafening as the three mares continued to sprint together, stride for stride. With just one hundred meters to go, Robles snapped the whip on the mare's rump, imploring her to keep up her speed. The lady did not disappoint—she maintained her speed through the finish line, while the other two mares faltered in the last several strides of the race.

She won the race by a length.

Gallo breathed a sigh of relief, but also felt a sense of accomplishment. He'd worked hard to develop the endurance of this horse, and she was a cooperative thoroughbred to train. Now that she had won a stakes race as a four-year-old, her future as an attractive brood mare was significantly enhanced.

After the race, Gallo joined the owners, the jockey, and the horse in the winner's circle for a photograph, and a presentation of a trophy paid for by the race sponsors. There were smiles all around the winner's circle—but in the stands, most patrons ripped up their betting tickets and threw them on the ground with disgust. Ultimately, every race ends the same way—there are far more losing bettors than winning bettors.

Once his ceremonial duties were complete, Gallo turned the mare over to Jimmy, who took her for a cooldown walk, a thorough examination, a body wash, and a dinner of hay and oats. He then began to make his way out of the clubhouse towards the paddock, where he was hoping to meet a couple of old friends for a few beers at the Paddock Tent. As he was about to go down the escalator, someone called out his name and he turned to see Channing Jamieson waving at him. A beat later, she was standing before him—smiling and giving him a hug.

"Congratulations, Ritchie!" Her eyes danced—he almost couldn't look away. "You've had a pretty good day. Your horses performed well."

"Thanks, Channing. I'm pleased with how things have worked out. What are you up to? Is Crawford here with you?"

"No, he had to go to California for some business meetings, but I hope to have him back in Saratoga in a week or so." Channing paused for a second, the rustling of patrons making a mass exodus filling up her silence. "Say, have you got a minute? I've got something I'd like to discuss with you."

Gallo walked Channing to a bench that looked out on the Saratoga Racetrack grounds. Several large tents painted with red and white stripes hosted businesses that sold food, works of art, clothing, and other merchandise specific to thoroughbred racing. A large crowd meandered around the tents and the green and white wooden buildings, where tellers accepted money to be bet on each race. In the distance, they could see the paddock, walking ring, and saddling sheds where the horses were prepared prior to stepping onto the track. Spread throughout the area were tall Adirondack pines, and maple and oak trees providing shade and a country fair atmosphere to this annual summer ritual in upstate New York.

"What's up?" he asked after a moment of taking in the scenery.

"I've been talking to CJ over the last few days, and it seems that she's struck up a friendship with a young man who lives here in the local area. I guess his parents own a house on the lake and he works in Albany. She's been talking to him on the phone *every day*." Channing paused to look up at Gallo through her pinched brows, smiling but suspicious. "His name is Elliot, and I got the impression that you introduced him to CJ."

"Uh, well—not exactly. He came up to us in a restaurant and introduced himself. He was obviously very interested in your daughter, and she seemed to like him. He's a heck of a nice guy, Channing. I didn't know that the two of them have been communicating with one another, but I don't think there's anything nefarious going on here. They're probably just getting to know each other."

"Well, evidently, they have their first date set up for tonight. He's going to take her to dinner at the Saratoga National Clubhouse."

"That's great. Prime at Saratoga National is one of my favorite restaurants here in town. Its steaks are terrific."

"Ritchie," she said with a sigh—so like the way she used to say his name, all those years ago. "It's not the food that I'm concerned about. CJ has never had a boyfriend. She's never even had a real date. She's not prepared for social encounters like this."

"Look, Channing, you're her mom. You get to call the shots on this—it's not my business. But I have to tell you, I've seen CJ grow as a person over the three weeks I've known her. She seems to be thriving in this atmosphere and has started to really come out of her shell when it comes to dealing with people. She still does things that drive me and Jimmy nuts, but she's starting to figure it out when it comes to personal relationships. She's smart, and this friendship with a guy may be more intellectual than emotional. She's just trying to figure out how these things work."

Channing sat back and sighed; she had the look of a worried mother on her face. "I don't know. Sometimes she's so fixated on being in her comfort zone, it's difficult to communicate with her. If this young man doesn't understand *why* she talks or acts the way she does, he may get frustrated and just figure he doesn't want to see her again. I can tell she kind of likes this guy—which in and of itself is very unusual for her—but I'm afraid she might be hurt if he rejects her. She never went through that romantic boy stuff like most teenage girls. She was too busy riding horses." Channing was silent for a few moments while she gave some thought to the situation. "Does this fellow know that she suffered a traumatic brain injury as a child?"

Gallo shook his head. "I really don't know. I didn't tell him, and I'm not sure CJ would say anything about that. The evening we met Elliot and his parents, she seemed like a normal—but shy—young woman, so I'm guessing he doesn't know she struggles with this."

69

Channing reached out and took his hand. "Ritchie, I realize that this isn't your business or your responsibility, but would you do me a favor and talk to this young guy about CJ? Make sure he understands that the cause of her behavioral or communication issues is just the legacy of a terrible accident. She's not mentally ill or a weirdo—she's just a little different."

Gallo wasn't sure he should get so involved with another family's issues, but his growing affection for CJ made him sympathetic to this circumstance. "Okay, Channing, I'll talk to him. But I've got to tell you something—I'm not a doctor, and I don't know diddly-squat about how the brain is supposed to work in a twenty-year-old young lady. I just know that the more my guys and I treat her like a *normal* woman, like a member of our team who must measure up and do her part, the more *normal* she behaves. I know it's tough, but you can't be a helicopter parent for her entire life. You've given her a lot of freedom since she's been here at Saratoga, and I think it's paying off."

"Ritchie, I hope you're right. I'm so grateful for the interest you've taken in her, and I'm sorry for sticking you in the middle of this, but with Crawford not being here and my inherent worries as a mother . . . I just don't know how else to deal with this before things go too far and she gets hurt."

"No sweat. Elliot is probably here at the track, seeing as it's Saturday, and he normally hangs out in the clubhouse. I can find him if he's here, and I'll have a talk with him. Believe me, I won't let anything bad happen to her if I can possibly do anything to avoid it."

They stood, and Channing gave Gallo a hug. "I'm sorry to seem like an overprotective mother, but I've spent the last fifteen years being her most important advocate. I'll never give up on her or prevent her from growing as a person, even if it scares me to death. I know how fast those horses are moving on that track and how much they weigh. I've seen my share of accidents, and I pray for her safety every time she races. I wish there was an easier way to do this, but her savant skill with horses gives her a unique channel to emerge as her own woman." She smiled at him, still holding his hand. "I guess when you put it in perspective, a smitten young man is probably not as dangerous as an out-of-control stallion."

"Yeah, well, it kind of depends on the situation. She's pretty good at handling stallions—let's hope she has the same talent for handling a guy." Gallo released her hand and gave her a pat on the shoulder as she began to walk away. "I'll call you later tonight and give you an update on my discussion with Elliot Monkmeyer."

Channing only nodded and smiled, leaving him to find Elliot. *If I was a young guy, in love with a beautiful female jockey, and I knew she was going to ride in the next race of the day, where would I find her?*

At the paddock, of course!

He left the clubhouse and walked to the paddock where the horses were being saddled for the final race on the card. Since he was wearing his photo I.D. and access pass on a lanyard around his neck, the security guards allowed him immediate entry into the secure area. He walked into the treed section in front of the saddling stalls and scanned the faces of several hundred people leaning on the fence watching the horses, owners, trainers, and jockeys. Off to his left, he could see CJ entering the paddock accompanied by a security marshal. She was making her way to the number seven stall, where her mount for the race was being saddled. He returned his gaze to the crowd until he spotted Elliot leaning over the fence, completely focused on the lady jockey.

He walked over to him and said, "Elliot, how you doin' buddy? Looks like you're checking out our favorite jockey."

"Oh, hey, Mister Gallo. Yeah, I wanted to watch her mount up before she hits the track. It's really nice to see you again."

"Look, once they start the parade to the post, let's go upstairs to the Club Pavilion Bar and watch the race together. I have something I'd like to discuss with you."

Elliot agreed to the proposal, and as the contestants for the last race filed out of the paddock toward the dirt oval, the pair found two seats in the clubhouse bar where they had a good view of the race-track. They each ordered a beer, and once the time was right, Gallo initiated the conversation.

"So," he began, taking a swig of his IPA. "I have it on good author-ity that you will be taking CJ out tonight on a date."

Elliot gave Gallo a sheepish grin. "We've been talking on the phone for the last couple of weeks, and it looked like tonight was a good time for us to get together. I'm only here on the weekends and she doesn't ride until the fourth race tomorrow, so she didn't have a problem with staying out a little later than usual. I didn't think to call you and let you know what we were doing. I hope you don't have a problem with this. . . ."

"Nah, you're an adult, and she's a big girl. I don't have any prob-lem with her going out with a local guy. I just want to be sure I un-derstand your intentions. CJ is very important to me, and her mother is a close friend."

Elliot became very animated. "Oh, gee, Mister Gallo—I could *never* have any bad intentions toward CJ! She's so sweet and nice and talented. . . . I would never do anything disrespectful. Honestly, Mister Gallo, I'm going to be a gentleman all the way. I just want to get to know her!"

"Okay, Elliot, calm down. I'm not accusing you of anything. I just want you to be aware of something that's very important, if you're going to have a relationship with CJ."

Gallo went on to explain that CJ suffered a serious injury as a child that resulted in traumatic brain damage. The injury left her with behavioral problems that impaired her ability to communicate and relate to other people. However, the trauma to her brain also enhanced her ability to communicate with horses, and her obsession with the animals provided a pathway for her to grow as an individual and function normally in society. Despite the obvious confidence and poise she demonstrated riding racehorses, in her personal life, she struggled with the process of building relationships with other people.

"When you spoke to her on the phone, didn't you notice that she communicates in an awkward fashion?"

Elliot shrugged his shoulders. "When I talk to her, she seems like she's shy. Normally, *I'm* the one acting shy around somebody I think is cool. I know what it's like to be on that end of a conversation, so when I speak to her, I try to make her feel comfortable. I want her to understand that I'm really interested in her as a person and that it's a real privilege for me to be able to talk to her. She's really beautiful, so I'm sure most guys are after her because of her looks, but . . . that's not me."

Gallo smiled and momentarily placed his head in his hands. Serving as a personal relationship coach was not his area of expertise. "Look, Elliot—I just want you to understand that she is a little different. Let me put it to you this way, what do you see when you look in a mirror?"

"I see me."

"Yeah, yeah, I know you see *you*, but I mean . . . do you see a tall, handsome stud with movie star looks that women just drool over?"

Elliot slowly answered, "No, I see a portly guy with glasses who is more comfortable with computers and numbers than he is with people." Elliot paused—apparently to think more about the question—and then, with more determination, he added, "I also see a guy from a great family who loves his parents and is loyal to his friends. I see a guy who is honest and thoughtful and who tries to treat people the way I wish people would treat me. I'm a good guy, Mister Gallo."

"That's right. You see the guy in the mirror—but you also see the *real guy* behind that face in the mirror. Now, what do you think CJ sees when she looks in a mirror?"

Elliot smiled. "She sees one of the most beautiful girls in the world."

"Okay, she's a great looking young lady, but just like you, she knows that the image is superficial. *Unlike* you, she isn't sure who that person is behind the pretty face. There are some spaces that aren't filled in yet when it comes to defining who she really is. You understand who and what you are, you know what's behind the face. She doesn't. Do you see where I'm going with this?"

"Yes, sir, I think so."

"Look, I'm no expert on psycho-babble stuff like this, but one thing I can tell you about CJ is that she's capable of moving forward in life and becoming a more rounded person. It isn't easy for her, and she doesn't do it quickly, but she can make slow and steady progress if she's patient and if she challenges herself. She needs a friend that can help her do that. She needs a guy who can help her fill in the blanks."

Elliot took a moment to ponder what he'd just heard. "So, what do I do?"

"Jeez, Elliot, I don't know the answer to that. I guess you just treat her with kindness and understanding but still treat her like she's a normal woman. Hell, Jimmy and I give her a hard time every day. The more we treat her like she's one of the guys, the happier she seems to be. Now, I don't recommend you treat her like she's one of the guys but . . . Well, you know what I'm saying."

"Yes, sir, I think so. Even though I tend to think in terms of numbers and logic trees, I'm pretty good at being nice to people. I've never had a real girlfriend before. I guess this is my chance to see if kindness works with women."

"Well, women are definitely not computers. Love isn't visible or measurable, and it can't be quantified. I don't think your training as a software engineer is going to be very helpful. You must lead with your heart but be thoughtful and patient with regard to her actions. Just be a good guy, and it'll work out."

The two men heard the bell go off in the starting gate, and the crowd came alive as the horses sprinted down the track. Gallo and Elliot watched intently as CJ rode her horse to a fourth-place finish, just out of the money. Elliot pulled out his para-mutual ticket, tore it up and threw it on the floor. "I was hoping that was going to pay for dinner."

CHAPTER TEN

E lliot's heart rate increased as he drove down Ludlow Street.
He was already sweating too much—it was a problem for him, the nervous sweating—so he cranked the air conditioning in his father's BMW up to a level that generated a swirling blast of frigid air straight to his face.

As he pulled up to CJ's apartment, he could see her standing on the steps waiting for him. She was wearing an Iris short sleeve flare dress from Ann Taylor, and her shoes were Jaida flats from Jimmy Choo. The color of the shoes matched the floral pattern of the dress. Her hair and makeup were perfect.

Elliot got out of the car and started up the walk toward the front of the house. CJ stepped forward and met him halfway. "Hi, CJ. You look really beautiful tonight."

"I know, thank you for saying that. You look really beautiful tonight, also."

Elliot laughed. "Thanks, no one ever referred to me as beautiful before."

"Well, I've learned recently that when a man compliments you, it's important to compliment him back. Besides, I like your face."

"Cool! Are you ready to go? We've got a reservation for seven o'clock."

"I am ready, but first I think we should set some rules for our date."

"Rules?"

"Yes. I did some research on a website that offers advice on successful dating, and it recommended that first dates have rules. So, here's the first rule: I don't want to discuss my condition during the date; I just want to act like a normal girl."

Elliot decided to play it safe. "What condition are you talking about?"

"Well, if you haven't figured it out already, I have some issues. I suffered a bad accident as a kid that resulted in damage to my brain. I've tried all my life to recover from that, and I seem normal most of the time, but I do struggle with personal relationships. I don't make friends as easily as I would like, and I don't communicate with people as well as I do with horses, but I'm really working on it."

"No problem. You seem perfectly normal to me. I don't need any explanations."

"Thank you. Now we can move on to rule number two, which is that you will be the lead on the date. In the movies and on television, it always seems that dates are more successful if the man is the leader."

"Okay," Elliot said with a chuckle. "I think I can handle that."

"Great! Now rule number three is that we have to take it slow on physical intimacy."

Elliot began to fidget and the smile left his face. "Like . . . What do you mean by *physical intimacy*?"

"When I was little, I didn't like having people touch me. Then I found I loved the touch of horses, and after that, I really enjoyed hugging my mom. The crazy thing is that I now seem to be comfortable when certain men touch me. The day I won the American Oaks, Mister Gallo put his arm around me in the winner's circle and told me he was proud of me. I really like it when he puts his arm around me. It makes me happy. And when Mister Jimmy thinks I've done a good job exercising our horses, he'll give me a high five. He can be a crotchety old guy sometimes, and he tells me to get out of his way—but when he smiles and tells me I did a good job? It makes me feel good."

The smile returned to Elliot's face. "CJ, I will be a perfect gentleman tonight. We'll just take it slow."

CJ looked directly into Elliot's eyes and smiled. Elliot thought that he'd never had a happier moment in his life. "I only have one more rule: If I go to the ladies' room and it seems like I've been gone for a long time, it isn't because I've left the building or because I'm sick, it's just that sometimes when I'm in a crowded or frenetic place, I need some alone time. I'm going to try really hard not to do that tonight because it isn't fair to you. I want to make this night about you, not about me."

"Are there any other rules?"

"No, that's it."

CJ stepped toward Elliot and took his arm. They turned, and he walked her to the car and opened the door so she could get in. When she sat in the passenger seat, she smiled at him through the windshield as he made his way to the driver's side.

Within ten minutes, they pulled into the clubhouse at Saratoga National Golf Club. Elliot left the car with the valet under the large stone portico that sheltered the main entrance to the building. Once inside, the maître d asked if they preferred to sit in the dining room or outside on the veranda overlooking the eighteenth green. CJ asked Elliot to make that decision since he was the lead on the date; he chose the veranda. Once seated, they ordered tea and began to have a conversation that allowed them to learn more about one another. They didn't talk about computer software or horses, but instead addressed various topics outside of their chosen professions. Since Elliot's life experiences were much broader than CJs, he was often answering her questions about places he had been and the things he enjoyed doing.

"This golf course is so beautiful," she said. "Do you play golf, Elliot?"

"Yeah, I do. I'm actually pretty good at it since I started playing with my dad when I was only seven or eight. We usually play here at Saratoga National once a month, but we also belong to a country club down near Albany where we live."

"I think I would like to play golf," said CJ. "It's a game you can play by yourself. It must be wonderful to walk along in the evening, just enjoying the view and being outdoors. Then, when you want to be with someone else, you can play the game as a group. I like having those options."

"Well, maybe next weekend I'll bring you over here one morning, give you a quick lesson, and then let you hit balls on the driving range. Who knows? Maybe you're a natural."

"Thank you, Elliot. That would be fun."

Elliot was delighted to find that talking with CJ was much easier than he anticipated. She was an attentive listener, and when she did respond to something he said, she spoke in a clear and direct manner. There wasn't any subtlety with her—she said just what she thought, which he appreciated. Most women were confusing or impossible to read, he'd found. But not CJ.

Elliot noticed from time to time that other diners seated near them would look at CJ. He figured they were impressed by her good looks, or they could be fans who recognized her. Her picture and awkward interviews had been all over the local media for the last few weeks. He was so *lucky* to be the guy she was on a date with tonight. He'd never been at a social event where other people envied his situation. The thing that made this even more rewarding was the fact that, so far, they seemed to truly enjoy being with one another.

The couple finished their meal by sharing a decadent dessert. "I'm going to have to jog an extra half mile tomorrow before I go the track," said CJ. "I'm usually a few pounds lighter than the male jockeys. With the weight allowance I get as an apprentice rider, I think it gives me a bit of an advantage."

"Well, you look pretty good to me, CJ. I wouldn't lose too much sleep over a small piece of cake. Besides, you're eating it so quickly, it doesn't look like your guilt is overriding your enjoyment!"

He was glad to see her reaction to that comment was a devilish laugh. She held still when he reached across the table to wipe a speck of frosting from her chin. "There you go–now you look perfect."

After he'd paid the bill, they stood and walked down the veranda towards the eighteenth green. Dusk had collapsed over the landscape, painting the sky periwinkle. It was a comfortable August evening and they could hear the cicadas singing on the golf course. Elliot wasn't ready for the date to be over. "Do you want to take a little walk around the grounds? It's a beautiful night."

"Sure," said CJ. As they started down a golf cart path in the direction of the driving range, CJ reached out and took Elliot's hand. They smiled at one another and then walked along in silence.

As the darkness drew near, Elliot retrieved his car from the valet and drove back to CJ's apartment. He walked her to the door, and once again, the butterflies in his stomach started doing aileron rolls. He had no idea how to handle a good night kiss.

CJ stood on the second step leading up to the porch and turned around. They were now standing eye to eye—even though he was eleven inches taller than she was—when she asked him a question. "Elliot, have you kissed many girls?"

"Who—me? Oh yeah, I've kissed a ton of girls . . . Well, you know—not a *ton*, but a few. Uh, actually, I'm not that experienced at kissing."

"Nor am I. In fact, I've never romantically kissed a guy in my whole life. Until recently, I never really thought about it. But now I think about it all the time."

"What made you get interested in kissing?"

"I saw your kind face that night at the Brook Tavern, and I just thought you were very kissable."

"Really?"

"Yup, so now we're here face to face, and you need to put your arms around my waist while I place my arms around your neck."

Elliot did what he was told and gently pulled her close to him. He was amazed at how petite she was. She didn't seem to have a waist, but he could tell she had breasts when her body touched his chest. CJ wrapped her arms around him and moved her face within an inch of his. "What are you thinking right now, Elliot?"

"I think that you're amazing—and I really, *really*, like you."

"That's good, because it gives me the ability to tell you that I really like you also. When another person tells me exactly what they're thinking, I don't have to guess. Which is helpful. I've spent a lot of my life in my own little world. I'm used to being alone, even if I'm physically near other people. Right now—right at this moment—I'm in a little world with you, and I love not being alone."

CJ placed her lips on Elliot's, and they kissed softly for several seconds. They smiled at one another and kissed again, this time with more passion and energy.

"Was that okay?" asked Elliot.

"It was *more* than okay—it was precious."

CJ gave her suitor a peck on the cheek and released her grip on his neck. "I better get to bed. I've got to jog a longer distance tomorrow, and I'm supposed to work Hit the Bid and T-three before I ride in the fourth race of the day. Besides, I need to go on the computer and research what you do after you start kissing. I know it eventually leads to sex, but I've had a lot of religious training in my life, and I think I'm *supposed* to be a virgin on my wedding night. I really need to determine how best to run this race."

"Okay, when you figure it out, let me know. I'm up for anything!"

CHAPTER ELEVEN

The eighteenth hole at Saratoga National Golf Club is a 412-yard par four from the championship tees. Its large, oblong-shaped green is bordered by Owl Pond on the east side, and a slope extending from the clubhouse veranda to the green on the west edge of the putting surface. As Gallo and John McCann approached the green, they smiled at one another.

"Great shot, Rich. We're all square going into the last hole, so if I miss my putt and you make the short putt for birdie, you'll win. How much did we bet on this? Wasn't it five bucks?"

"Nice try—it's *ten* bucks, big spender!"

The caddies handed the two men their putters, and McCann rolled a beautiful putt that just lipped out of the cup. He tapped in for par. Gallo looked at his putt from above and below the hole and then addressed the ball.

"That looks like a slippery downhiller to me," said McCann. "But, hey, no pressure."

Gallo looked at his competitor and smiled before refocusing and stroking a well-measured putt that dove right into the jar. "I guess I'm ten dollars richer, Mister McCann, so I can afford to buy you a beer."

After tipping the caddies, Gallo and John walked up the steps to the veranda behind the clubhouse and headed for the outdoor bar. As they were about to place an order with the bartender, they heard someone calling their names and turned to see Crawford Jamieson waving at them from a table.

"Hey, Ritch and John! Come over and join us. I need to buy you guys a drink."

"Thanks, Crawford—don't mind if we do," said McCann.

When they reached the table, Crawford introduced them to three other people sitting there, one of whom was Channing Jamieson. This was the first time Gallo had been with both of CJ's parents at the same time, and he immediately felt a bit uncomfortable. When he shook her hand, they traded tentative smiles. "Nice to see you again, Mrs. Jamieson."

Crawford was in a jovial mood as he explained to his guests what a great trainer Gallo was and how grateful he was to John McCann for getting CJ licensed as a jockey and guiding her career. Gallo was a bit surprised at his amiable manner. His partners at Stone Fence Farms had advised Crawford that they would not sell Tackle Tim Tom, and the businessman's reaction to that news hadn't been particularly graceful. Nonetheless, the discussion around the table was lively and friendly.

Gallo decided he wasn't going to sit there for longer than the consumption of one beer. He tried not to look at Channing and sensed that she was also avoiding his gaze. It just didn't feel right, and he thought he would make his exit as soon as he could. Crawford, on the other hand, was happy and convivial, and he began to direct the discussion into the business side of the thoroughbred racing industry.

"You know, Ritchie, recently I was over in Dubai where I visited a sheikh who has a major investment in one of my limited partnerships. Believe it or not, this guy is the Prime Minister of the country and was one of the major underwriters of the Meydan Racecourse. You ever been there?"

"No, I've never been to Dubai, but I've heard that Meydan is a heck of a place."

"Oh, my God, you wouldn't believe it. Besides the most luxurious and beautiful horse racetrack in the world, it's a complete entertainment center. Hotels, restaurants, nightspots, tennis, golf, pools—you name it. Just off-the-charts fabulous."

McCann smiled. "We should go over there some time, Ritchie. Maybe I can beat you on that golf course."

"I doubt it," said Gallo.

Crawford continued to talk. "Anyway, this sheikh owns 80 percent of a limited partnership I formed that owns a horse named Tamerlane."

"Tamerlane? You own *Tamerlane*?" Asked John McCann.

"Well, actually, I only own 5 percent. The other 15 percent is owned by three other investors. The sheikh, however, initiated the interest in buying the horse when it was foaled in Ireland. As a yearling, we moved him to England to be trained and he began racing in France and Britain as a two-year-old. The big jump came when we brought the horse to Dubai. He won a big stakes race last January, and then he won the Dubai World Cup in March. That was a twelve-million-dollar purse. We really banked some money over that three-month period."

"Some guys in the business have told me that he's the fastest horse in the world," said Gallo. "I'm not sure how you can say that without racing in the States. Our purses may not be as big as the oil money available in Dubai, but we still have the best horses."

"That's an interesting statement, Mister Gallo. Would you be interested in proving it?"

"What do you mean?"

"Well, let's say that my partners and I brought Tamerlane to the United States after the Breeders' Cup races in November. We could bring him over in December, or even January of next year. At that point, we set up a match race with the top thoroughbred in the U.S. It would be a huge sports event that would attract horse racing fans all over the world." Crawford paused before adding, "Just imagine how broad the television audience for this race would be if the great stallion Tamerlane was racing against an American bred filly with a female jockey."

At that point, an inescapable thought came into Gallo's head: *No wonder you wanted to buy Hit the Bid.*

"Mister Jamieson, we have two big races to win this year before I can make a claim that Hit the Bid is the top horse in the United States. The Travers is this week, and if we win that race, we still have to win the Breeders' Cup Classic at Churchill Downs in November. As you've mentioned to me before, there are no guarantees in this business. We may not get there."

"Maybe not, Mister Gallo. But I have faith in you, and I have faith in Hit the Bid and her jockey. We're going to try and put a deal like this together. If you get to the finish line first at Saratoga and Churchill Downs, I hope you will consider my offer to participate in a match race that people will remember for years."

Gallo finished the last few ounces of his beer and stood up. "Well, I appreciate your offer, Mister Jamieson—but at this point, it's just speculation. Right now, I have to concentrate on the Travers Stakes, so if you will excuse me, I need to get back to the stables and my office. It was great meeting you folks and nice to see you again, Mrs. Jamieson." Gallo shook hands all around and made his way through the bar to the entrance foyer of the clubhouse.

Gallo stopped in the men's locker room and, while relieving himself, thought about what he had just heard: *This guy's had a plan to bring the Dubai stallion to the U.S. for a while and figured he could make more money on the horse by setting up match races with the best-known American thoroughbreds. If he owned Hit the Bid and T-three, he'd have a corner on two of the top racers in the business. Playing the female angle with Hit the Bid and CJ would be a no-brainer for a national television audience. This dude's a shrewd businessman. He's even willing to bet against his own daughter to make a buck.*

Gallo washed his hands and left the locker room, only to find

Channing Jamieson waiting for him in the lobby of the clubhouse. "Hi, Ritchie, I'm glad I caught you before you left the club."

"That's okay; what's up?"

"Well, I could tell you were a little uncomfortable sitting there with Crawford and myself. Candidly, I felt the same way. I want us to be friends, but it's not likely we will be able to spend a lot of time together. It just feels too awkward."

"Yeah, I get it. That's why I'm on my way out the door right now. Does your husband know that you and I had a relationship many years ago?"

"No, I've never told him or CJ, and I think it's best to keep it that way. In addition, I wanted to apologize on behalf of Crawford. I sense you're a bit put off by his interest in your horses. Crawford is always thinking like a businessman. That's just how he's wired—*everything* is viewed as an asset, a liability, or a source of revenue. He doesn't mean to be pushy or aloof. He just comes across that way sometimes."

Gallo laughed. "I know where he's coming from and understand that this is a business. We live a privileged life by participating in this sport—but people have to be paid for their time, and investors need to get a return on their capital if they can. When it comes to these horses, I have an emotional attachment to all the thoroughbreds I work with, especially to Hit the Bid and Tackle Tim Tom. They aren't just assets to me. They are my family and I want what's best for them. I realize that's a hopelessly romantic and naive viewpoint, which will probably prevent me from making the kind of money in this business I would otherwise make, but if I'm happy with the outcome, I'm good with that."

Channing smiled at Gallo. It was the smile he remembered from twenty years before. A smile on a face that went beyond beauty. A smile that told him he was looking at a woman who possessed a heart imbued with kindness, sincerity, and forgiveness. The smile of a loving mother and a loyal wife. A smile on a face that he was still in love with, all these years later. He wanted to embrace her, but that was an impossible reaction both physically and emotionally. It was time to leave.

"I better get going."

"Goodbye, Ritchie. Good luck in the Travers, and please take care of my daughter."

"I'll do my part—but trust me on this, thanks to a mom that never gave up on her daughter, she can take care of herself."

CHAPTER TWELVE

Crawford Jamieson slowly drove his Mercedes out of the parking lot of the Gideon Putnam Hotel and turned down the narrow entrance road that led back to South Broadway. Staring out the window on the passenger side, Channing took in the beauty of the tall Adirondack pines that lined the thoroughfare. They had just finished dinner in the main dining room of the hotel, where they were joined by CJ and her new boyfriend. Channing had arrived at the hotel two hours earlier with some degree of anxiety about meeting Elliot Monkmeyer. But now, surrounded by the beauty of Saratoga Spa State Park, she was happy and delighted that the evening unfolded so well. Her husband wasn't saying much, so Channing knew she was going to have to drag his opinions out of him.

"Tell me, Crawford, have you ever seen our daughter as happy as she was tonight? Other than when she is on the back of a horse, of course. She was completely engaged in the discussion at the table for two hours, and constantly traded smiles with this young fellow. No one could have sat there during that entire meal and thought that she was anything other than a young, intelligent, and ambitious young woman. She just sparkled. I've never seen her like that before. It was so great—so cool."

Crawford continued to drive along in silence. "Crawford, I'm *talking* to you! What did you think of Elliot? Talk to me!"

The man shrugged his shoulders and reluctantly opened up to his wife. "He seems like a nice enough kid. He's not the most handsome guy I've ever met, but he seems okay."

"*Okay*? Jesus, Crawford, give the kid a break. He adores our daughter, he's respectful and kind when he deals with her, he's able to make her laugh easily, he comes from a great family, and he's obviously very smart. Who the hell cares what he looks like? CJ thinks he's attractive, and that's all that matters."

"Yeah, I guess I just envisioned her with a more athletic, California type of guy. I agree he's smart, but he kind of lost me with all that computer mumbo jumbo."

"Well, I, for one, never thought she would end up with a guy at all, so to find someone who is so gentle and understanding with her is just a blessing."

Crawford continued to drive north in the direction of their condominium on Union Avenue, just east of Congress Park. Channing gazed out of her window, thinking out loud: "We took a big risk earlier this year, allowing her to get her jockey license and to ride at Santa Anita. As she started to get better and better results on the track, you could see her confidence increase, and her belief in herself improve. She even began to come out of her shell a bit when dealing with people. And then when we let her come to Saratoga and live on her own, we took another big risk, which seems to be paying off. The people she's met here, the horses she works with, and the entire situation seems to be allowing her to unfold more of her personality each week. Today I went down to the paddock to watch her mount up for the fifth race. As she walked from the jockey room to the paddock, people lined up at the fence and called out to her. Her first week at Saratoga, she made that walk with her head down and didn't say a word. Today, she smiled, signed some autographs, and talked to the people who had come down there just to see her. Most of them were women. Ever since she's been on national television, she's somewhat of a celebrity."

"Yeah, I didn't really like that piece they did on the nightly news. That was shown all over the country."

"What didn't you like about it? It was an endearing story about her affiliation with Ritchie and Hit the Bid. The Travers is tomorrow afternoon. It's the most widely anticipated race of the year because of the segment they did about her on a national network news show. The New York State Racing Commission must be ecstatic. The betting handle for the race is going to be off the charts."

"Well, I didn't like the fact that she admitted to the interviewer that she has a mental deficiency."

"Crawford, it's not an admission! She didn't do anything wrong. It's just a fact. She's still recovering from a traumatic brain injury, and she isn't ashamed to say so. Maybe the experience she's had will provide some hope to other disabled kids or their parents. We found something that's made a huge difference in her life; maybe other families can find something that will make a difference for their kids. I think she was very courageous to talk about it on a nationwide broadcast."

Crawford continued to drive along in silence, so Channing began to speak again. "I ran into a woman I know from New York who is in the publishing business. She said that *Sports Illustrated* has sent an editor, a writer, and a photographer here to cover the Travers. If CJ and Hit the Bid win, they will be on the cover of the magazine next week. Isn't that incredible? Who could have envisioned this seven months ago?"

"Yeah, I guess that's okay."

"Damn it, Crawford, what the hell is wrong with you? What's your problem with all this?"

Her husband turned from Broadway to Circular Street and then pulled over and parked. He turned off the engine and then looked over at his wife. "I'll tell you what my problem is. I see her growing and becoming a more complete person just like you do. But I see her doing it around *other people*. She's only known this guy Elliot for a few weeks, and they're crazy about each other. You go over to the backstretch and the paddock when she's with Gallo and his groom, Jimmy, the black guy—they're great buddies. They smile at one another, high five each other, and act like they are on the same football team."

"His name isn't 'Jimmy, the black guy,' it's Jimmy Crowder."

"Whatever! She still has a closer relationship with this groom than she does with me, and I'm her goddamned father! I *never* see her act that way with me." He was quiet for a moment, and Channing let the silence funnel in. He was right. "I'm the head of this family. She's my daughter, and it's my responsibility to make this right. I didn't want her becoming a jockey to begin with, but you and CJ talked me into it. Just think about this—she's in this mental state because she fell on her head, and we now have her working in a job where head and back injuries are common among jockeys. Does that make *any* sense? Why the hell couldn't we just keep her working with a psychiatrist while she went to school at Pomona full-time? Why can't she just act like a normal young woman?"

"Crawford—she's *not* a normal young woman. The only way she will ever be normal is if we allow her to grow as a person in a way that makes the most sense for her. I know this is tough for you. All her life, you've been there for her and me. CJ and I are so lucky to have you. But it's difficult to predict or anticipate how she will emerge from that shady world she used to live in and acclimate to the real world around her. You're a very personable and outgoing guy when you're in a business or social setting, but sometimes—" Channing stopped, simultaneously looking for the right words and wondering if she should say them at all. "Sometimes, when you're dealing with someone on an individual basis, you have the aura of a king who rules the roost. You don't make yourself emotionally available to her—and frankly, you're not always emotionally generous with me. Sometimes we can't quite figure out how to approach you or determine what it is you need from us. She's accomplished so much in the last six months; I don't understand why you can't be proud of her and appreciate the changes she has made in her life."

Crawford sat back in his seat and leaned his head against the headrest. "I don't want to have this argument again with you, Channing. I know I'm a really *terrible* guy because I don't slobber all over you with hugs and kisses each day, but I'm running a major bank and a successful business in a very risky thoroughbred racing industry. I have never shirked my responsibility to take care of you and CJ and our family. That's my job in life, and I think I do it well." The couple sat there in silence for several moments. Crawford clearly didn't want to continue this discussion, and Channing didn't know what to say. "Truth be told, I guess I'm a little envious of the relationship Gallo has with CJ. It seems like he's more of a father figure than I am."

Channing said nothing and patted her husband's hand.

"Ah, what the heck," said Crawford. "This thing with the young engineer is probably just a summer fling. I hear there's a lot of summer flings here in Saratoga."

"Yeah, that's what I've heard," said Channing. "It is a very romantic place."

Crawford started the car and resumed the drive toward their condo. "Man, look at these clouds. We may get some rain tonight. I hope we don't have a sloppy track for the Travers tomorrow."

"Me, either," said his wife.

———————◆———————

CJ and Elliot held hands as they walked to Elliot's car in the parking lot of the Gideon Putnam Hotel. They continued to engage in their two-hour marathon of smiling at one another, and began to discuss the dinner event they had just completed with her parents.

"Your mom is so cool. I really enjoyed talking to her—she is just so *personable*. You look a lot like her. You're both beautiful."

"Thanks, Elliot. I'm sure she thinks you are beautiful also. What did you think of my dad?"

"He's obviously a very smart and successful man. He carries himself like a CEO, which I think is neat. He was checking me out pretty well—hopefully, he thinks I'm a good guy and realizes how much I like you."

"Yes, my dad can seem tough at times, but he's been a wonderful father, and he takes good care of my mom and me."

Once inside Elliot's car, they began to make their way back to CJ's apartment on Ludlow Street. "Did you notice how many people at the restaurant recognized you? You're a local celebrity since the nightly news did that story about you and Mister Gallo. Of course, all the race fans around here know who you are, based on the success you've had on the track."

"I did notice that many people were staring. It makes me uneasy. I feel like I want to go to the ladies' room for some alone time, but I realize that I have to be more comfortable around people in social situations like this if I want to continue to be a jockey. I'm going to be in the public eye whether I like it or not, and I have to deal with it." She looked over at Elliot. "Do you know what helps me deal with it?"

"No, what?"

"My relationship with you. If I can have a great guy like you fall for me, I know I can relate to lots of other people. You give me confidence."

"Jeez, CJ. That's so nice of you to say that. No girl has ever told me I'm a great guy."

CJ smiled. "Then you've clearly been hanging around with the wrong girls."

They drove along for a while in silence. Elliot was feeling emotions for this young woman he had never felt before, and it was amazing to him how easily she accepted and cherished his attention and kindness.

"After tomorrow, there's only one week left of the meet here at Saratoga. I guess you're off to Churchill Downs at that point."

"Yes," said CJ. "We'll go back to California for a while, but then I plan to ride in Kentucky for about six weeks. If all goes well tomorrow in The Travers and next week with T-three in The Hopeful, I'll return to Churchill Downs again in November for the Breeders' Cup races. That would be a really cool experience."

Elliot said nothing, lost in thought. He'd been so swept up in this new romance, he hadn't allowed himself to consider what it'd look like once CJ left—and *of course* she would leave. He should've seen this coming.

"I'm going to really miss you, Elliot," CJ said, cutting the silence. "We must talk every day on the phone and use Skype to see each other. Do you think you can come and visit me while I'm in Kentucky?"

"Absolutely," he said—and he meant it. "I'll fly to Louisville so I can see you race and so we can be together. Then, if you make the Breeders' Cup, I'll definitely come out again to see you win those races."

"Oh, that would be so much fun. Hit the Bid and Tackle Tim Tom will also be happy to see you again."

Elliot laughed, a sense of relief sweeping over him. "Hit the Bid likes me because I bring her apples, but Tackle Tim Tom sees me as a competitor. He wants to be the only male in your life, and I have the feeling he would run me over if he had the chance."

"Yeah, he is a stubborn young stallion, but he's really starting to show great heart on the track, just like Hit the Bid."

"Have you thought about riding T-three next year when he's a three-year-old? Has Mister Gallo discussed that with you?"

"Yes, he has. I promised my parents I would attend the Spring

Semester at Pomona College near our home in Pasadena, but I'll get in some exercise riding at Santa Anita in order to stay in shape. If Tackle Tim Tom qualifies for the Derby, Mister Gallo wants me aboard."

"Wow, can you imagine what it would be like for you to win the Triple Crown on Tackle Tim Tom? Heck, you'd be the most famous female athlete in America! You'd make a ton of money, and everyone would want to get to know you. I bet you would even be invited to the White House."

"Would you still want to be my boyfriend if I was a big celebrity?"

"Well, of course. The question is, would *you* still want to be my girlfriend?"

"Why wouldn't I?" she asked in a quizzical voice.

Elliot smiled to himself. This beautiful and talented woman was too good to be true.

As Elliot pulled into the driveway next to CJ's apartment, he looked up at the sky. "Man, look at these clouds. We may get some rain tonight. I hope we don't have a sloppy track for the Travers tomorrow."

"Me, either," said CJ.

CHAPTER THIRTEEN

The thunder generated by lightning bolts clashing between the rain-soaked clouds above Saratoga Springs startled Gallo from a deep sleep and brought him upright in his bed.

He walked to the window, only to see torrential rainfall cascading from the sky. Not a sight he welcomed on the night before the biggest horse race of his career. He tried to go back to sleep, but the violence of the storm, and his anticipation of a trying day, negated any chance he had of getting the rest he needed. It was already nearly 4:00 a.m.

Giving up, he got out of bed, took a shower, and put on his work clothes. He grabbed a hanging bag that contained a suit, shirt, and tie he would wear later in the day before the Travers Stakes was broadcast live on national television. Just in case the mud was still ankle-deep at four o'clock that afternoon, he took along his L.L. Bean duck boots, figuring it didn't matter—the television cameras wouldn't see what he was wearing on his feet.

By the time he arrived at the stables on the backstretch of the track, it was 5:00 a.m. and the early morning activity was frenetic. Heavy rains were notorious for screwing up *everything* in the racing business, and today was no exception. The trainers, grooms, riders, and horse attendants were all trying to figure out how to prepare for an important day of racing without carrying out the normal ritual of tasks contained in their daily work cycle.

As predicted, the Oklahoma training track was sloppy and muddy. Most trainers didn't want to exercise or prep the horses in such conditions. The thunder and lightning—which continued to blanket the area—were spooking many of the thoroughbreds, disrupting their eating habits, and making them reluctant to leave their stall or be walked from one area to another. Several farriers were busy moving from stable to stable, reshoeing horses with aluminum shoes designed for racing in the mud. Everyone on the backstretch, both humans and animals, were feeling the anxiety caused by the challenge of bad weather on race day.

Gallo went into the trainer's trailer where several anxious trainers were hovering in front of a television tuned to the Weather Channel.

"How does it look?" asked Gallo, not feeling too hopeful.

"It looks like a fast-moving front, but it's still going to drop a lot of rain over the next few hours," said a trainer with a perplexed look on his face. "Even if the sun comes out by noon, the track is going to be slow, especially through the first five or six races. The Travers is the tenth race—maybe we get lucky by then, and it's a bit drier."

Gallo hung up the travel bag that contained his suit and left the trailer to join Jimmy at the stalls where his horses were stabled. Jimmy was exhibiting his usual state of concern but wasn't as freaked out as Gallo expected. The rain would prevent them from conducting their normal training routine, so the key for the day was to get a pair of horses ready for two important stakes races.

Jimmy gave his boss an update. "The gelding that's going to run in the Saratoga Stakes seems to be taking it in stride. He's eating okay, and I've got two grooms giving him a good brush down. In a little while, we'll take him out to the walking ring and let him walk around in the rain and mud to see how he reacts and try to get him acclimated. Hopefully he'll be okay, and since Miss CJ is his jockey, I'm not that concerned. She's really good at keeping horses calm."

"How about Hit the Bid?" asked Gallo.

"Ah, she's as happy as a clam. Nothin' bothers that filly. I have been singing to her all morning, and she just wants to play with her food and nudge me in the butt whenever I turn my back. She'll be even happier when CJ shows up."

"Okay, I'm going to walk across the street to the main track and see how things look. I also have several meetings to attend in the administrative offices. There's a special briefing for all the trainers and owners participating in the Travers, and there's a production meeting with the folks from ABC TV to plan the broadcast of the race this afternoon. I might be over there for a while."

"No sweat, boss. I got it covered."

Gallo crossed Union Avenue and entered the main track through a gate manned by security guards dressed in rain jackets. "Ain't looking too good here, Mister Gallo. Several inches of water on the track, especially down by the rail. Sure hope Hit the Bid's a mudder!"

"Well, we'll find out today. She's never run in the mud before, so this should be interesting."

Gallo entered the main building and made his way to the offices on the third floor. For the balance of the morning, he met with track officials and stewards, horse owners and trainers, and producers from ABC TV who would choreograph the nationwide broadcast of the Travers. He also accompanied CJ to a press conference, where the two of them fielded questions from print, cable, and national news organizations. For the previous five weeks, CJ had increasingly been made available to the press and had become better at handling the questions thrown in her direction. A major network had broadcast a human-interest piece about her on a national nightly news program, so everyone present knew she had some communication issues. The reporters typically tried to ask questions in a straightforward and direct fashion. They seemed to understand that she often didn't comprehend subtle, sarcastic, or oblique references, and most were okay with the fact that Gallo would occasionally step in and help with her responses.

Once the press conference was over, Gallo took CJ aside, and they walked into an empty booth where race officials watch each race. It was at the highest point in the building and, as such, had a complete view of the track.

Gallo glanced at the clock—it was 11:00 a.m., and thankfully the rain had tapered off to a drizzle, but the dirt track was very wet and sloppy, with water pooling down near the rail. Several tractors pulling large rakes began to drive around the track in a counterclockwise direction, overlapping the areas they were raking. This raking process would accelerate the drainage of the water and smooth out the running surface—but without several hours of direct sunlight and some wind? Gallo shook his head. A dry and fast track couldn't be anticipated.

"These are tough conditions, CJ. It's going to be a challenge for both races. The gelding has run in the mud before, and it didn't seem to bother him. The disadvantage you've got in the Saratoga Stakes is that you're coming out of the lowest post position, and you'll be on the rail as the race begins. That's the slowest surface on the track—you've got to get him out of there and into firmer dirt so he can use his speed. It's only a seven-furlong race so there's no room for errors here."

"I know, Mister Gallo. I'll do my best, and I think the gelding will do okay. He's responsive to me and we just have to hope he has the ability to finish in a short race like this. All the horses in the race are mature stallions and mares who are successful sprinters. There's some real talent in the field."

"Yeah, I know. You just give him the best ride you can and be safe out there. Sloppy tracks make it more difficult to anticipate the movement of the horses around you. I want you and the horse to come back in one piece."

Gallo and CJ smiled at one another in a way that prompted Gallo to realize something—they had become *more* than colleagues. They were friends who enjoyed being together at work or off the track. He admired the way she had matured as a rider and as a person. Theirs was a connection that Gallo hoped gave CJ the ability to develop social relationships with people that surrounded her on a day-to-day basis. He knew connecting with people had always been an arduous task for her, but he dared believe she was becoming more accomplished at this process *since* they'd met. Either way, her steady improvement filled him with a sense of pride he didn't often feel.

"I gotta head back to the stables," Gallo said. "Where are you going right now?"

"I'm going to go back to the jockey room and sit in the corner. I need a little alone time after being bombarded with so many questions."

Gallo laughed. "To tell you the truth, I could use some alone time myself. Unfortunately, between Jimmy and the horses, I don't think that's going to happen. I'll see you in the paddock when we saddle the gelding for the fifth race. Hang in there, kid."

By the time Gallo got back to the stable area, the rain had stopped, the sky was clearing, and sunlight began to replace the dreary atmosphere that had blanketed the track for the last nine hours. Racing fans started to stream into the track, and it looked like the enormous crowd expected for Travers Day would arrive due to the welcomed return of the sun. The first race would go off as scheduled at 1:00 p.m., followed by nine more races that included seven prestigious stakes races. The final race of the day was the Travers Stakes, with a total betting handle from the race expected to exceed fifty million dollars. Most of that money would be wagered in the Off-Track Betting system regulated by New York State, but the cash funneled through the machines at the track would still total around twelve million. As the day brightened, the spirits of fans, track officials, trainers, and jockeys began to lift, but the 800-pound gorilla in the room was the sloppy and slow racetrack. Sloppy tracks produced unpredictable results.

Gallo met up with Jimmy and reviewed the preparations for the two horses that would compete that day. His entry in The Saratoga

Stakes was a chestnut gelding named Backboard. This was the same horse that performed well in an allowance race several weeks earlier. For this race, he decided to replace the horse's previous jockey with CJ. She had worked the horse on several training runs and developed a good rapport with the thoroughbred. Once again, the special touch she had with horses seemed to be in play as Backboard continued to improve on the training track with CJ in the saddle.

The horse was owned by a syndicate of ten working-class men who loved horse racing but could never afford an animal worth sixty thousand dollars without pooling their resources. They were delighted to have CJ aboard—based on her excellent results throughout the Saratoga Meet—and were ready to have their picture taken with her in the paddock and *hopefully* in the winner's circle. This was a group of blue-collar guys having fun and enjoying the day rubbing shoulders with the gentrified class that owned the athletes participating in the sport of kings. The Saratoga Stakes had a purse of two hundred thousand, with 60 percent of that amount going to the winner. If Backboard won, this would be a day his owners would never forget.

At 2:45 p.m., Jimmy led Backboard by the reins and joined a parade of nine horses that walked across Union Avenue into the racetrack. On a muddy dirt path, the horses passed several thousand onlookers who gathered there to admire these sleek racers. The saddle, saddle cloth, harness, and girth straps that would be placed on the gelding's body were already in the jockey room where CJ would hold these items in her arms while being weighed before the race. This procedure, conducted prior to every race, assured the stewards that each horse was carrying the required weight. When Jimmy and Backboard reached the paddock, Jimmy walked the horse around the walking ring several times before bringing him to the number one stall where Gallo waited with ten excited owners. He helped Jimmy prepare and saddle the horse, as CJ arrived along with the other jockeys scheduled to ride.

When CJ first began to race at Saratoga, she didn't enjoy her introductions to owners in the paddock. She never knew what to say, she didn't like looking people in the eye, and she was anxious to mount her racehorse. But after five weeks of being badgered, cajoled, and encouraged by Gallo and Jimmy, she learned how to handle this important event. She quietly shook hands, smiled, and looked into the eyes of all ten men who surrounded her when she approached the stall. They returned beaming smiles, words of encouragement, and wishes of good luck. Before boosting CJ into the saddle, Gallo gave her his instructions on running the race. All ten of the owners huddled about the trainer and jockey, trying to hear every word they exchanged.

"The dirt down near the rail is still really wet and sloppy. Farther out from the rail, the track appears to be drying out. You're coming out of the one slot, so every other jock is going to do his best to keep you down in the slop. You've really only got two options, CJ. You can pull him back right out of the gate and try to go around the pack, or you can try to get a jump on the field at the start and take him right to the front. If you lag back, you're going to get a ton of soft dirt kicked up into the horse's eyes and chest as you try to work your way to the front. That's going to take a lot of energy out of the horse, and we're only racing seven furlongs against a field of strong sprinters. Since we're coming out of the number one gate, I think the only chance we got is to take him to the front and see if they can outrun him to the finish. He's been breezing really well lately, so I think he can do it. The key is to get good dirt under his feet and not the soft stuff."

"I understand, Mister Gallo. I don't have a lot of time to work him around eight other horses from the number one position, so I'll try to go right to the lead and then get off the rail into a firmer track surface. He's been running very fast split times in training, so I think we've got a shot."

"Okay, kid, be safe."

Once in the saddle of the number one horse, CJ followed the outrider who led the parade to the post. As Backboard approached the track from the entry lane, an escort rider on a track pony came alongside and took control of Backboard's reins so CJ could get settled in the saddle and relax for a few moments. After walking side by side for an eighth of a mile, CJ asked the escort rider to kick it up to a trot and then to a canter. She wanted to get the horse loose for the run and to see how he reacted to the soft track. She was pleased to see that Backboard was handling the situation quite well. His ears were up. He wasn't sweating profusely and didn't seem nervous or skittish. He wasn't distracted by the large, noisy crowd of people watching the race and hanging off the outside rail.

After moving clockwise along the outer periphery of the track, the escort rider turned Backboard around and brought the horse and jockey to the starting gate where two attendants came out and took over the reins. They walked Backboard into the first compartment of the starting gate. One attendant pulled the horse into the enclosure, and then jumped up on a platform next to the horse and jockey. The other attendant closed the doors of the gate behind the horse. Since CJ and her mount were in the first slot, she would have to keep Backboard calm while the other competitors were inserted into the gates one by one.

She talked to the horse and stroked his neck while giving him a little pep talk. "We're really going after this, big boy. I'm going to smack you a couple times on the butt, because I want you to sprint to the front. We don't want all that bad stuff getting kicked up in our face now, do we? Once we're at the front, we're going to be smart—no mistakes—just show 'em your speed."

When the last horse was positioned in the starting gate, CJ heard the starter say "Riders Ready" from a speaker above her head. Backboard heard it also. He knew what was coming. CJ lifted her butt off the saddle and put all her weight on the balls of her feet in the stirrups. She was leaning forward so the racehorse would have as little weight as possible on his hind legs, giving him the ability to push off quickly. The starting bell rang, and the gates opened, initiating a rush of adrenalin, power, and controlled chaos that would last for the next seven-eighths of a mile.

Backboard made a clean and fast start. When they cleared the gate, CJ snapped her whip three times on the horse's rump, giving the gelding a message that she wanted him to take the lead. He responded accordingly, and after sprinting one hundred yards from the starting gate, she had the horse at the front of the pack and fifteen feet away from the soft dirt at the rail. Since the distance of the race was only seven furlongs, the starting gate was on a straightaway at the opposite side of the track from the grandstands and the clubhouse. Consequently, there was only one turn to be run by the horses. Since every horse in the race was trained to be a sprinter, CJ continually urged her mount to run in order to hold on to the lead. Every horse was running flat out for seven-eighths of a mile.

Halfway down the backstretch, CJ sensed two horses on either side of her challenging for the first position. She felt that the track surface on the line she was running was reasonably dry, so she moved Backboard a little to his left in an effort to drive the horse on her inside deeper into the softer dirt. As they entered the far turn, she had maneuvered the inside horse into the wettest part of the track, and as they ran through the turn, the horse mired by soft dirt couldn't keep the pace. With Backboard still in the lead, the field turned for home at the top of the stretch. The horse to her right had maintained its position all the way through the turn, and she could hear the jockey urging his mount to run and snapping his whip. The challenger moved up next to Backboard and both horses thundered for home with the other seven horses in the field only a few lengths behind.

CJ had participated in over one hundred races in her short career, but she knew she was now experiencing one of those special moments with a horse that only came along once in a while. She could feel the horse's desire to run; she could sense it in her hands, her body, and her mind. More than that, she knew this horse wanted to *win*. All thoroughbreds are runners, but only a handful are truly winners—combatants who understand the purpose of the race. She stowed her whip and continued to concentrate on moving her body in perfect harmony with the horse. She didn't need to hit him to get him to run. She only needed to give him his freedom and let him know she was there to help.

"Come on, big guy! You got him, you got him!" Backboard was breezing as fast as he could, and yet he did it effortlessly. The weight of the jockey meant nothing to him, nor did the softness of the track. It was as though he understood that the lady rider on his back had given him the green light to do what he was born to do—to win.

When Backboard's nose crossed the finish line six inches ahead of the second-place horse, ten men who worked as plumbers, mailmen, carpenters, truck drivers, and cops, jumped up and down like teenagers who had just won a football game. They hugged each other, their trainer, and anyone else within reach—and then they cried. There is something magical about a racehorse and what it can accomplish on a track. Some people see it as entertainment, and some see it as human cruelty to an animal. But some people get it. These ten men got it. This was an experience that would remain with them for the rest of their lives.

Someday, when Backboard is too old to race and suffering from a fatal disease, he would be euthanized. On that day, the ten men who owned him would feel that loss as though the animal was a member of their family. They would remember the chestnut gelding's courage and determination to give everything he had to win that race in front of 50,000 human beings and ten men who loved him.

These ten men got it—so did their trainer and jockey.

CHAPTER FOURTEEN

Dave and Becky waited for the director to give them the signal that the program was on the air, and Dave initiated the dialogue.

"Welcome, everyone, to the one hundred and fiftieth running of the Travers Stakes at beautiful Saratoga Race Course. We are delighted to be here with ABC Sports, televising what is considered to be the third most prestigious thoroughbred race in the world. The Travers, a Grade One stakes race, dates back to 1864 and has a purse of $1,250,000. The finest three-year-old thoroughbreds from around the globe are here to compete over a distance of one-and-a-quarter miles. The field today includes the winners of this year's Kentucky Derby, The Preakness, and The Belmont—and to the delight of many racing fans, the fastest filly in the business, Hit the Bid."

Becky then took over the narrative. "That's right, Dave. We have a terrific field of super horses here ready to compete in a race that is often referred to as the midsummer derby, because of the superior quality of the contestants in the race. But Saratoga is also called 'the graveyard of champions,' because we routinely see the marquis horses beaten when they come to upstate New York and run on the oldest major horse racetrack in America. In the past, we've had champions like Secretariat and American Pharaoh lose in the Travers to upstarts that were ready to take on the big boys. It will be interesting to see if the big boys get beat today by a filly who has been turning heads throughout the racing year."

"Well, now that you mention it, Becky, it's interesting to note that colts in this race are required to carry 126 pounds, but the fillies are allowed to run with 121 pounds on their backs. When you consider the fact that CJ Jamieson is still classified as an apprentice jockey, Hit the Bid will only be carrying 114 pounds since Jamieson gets an additional seven-pound allowance. That could be a real advantage for the filly. She is a very big and strong horse, even though she is a female, and Jamieson is certainly not your typical apprentice. The young jockey has notched eighteen wins thus far in her five weeks here at Saratoga."

"I think you've got that right, Dave. The weight advantage could mean even more today because we won't have a fast track when the race begins. The track surface right now is classified as 'slow.' The racing surface has begun to dry out from the heavy rains we experienced last night and early this morning. Although the top level of dirt looks to be dry, the base of the track is still very moist. This will generally result in times that are slower than on a fast and firm track."

"You know, Becky, despite the rain we had earlier in the day, the sunshine has brought out the crowds and the attendance is about fifty thousand. I think everyone is excited to see the three colts that won the Triple Crown races go against the talented filly that won the American Oaks here in July. It should be a great race."

"I agree, it should be a lot of fun. Right now, let's go down to the walking path where the horses are being led to the paddock and check in with our on-track reporter, Mary Tierney. Take it away, Mary!"

The picture changed to the path leading from the stables to the paddock where the grooms, trainers, and owners were walking with their horses. "Thanks, Becky, I'm here on the walking path and as you can see behind me, each horse is on its way to being saddled and prepared for the race. If my cameraman can point down at my feet"—she paused, waiting for the camera man to, indeed, pan downward—"you can see that this dirt path is still a bit muddy, and the layer under the top layer of dirt is still pretty soft." The camera whipped back up to Mary's wide-smiling face. "I suspect that the racetrack is in the same condition, so the race will be a little more challenging for the contestants and their jockeys. Sometimes, in these conditions, it isn't the fastest horse that wins but the horse that's the best athlete."

Mary changed her position from the side of the path and moved out to the middle where the horses were walking. "I've just been passed by Find That Bird, the winner of the Kentucky Derby—and now I'll move back down the line of horses, trying to get to number eleven, Hit the Bid. Hopefully, I can get a quick interview with the filly's trainer, Ritchie Gallo."

As Gallo, Jimmy, and Hit the Bid approached Tierney's position, the reporter smiled at the trainer and thrust a microphone in his face. "Ritchie, your filly looks happy this afternoon; she's already dancing for the crowd! Do you think she's ready to run?"

"Oh, yeah. She's in good shape and well-prepared to go a mile-and-a-quarter against the colts. We're really pleased with her conditioning at this point."

"Ritchie, the track is a little slow. Do you think this is a problem for your horse? Did you fit her out with different shoes?"

"No, she was re-shod five days ago with standard shoes. We decided not to go with mud caulks today. Her stride is good, and she's such a great athlete, I didn't want to do anything that might change her running style. Before each race, she plays to the crowd with the dancing and the posing but once the gates open—she's all heart. I don't think the conditions are going to slow her down much."

"Talk to me about your jockey, CJ Jamieson. I'm sure the public was surprised a few weeks ago when she announced on a national news program that she still deals with mental challenges caused by a terrible accident she experienced as a child. Most people might assume that she would have some physical issues with this condition, but she certainly doesn't have any disability when she's riding a thoroughbred."

Gallo smiled as he answered the question. "CJ is a very special woman. Physically, she's a great rider, but she is much more than that as a person. She has an almost mystical talent for connecting with horses—and with regard to Hit the Bid, their connection is really unique and special. She and the horse seem to be thinking the same thing as they move around the track, and Hit the Bid really responds to her. It's just great to watch. I'm very grateful that she helps me to train Hit the Bid as well as a two-year-old colt I have that's a future superstar. I really love working with her."

"Ritchie, thanks for your time, and good luck."

The reporter turned to face the camera as she prepared to send the broadcast back to the anchor desk. "Dave and Becky, you can feel the anticipation down here near the track. The crowd is huge, and there is a large number of female fans rooting for Hit the Bid and her lady jockey. When you consider that they are going up against the three colts that won the Triple Crown races, this is shaping up to be a race that fans will remember for a long time. Back to you."

As the television broadcast continued to inform viewers about the horses, trainers, jockeys, and owners entered in the Travers, Ritchie and Jimmy plodded their way to the paddock where they met up with CJ. Jimmy took Hit the Bid by the reins and guided her around the walking ring to the delight of nearly one thousand fans assembled outside the fence. Hit the Bid looked bright and alert with her ears moving straight up, as if to listen for the compliments provided by an adoring fanbase. The horse puffed up her chest and looked left and right, surveying the throngs that surrounded the paddock. Every few yards, she would make a prancing move with her front legs followed by a swaying movement in both directions with her hips. To make it even more entertaining for the crowd, Jimmy was singing a song recorded by Smokey Robinson and the Miracles. He bobbed his head to the rhythm of the song and the horse seemed to be doing the same. All of this was captured on hundreds of cell phones, with many of the pictures and videos going viral within a matter of minutes.

Although the filly and the groom appeared to be enjoying themselves, Gallo was getting a little nervous. "What did you think of the track conditions, CJ?"

"The sun's been out, so it must have improved since I ran in The Saratoga Stakes. We're coming out of the eleventh gate in this race, so I think we will have pretty good dirt out to the first turn."

"Look, all the colts that ran in the Triple Crown races are strong and fast. Take advantage of the good dirt in front of you and move towards the front before the first turn. I'll bet my shirt that Find That Bird is going to take the lead right out of the gate. Just stay on his right flank all the way through the backstretch and the far turn. At the one-mile marker, let her run. At that point, it's up to her—can she beat the boys, or can't she? Is she a champion, or isn't she?"

CJ smiled back at him, "I think we both know the answer to that question, Mister Gallo." She reached into her pocket and pulled out two one-dollar bills. "Do me a favor. Put two bucks on the nose for the eleven horse. I'll pick up my winnings from you after the race."

"No sweat, kid. You got it."

Television coverage of The Travers Stakes continued showing the eleven horses parading to the post and being placed in the starting gate one at a time. Earlier in The Saratoga Stakes, CJ's mount was the first horse in the gate, but for this race, Hit the Bid was the last horse to be enclosed in the mobile starting gate. From a speaker above her head, CJ heard the starter boom, "Riders ready!"

Hit the Bid heard it also. She knew what was coming.

As horse racing fans all over the world focused on their television screens, the audio switched over to the track announcer:

"The last horse has just settled into the starting gate, and they are ready to run."

"AND THEY'RE OFF! It's the start of the one hundred and fiftieth running of the Travers Stakes!

"The bay colt, Wonder Boy, has made a fast break, but it's the Kentucky Derby winner Find That Bird set to take the lead and now grabbing the early advantage. And then it's Hit the Bid followed by Fivefold, Musketeer, and Storm Warning. Bad Magic is outside of horses, five lengths off the lead, and then comes Vino Tinto as the field enters the clubhouse turn. Grabowski, King Avery, and Mastermind are at the back of the pack.

"Jockey, Ryan Morehead, hustles Find That Bird out of the turn, running full steam ahead and covering the first quarter-mile in a surprisingly swift time of twenty-three and one-fifth seconds.

"Find That Bird is on top by half a length with Hit the Bid pressing the pace on the outside in second place, and Wonder Boy moving down towards the inside as they head to the backstretch. Then it's Fivefold with Musketeer just behind him, and Bad Magic still five lengths off the lead. Storm Warning, Grabowski, King Avery, and Mastermind continue to trail by six to eight lengths. The speed continues to be excellent for a slow track with the half-mile covered in forty-eight seconds.

"They're moving up the backstretch where Hit the Bid confronts Find That Bird, but Find That Bird keeps his lead by a neck. Wonder Boy is two-and-a-half lengths off them, with Fivefold outside of Storm Warning, who is moving down to the inside rail. Bad Magic is still about five lengths behind—just ahead of Grabowski, King Avery, and Mastermind, who are all trying to keep the blistering pace being set by Find That Bird.

"They've now run the first six furlongs in one minute and twelve seconds, a very fast time considering the softness of the track. Find That Bird is on top, but CJ Jamieson is keeping Hit the Bid on his right flank. They begin to move into the far turn with the Kentucky Derby winner continuing to maintain the lead, but Hit the Bid is still running with him. They've been one and two throughout the race.

"Coming through the far turn, Fivefold, Musketeer, and Wonder Boy are trailing the leaders by two lengths, but the rest of the field is faltering and having trouble staying in contact with the leaders who seem to be accelerating out of the turn.

"As they come out of the turn, Cicely Jamieson is asking Hit the Bid to run and make a move on Find that Bird.

"DOWN THE STRETCH THEY COME! IT'S HIT THE BID TAKING THE LEAD ON THE OUTSIDE! FIND THAT BIRD IS FULL OUT ON THE RAIL— IT'S FIVE LENGTHS BACK TO MUSKETEER, WHO IS NOW THIRD WITH VINO TINTO AND KING

AVERY THREE HORSES WIDE TRYING TO MAKE A MOVE!

"THEY'RE COMING DOWN TO THE SIXTEENTH POLE! FIND THAT BIRD IS GIVING IT EVERYTHING HE'S GOT BUT HIT THE BID IS PULLING AWAY! JAMIESON JUST SHOWED HER THE WHIP, AND THE FILLY IS EXTENDING HER LEAD! SHE IS MOVING EFFORTLESSLY TO THE FINISH LINE; IT LOOKS LIKE SHE COULD GO ANOTHER MILE AT THIS PACE IF SHE WANTED TO. THE FILLY IS SO IMPRESSIVE TODAY, THE OTHERS DIDN'T EVEN HAVE A PRAYER!

"Hit the Bid rolls in the Travers Stakes, crossing the finish line three lengths in front of Find That Bird, with Musketeer running third. Despite a slow track, the talented filly finished in two minutes, two-and-five-tenths seconds. What a great performance. This lady is a champ, impressively beating a field of colts that included the winners of the Derby, the Preakness and the Belmont. The filly and the lady jockey ran one heck of a race!"

CHAPTER FIFTEEN

Elliot Monkmeyer helped his father flip burgers, Italian sausages, and marinated chicken breasts on the large bricked-in barbecue grill behind their summer cottage on Saratoga Lake. His mother was busy moving about the backyard, serving drinks to their guests, while the television crew from *Sixty Minutes* interviewed Ritchie Gallo and CJ Jamieson.

John McCann and Jimmy Crowder relaxed in folding chairs positioned to give them an unobstructed view of the boats zooming around the lake, pulling water skiers or inflated inner tubes. Mrs. Monkmeyer delivered a scotch on the rocks to McCann and a whiskey sour to the groom. The men clinked their glasses and sipped their drinks.

"Well, Mister Jimmy, you certainly look like you are enjoying yourself after six weeks of hard work here at Saratoga," said Elliot's mom.

"Oh, yes, ma'am," said Jimmy. "We put all our horses on a sixteen-wheeler today and they're headed back to Stone Fence Farms. I got a couple guys traveling with them, but Mister Gallo and I will hop on a plane headed for Louisville tomorrow. We should be there by the time they arrive."

"Good for you! You gentlemen call me if you need anything else to drink. We'll be eating in about twenty minutes."

McCann and Crowder continued to enjoy their drinks while watching Gallo and CJ being interviewed on the dock where the

Monkmeyer's speed boat was moored. Several cameras and lights, along with a plethora of intertwined wires and cables, were behind the interviewer as she peppered the trainer and the jockey with questions.

"I'll tell you something, Jimmy—you know you've hit the big time when they're doing a story about you on *Sixty Minutes*. That TV crew has been following Gallo and CJ around all week since the Travers. Next Sunday, CJ will be a headliner on a national news show. My phone is already ringing off the hook from owners and trainers that want her to ride for them. This has been a good summer for all of us at Saratoga."

"You got that right, Mister McCann. Couldn't have ended better than yesterday with Tackle Tim Tom winning the Hopeful Stakes on the last day of the meet. My God, I never have seen a colt accelerate out of the turn like that young stallion. When CJ asked him to break for home, he looked like a missile coming off a launching pad. Man, I think we got us a shot at the Derby next year when he's a three-year-old."

"Yeah, I don't doubt it. CJ has already told me she will ride any horse I think is good for her career, but her heart is with Gallo and your two stars. Hit the Bid and T-three are her priority assignments. If Tackle Tim Tom is in the Derby next year, you know she'll be there."

"Hey, tell me something, Mister McCann. With all the races she won at Saratoga this season, how much money did that girl make?"

"Jimmy, I can't tell you that. I'm her agent, it's confidential." McCann looked around and then leaned over to speak softly into Jimmy's ear. "She made north of a two handle."

"North of a two handle? What's that mean?"

"Two hundred thousand. She made over two hundred thousand dollars."

"Dang! I have been buying that little lady a coffee every day for the last six weeks, and she's making big-time money like that. Hey, from now on, *she's* buying the coffee every morning, and I don't give a damn how many sugars she puts in it!"

McCann laughed and took another sip of scotch.

Elsewhere in the Monkmeyer backyard, Crawford and Channing Jamieson watched their daughter being interviewed from a distance. Channing was holding a copy of *Sports Illustrated* magazine. The cover photograph was a picture of Hit the Bid crossing the finish line at The Travers with a determined and focused CJ in the saddle. The amount of national attention aimed at CJ was overwhelming, but Channing was delighted to see how calmly and maturely her daughter was handling the exposure. She was also pleased that her husband was on his best behavior on this day when they had the chance to meet Elliot's mother and father. Crawford was friendly, considerate, and polite. In addition to charming the Monkmeyers, he was doing his best to be friendly with Ritchie Gallo and to be a proud and loving father to CJ. His efforts brought a smile of happiness to Channing, but she was a bit concerned about Gallo. It may have been her imagination, but she thought she caught the trainer looking at her too intensely, and she was concerned that her husband may have noticed the man's attentive stares. For the rest of the afternoon, she would do her best to avoid looking Ritchie in the eye.

The CBS interviewer speaking with Gallo and CJ was asking random questions that could be edited into the hours of video shot earlier in the week in order to finalize a twenty-minute program. She and her producer could sense that CJ's concentration and attention to the questions was beginning to wane, so they decided to wrap it up with a few general inquiries.

"So, CJ—I understand you're heading for California tomorrow for a short vacation, and then you will go to Churchill Downs in Kentucky for more racing."

"Yes, that's right. I'm going home with my mom and dad for a week and then will go to Churchill Downs for the fall meet."

"I see. And Ritchie—you will be in Kentucky also, isn't that right?"

"Yeah, with Stone Fence Farms being so close to Churchill Downs, we'll have five or six horses running each week of the meet. The logistics there are so much easier than coming here to Saratoga, so it gives us a chance to develop more of our younger horses and enter some of the older thoroughbreds in races where they can be competitive."

"And will CJ be riding for you there?"

"Yes, I'm currently negotiating with her agent to get her aboard some of our horses. She is in big demand now from many owners—so we won't have a monopoly on her time—but this is a great career move for her, and I think she's just going to get better and better as a jockey."

"Will she be riding Hit the Bid at Churchill Downs?"

"Yes—she will be riding Hit the Bid and Tackle Tim Tom at the Breeders' Cup races early in November. This year, those races are being held at Churchill Downs after the conclusion of the fall meet."

"Those are very prestigious races, and my understanding is that there is a lot of money on the line."

"That's true," said Gallo. "Tackle Tim Tom will run on the first day of the two-day event in the Breeders' Cup Juveniles race. It's a race for the fastest two-year-olds in the country. The horse racing equivalent to the Super Bowl is the Breeders' Cup Classic, which takes place the following day. The horses in that race are at least three years old, and they are basically the fastest thoroughbreds from all over the world. It's a six-million-dollar race, so it's really a big-time competition. Hit the Bid will be competing in that race."

"Do you think your horses can win those races?"

CJ and Ritchie smiled at each other, nodding their heads. "We've got two great horses here and a talented jockey, so I think the odds are good," said Gallo. "But it is horse racing, after all—you never know what will happen."

———————◆———————

The producer from CBS informed Gallo and CJ that the interview was over.

As the television crew began to pack up their equipment, the trainer and the jockey joined the Monkmeyers, the Jamiesons, John McCann, and Jimmy at a long picnic table covered with bowls filled with salads and platters piled high with cheeseburgers, Italian sausage sandwiches, and barbecued chicken. The chatter around the table was lively and friendly, with everyone commenting on an enjoyable summer at Saratoga and the bit of sadness they all felt since the meet had come to an end. Soon, the seasons would change, and the lake would be surrounded by a kaleidoscope of multi-colored leaves heralding autumn. By November, the trees would be bare, and the nightly temperatures would generate a frost on the grass, giving the residents of upstate New York a quick reminder of how lovely the summer is in this region, and how much excitement and fun is generated when the thoroughbreds come to town.

Elliot's mother inquired into an activity her son and CJ had completed earlier in the day. "So, CJ—I hear you held your own at the golf course today?"

CJ smiled broadly. "Yes, I really enjoyed hitting golf balls with Elliot. I think I did pretty well."

"Pretty well?" said Elliot. "You wouldn't believe it, Mom. I gave her a quick lesson on how to grip the club and set up in her stance. I showed her the basics of the golf swing, and then I let her try to hit balls with a seven iron. She sprayed ten or fifteen balls all over the place, but once she hit one straight, it seemed like she had been playing the game her *entire life*. She just kept striping shots straight down the middle until we ran out of balls. I was amazed!"

"I like it," said CJ. "Once I got the sensation of squaring up the clubface as I hit the ball, I was able to repeat it over and over again. I just had a feel for it. Kind of like I have with horses."

"How did you do on the putting green?" asked Elliot's father.

"Gosh, not so well," CJ confessed, cheeks blushing slightly. "On the putting green, I can't quite grasp the dimensions of space and motion that I sense when standing on the driving range. I feel like I'm standing on a giant green felt carpet—I don't recognize the subtle changes in the terrain or the grain of the grass. Putting is going to take some work. Just like learning to deal with people."

"Don't worry," said Elliot as he touched her hand. "You're conquering your reticence to deal with people, and I'm sure some day you'll be a good putter. You always overcome obstacles to achieve things that are important to you."

When CJ heard Elliot say that, she wanted to cry. What a blessing it had been to meet a man who treated her with such empathy, understanding, and affection. Saratoga had become a magical place for her, just as it had been for her mother, two decades in the past.

As dinner ended, Gallo gestured to CJ and got her to walk to the lakefront so they could talk in private. He pulled six dollars out of his pocket and gave it to her.

"What's this for?" she asked.

"Don't you remember? Before the Travers, you gave me two dollars and told me to put it on the eleven horse. Well, Hit the Bid won the race, so here are your winnings. You went off at two to one."

CJ smiled. "I think I am going to have this money framed. It will remind me of the first big victory of my life."

"Ah, you've got a lot bigger victories coming your way in the racing business. This one was just the start."

"I wasn't really referring to winning the Travers, Mister Gallo. Being *here* for the last six weeks has been the first big victory for my life. When I was racing at Santa Anita, I was having success, but it was still a success in my own little world. Since I met you, I've been able to share my life experiences with other people. It made my world bigger and happier. I mean, I've got a boyfriend now. A wonderful guy who treats me so well and has opened my eyes to so many things around me that I never recognized before. I've got good friends now—you, Mister Jimmy, and Mister McCann. I've been able to build a relationship with Elliot's parents and, best of all, my relationship with my own parents has gotten better. You've helped me a lot, Mister Gallo. You, Hit the Bid, and T-three have brought me into the real world. It's a beautiful world, and I'm very grateful."

CJ realized that she was a very different lady than the shy exercise rider Gallo first met a month-and-a-half earlier. For the first time, she was speaking in profound terms that accurately expressed her feelings and emotions. She still had some foibles and awkwardness in her interactions with strangers, but she knew she had come a long way.

"You know, I wouldn't discount your own determination to change and grow. You should be proud of yourself, CJ. You're a great jockey, but you've also become a great young woman."

CJ smiled and looked at the cash in her hand. "This is only six dollars, but in reality, it's a fortune to me."

"That's good," said Gallo. "It's going to take a fortune for you to pay back Jimmy for all the coffee he bought you over the last six weeks."

Chapter Sixteen

CJ walked past one of the large white barns at Stone Fence Farms and approached a black wooden fence that encompassed two acres of Kentucky bluegrass. In the center of the field, a cadre of thoroughbreds ambled about, enjoying the warmth of the sun on a cool October day. CJ rested her arms on the top plank of the fence and smiled when she spotted Hit the Bid about a hundred yards away. The horse was casually grazing but, every once in a while, managed to produce a little dance step with her front legs. It had been seven weeks since she last saw T-three and Hit the Bid, but now she had come to the farm to prepare the horses for the Breeders' Cup races.

CJ called out to the filly, "Bid, it's me. It's CJ. Come over here, girl. Come on, Bid, it's me!"

The horse immediately raised her head when she heard the familiar voice and looked in the direction of the barn. She started to walk in CJ's direction and then broke into a gallop that enabled her to cover the distance in just a few seconds. Thrusting her head over the top of the fence, she welcomed CJ's affectionate pats and a hug around the neck.

CJ climbed over the fence, entering the enclosure, and produced an apple from her jacket—which was practically inhaled by the filly. "I haven't seen you since Saratoga, beautiful lady. You look great and I hear you've been working well on the training track. I've been busy at Churchill Downs since Saratoga, but now that the meet is over, I can concentrate on you and the Breeders' Cup. We've only got three weeks to get ready, but I know we'll be fine—we're going to win."

As CJ chatted away with Hit the Bid, another horse approached and moved in to nuzzle the jockey with his nose. "Hey, Backboard. How are you doing?" CJ pulled another apple from the inner pocket of her jacket and the chestnut gelding willingly ate the fruit from her hand. "Backboard, did you tell Hit the Bid that I rode you to another win at Churchill Downs last month? You've become a fine sprinter, and those ten guys who own you are just terrific. They love you so much and they're proud of you. Since you don't have a future in the breeding barn, I hope we can win a few more races together. C'mon, you guys, let's take a walk." CJ turned and began to move along the fence line, talking incessantly to the horses who dutifully followed behind her.

She hadn't gone very far when she heard someone call out to her. "Hey, Miss CJ! I got another old friend that wants to see you!"

Jimmy was standing at the entrance to the fenced field, holding the reins attached to Tackle Tim Tom. He opened the gate, disconnected the reins, and allowed T-three to burst into the field and sprint up to CJ and the two other horses. Luckily, CJ had a third apple, which the young stallion ate in the blink of an eye.

"Wow, T-three, you look like you've gotten even bigger since I last saw you. We're going to blow those other juveniles away next month, aren't we? C'mon, let's keep walking. I have a lot to tell you guys."

CJ continued to move along inside the fence with the three horses trailing behind. She explained, in great detail, her activities since she left Saratoga. The meet at Churchill Downs had been a big success from a career perspective. She'd won sixteen races there and was no longer an apprentice rider, seeing as her short career now included over forty wins. Her agent, John, had engaged her to ride for all the top trainers and horse farms, and she was now considered within the racing industry to be one of the most accomplished jockeys. She was a rider whose talents were in big demand.

"I get to ride a lot of really cool horses now, but you two are still my favorites," she said, and Backboard whinnied, as though outraged. "Oops! You're my favorite too, Backboard."

As CJ proceeded to move around the outside of the field, other horses gradually joined the parade. After no more than five minutes, every adult thoroughbred that had been grazing in the area was now walking along behind her as she talked non-stop to her attentive equestrian audience.

"Even though I only rode for Mister Gallo six or seven times during the meet, I was able to see him and Mister Jimmy almost every day. Lots of times we would go to dinner together, so that was fun. Oh, and I think you guys may remember my boyfriend, Elliot Monkmeyer. He flew here to Kentucky for several days to see me race, and he'll be coming out again for the Breeders' Cup. I really miss him. He's such a great guy." Tackle Tim Tom snorted and shook his head.

• — • — •

Back at the entrance gate to the pasture, Jimmy leaned on the fence and watched CJ and the horses from a distance. "I just can't believe it," he said out loud. "She's like the doggone Pie-Eyed Piper of Hambletonian, except it ain't rats and children that follow her around, it's horses. How is any jockey going to compete with her when she can communicate with these animals like that? I ain't never seen anything like this in my life."

As the parade of horses proceeded, a female foal born just six months earlier pranced in CJ's direction. CJ could see that the small filly was apprehensive when she came close. The youngster had only been touched by male grooms in her brief life and she had never had a bridle or a saddle placed on her body. Her training to be a racehorse had not yet begun. CJ correctly sensed that the juvenile horse was

123

checking her out and trying to understand how a small human like CJ could have such masterful control of all the mature horses in the field.

The curious little horse got within twelve feet of CJ, but appeared to be afraid to come any closer. CJ stopped walking and smiled at the foal. She held out her hand. "I don't have any more apples, but if you come here, I'll pet your neck and we can get to know one another. Come here, don't be afraid . . . Come here and touch my hand."

The filly came closer, inhaling CJ's scent. The jockey opened her hand, allowing the young horse to lick her palm, which CJ assumed still smelled like a fresh apple. She moved in next to the horse, rubbing her forehead, and stroking her neck. "You are a beautiful little lady. You know that, don't you?"

The foal moved up against CJ's body, and because she was less than half the size of Hit the Bid, it was easy to wrap her arms around the filly's neck, resting her head against her mane. "I can feel it. You're going to be a champion. You will know what it feels like to win, and you'll want to do it every time you race. Someday, you just may be as beautiful as Hit the Bid."

While CJ communed with the foal, Gallo joined Jimmy at the entrance to the field. "You been watching this, boss?" Said Jimmy.

"Yeah, it's just crazy, isn't it? It's something you can't explain. Do you think these horses really understand what she's saying?"

"Well, it ain't so much understanding in the book learning sense. It's more like an understanding of emotions or feelings. I mean, when I sing to Hit the Bid, nobody's gonna tell me that she don't get it. She may not know where Georgia is or what an ex-girlfriend is, but she understands happiness, sadness, and being lonely. She feels what I feel when I'm singing and that helps me as much as it helps her. So, I know that people can connect with horses. I just never seen anybody that can do it like Miss CJ. She can drive me crazy with her questions and antics, but she's a special girl."

"Yeah, she's special all right—but I have to sit down and talk to her about the training routine we need to refine over the next three weeks. When she's done parting the Red Sea and raising the dead, send her into my office so I can map this out with her."

"You got it, boss."

Gallo retreated to the small office he kept in the corner of the largest barn. Since bringing Hit the Bid and Tackle Tim Tom back from Saratoga in early September, he had been executing a training regime aimed at the Breeders' Cup races three weeks hence. The training plan included very specific daily routines that enabled the body of each horse to transform stored muscle energy into speed. For the first few weeks after the two champions returned from Saratoga, Gallo had them running long, slow gallops, allowing their bodies to recover from the stress induced by their respective competitions in The Travers and The Hopeful Stakes. Recently, however, he changed the daily form of exercise by alternating routine training days with heavy training days.

On routine days, the horses went out for a slow gallop, but their heart rate was kept below a hundred and sixty beats per minute to prevent them from burning up too much muscle energy. On heavy training days, the horses ran a series of three-furlong sprints at eleven to twelve seconds per furlong. Each sprint was separated by a short rest, to allow the horse's heart rate and respiration to recover. This prepared the body of each horse to store and use the glycogen stored in its muscles efficiently. Gallo intended to keep this alternate training day process going until a week prior to the Breeders' Cup races. From then until race day, Hit the Bid and T-three would be taken out for gentle gallops, where their heart rates would be kept below the a hundred and sixty beat threshold and their diets would be carefully monitored.

As Gallo reviewed his training plan, a quick knock on the door was followed by the entry of CJ.

"Hey kid, how's it going? How was the reunion out behind the barn?" he asked.

"Ah, it was great to see them again. Hit the Bid looks fit and firm, and T-three just gets bigger and stronger."

"Yeah, I'm really pleased with the shape they're in, but they've regressed a little bit in their behavioral training. Tackle Tim Tom isn't always cooperating with the exercise riders and Hit the Bid still wants to put the pedal to the metal when she should be running a slow gallop. The sooner you're back in the saddle, the better."

"No sweat, Mister Gallo. It only took fifty-five minutes for me to get here from my apartment in Louisville, so I can be here whenever you want me."

Gallo proceeded to give CJ a day by day description of the training for each horse, right up to the day of the races. Tackle Tim Tom was entered in the Breeders' Cup Juveniles race on Friday, November 2, and Hit the Bid would start in the Breeders' Cup Classic on Saturday, the culminating race of the meet. Gallo planned to transport the horses to Churchill Downs on the Wednesday before the races to give them an opportunity to become comfortable with the track and its surroundings. Since both horses were racing veterans and had competed in front of large crowds in the past, he didn't think they would lose their poise, but he still wanted them as calm as possible prior to the actual race.

"You know, CJ, your agent told me he could have engaged you to ride in all fourteen of the races held over the two days—but he said you declined and would only ride Hit the Bid and T-three. Why did you do that?"

CJ shrugged. "These are huge races that are really important to you and Mister Jimmy. I love these horses, and I just want to concentrate on bringing them to the finish line first in each race. In future years, I'll have plenty of opportunities to ride in the Breeders' Cup. If you retire Hit the Bid, this will be my last chance to ride this great filly. I want to spend as much time with her as I can prior to running in the Classic."

"Well, I know you're passing up on a lot of potential money by limiting your rides to my two horses. I'm grateful for your help, CJ. I really appreciate it."

"No problem, Mister Gallo. I know if we win, you will give Mister Jimmy a big bonus and this is my way of paying him back for all the coffee he bought me at Saratoga."

Gallo laughed. "He's never going to let go of that, is he?"

"Nope, he'll be extorting money from me for the rest of his life."

The two friends smiled at one another as Gallo sat back and put his feet on the desk. "Speaking of the rest of your life—how's Mister Elliot Monkmeyer doing?"

"He's doing great. We had so much fun when he visited me at Churchill Downs. He enjoyed seeing you, Mister Jimmy, and the horses again, but it was so special for me and him to have some quality time together. I think about him all the time, and I really do miss him."

"I think Elliot is a terrific young man, but you both are still pretty young. You're not getting too serious, here, are you?"

"It would be tough for me to be married to someone right now and to live with that person, because I still have this compelling need to bring order to everything that surrounds me. It wouldn't be fair to Elliot to have a wife that needed her environment to be as organized as she wants it, right down to where the bed and dresser sit. Whenever I'm with Elliot, I try hard to make whatever we are doing about him and not about me. It's not easy for me, though, and I haven't reached a point where I can make a complete compromise on how I structure my life. It's really kind of nuts, when you think about it. I have no problem dealing with the chaos of a horse race, but if Elliot replaces a pencil on my desk in a spot other than where I want it? Well, it just drives me *crazy*, and I have to immediately put it back where it belongs. If I can't learn to deal with things that aren't perfect, I'm afraid I will always be alone. No man will want to live with me."

"Look, CJ—you've changed dramatically since I met you four months ago, and I think you will continue to grow as a person. In addition to that, you've met a guy that's willing to wait for you until hell freezes over in order to get to a place where you can have the kind of relationship that you want. Don't give up on yourself or Elliot. Just be careful to let that relationship develop naturally and with a healthy level of respect for one another. If it's meant to be, it will be."

"Thanks for the advice, Mister Gallo. We'll take it slow, and having Elliot as a boyfriend makes me optimistic about my future."

"Well, it should. He's a great guy."

Gallo sat up in his chair and placed his hands on the desk, leaning in CJ's direction. "You know CJ, I've got to ask you a question. I just watched you walk around the pasture with all those horses following you. I've always thought I was pretty good at reading horses, you know? Figuring out when they're scared, or happy, or tired of training. I've also seen a number of jockeys who could make riding a thoroughbred look effortless, even though they were constantly communicating and controlling the horse. But I've *never* seen anyone do it as well as you. I've never asked you this, but . . . What goes on in your head, or in the horse's head, when you are in the saddle?"

Cicely shrugged and smiled. "I learned at a very young age that horses think in terms of images and emotions. From the very first time I touched a horse, I was able to receive a picture or image from the animal, along with the emotions the horse was feeling."

"You have to remember, Mister Gallo," she went on, "that much of what goes through a horse's head is instinct. In the hierarchy of animals, horses are the prey. They aren't predators, so they live in a state of curiosity that will quickly revert to fear if they believe there may be an ounce of danger present. If I sense that fear, I just communicate an emotion of peacefulness or safety in order to overcome the fearful instinct and get the horse to trust me. If I touch the horse, talk to it, and transmit a sense of calm and happiness, it generally responds to my directions. I'm not completely sure how I do it, and it doesn't work every time with every horse—but here and there, it works pretty well."

CJ walked over to the wall behind Gallo's desk and looked at several pictures of him in a winner's circle accompanied by the race winners and owners. "Humans are so much more complicated than horses. I wish I could relate to people the way you do. People respect you and like you. It doesn't matter if it's a groom working in the stables or a millionaire owner of a horse, you have a natural skill for gaining their friendship. I wish I could do that."

"Ah, you'll figure it out, CJ. You're getting better at it all the time, and just like you and horses, my interpersonal skills don't work with everyone. Heck, I'm forty-two years old and never been married. What's that tell you about my ability to relate to women? I'm clueless!"

CHAPTER SEVENTEEN

T
he grandstands and clubhouse of Churchill Downs erupted like a volcano as fifty thousand racing fans jumped up and down, emitting a crescendo of sound when Hit the Bid crossed the finish line one yard ahead of her closest competitor. The filly had come from eighteen lengths off the pace to run down the fastest colts in thoroughbred racing—claiming the title to the most prestigious horse race of the year.

Gallo watched as a trackside reporter working for ABC Sports pushed his way into the owner's box with a cameraman and a sound-man in tow. He would be the first to get a post-race interview with Ritchie Gallo.

"Ritchie!" he shouted, flashing dazzling teeth at the camera as he pushed a microphone into Gallo's face. "This place is going *ballistic* after that heart-stopping race. How are you feeling right now?"

"Oh man, what can I say? Right now, I have tears in my eyes. I just can't believe the performance of this filly for the last two years. She never gives up, she never quits—she just loves to run, and it's a blessing to be able to watch her."

"She got off to a slow start, and for quite a while, it didn't look like she had much of a chance."

"Yeah, she came out of the gate on the wrong lead, and it took CJ a few seconds to get her stride back in tempo, but CJ really knows what she's doing on this horse—she paced her really well right up until she asked her to run."

"Ritchie, I can't get over the fans' reaction to this filly." As he said so, the crowd went wild in the background, and the cameraman briefly panned sidelong to catch the countless women holding signs saying, "*GO HTB – GO CJ!*"

"It's got to be really rewarding to see so much support from the public, and especially so many fans who aren't normally into thoroughbred racing."

"Oh yeah, it's really amazing. They lined up an hour ahead of time to see her walk from the stables to the paddock, and fans were ten deep around the paddock watching her dance and pose for them. This horse really feeds off this stuff—she likes people, and she understands that people like her, and it just emboldens her to give it everything she's got."

"Ritchie, a lot has been said and written about your jockey, CJ Jamieson. She's been honest about the fact that she has some mental challenges, but it certainly doesn't seem to be something that prevents her from winning races."

"Nah, CJ is a great young lady and rider. She doesn't crave the limelight like Hit the Bid, but once she's in the saddle, the two of them seem to have some sort of mind-meld, and they just turn into superwomen. She's done a great job assisting me in training the horse as well as bringing the filly home to the finish line."

"This is the last big race of the year—the voting for the Eclipse Award will be held very soon. Is she the horse of the year?"

Ritchie smiled. "You tell me, brother!"

"Well, I think it's pretty hard to argue that she isn't. Congratulations, Ritchie Gallo, and now we will send it out to the track where Mary Tierney is catching up with our winner."

CJ watched as reporter Mary Tierney rode out to the backstretch, where an escort rider held Hit the Bid's reins in preparation for the interview.

"CJ, what a great race! It was an unbelievable ride. There was a real display of girl power here at Churchill Downs today! Hit the Bid was the only filly in the race, but she beat the most talented field of colts to run this year. How do you feel, now that you've won?"

Tierney extended a microphone in CJ's direction, holding it there while CJ bent over, hugging the filly. "I'm speechless; I just don't know what to say. She's such an amazing horse."

"You got off to a slow start, and as you came through the far turn, you were still eighteen lengths behind the leaders. You were dead last for three-quarters of the race. How did that happen?"

"Well, she was a little jumpy in the gate because there was some chaos being created by the colts on either side of us. Then, for some reason, she broke out on a left lead as opposed to the right. We gave up some ground right away, and I had to tap her on the right shoulder a few times to get her to change leads—but once she made the change, she was running effortlessly. I really hadn't planned on being that far back, but I just took my time and let her gradually move closer to the pack."

"As you entered the far turn, you were still last, but you began to reposition Hit the Bid in order to make a stretch run."

"Yeah, I was able to cut the corner and move down inside. She responded well to the maneuver—at that point, she still wasn't in high gear."

"CJ, I've got to take my hat off to you. You showed great calm and poise to hold your position and be patient rather than have the horse run farther than she needed to. Only when you reached the straight-away did you angle out so you didn't lose much ground."

"Thanks, Mary. I was actually thinking about splitting horses as we came through the turn, because she becomes more aggressive when she splits horses, but the colts came back together, shutting off the move. She's so agile, she just skipped over their heels and moved outside. At that point, we just accelerated down the stretch. It was kind of funny, because as the crowd began to roar, I thought she was going to stop in the middle of the stretch and pose for pictures, so I had to get on her a little bit and get her to focus on the finish line. If she hadn't lost her focus for a few strides, we would have won by a bigger margin, but then the finish wouldn't have been as exciting. She really knows how to generate drama and please the fans."

"CJ, do you think Hit the Bid is the horse of the year?"

"She's the horse of the year, by a long shot. The only race she ever lost was her maiden outing, and since then, she has consistently beaten the best fillies, mares, colts, and stallions in the country. To me, she's the horse of the decade!"

"Well, I think there are a lot of people in the racing industry who agree with you after the performance she put on today. Good luck, CJ! And enjoy the win. Back to you guys in the broadcast booth!"

The escort rider guided CJ and the filly back to the winner's circle in front of the grandstand where Jimmy was already waiting with a sponge saturated with water. He took the reins from the escort and began to wipe the horse's mouth with the sponge in order to begin the process of rehydrating the animal. The fans in the crowd were still clapping and yelling out to Hit the Bid and CJ as the horse was immediately surrounded by photographers, track officials, and racing industry dignitaries. Jimmy made sure he had control of the filly as he moved out a few yards into the middle of the track, continuing her cooldown walk and preventing anyone that wasn't a member of the inner circle from getting too close to the horse.

Once Jimmy had the thoroughbred under control, CJ jumped to the ground into the arms of Gallo.

"I'm proud of you kid," he said. "You gave her a great ride."

"Thanks, Mister Gallo, I'm so happy. Winning yesterday on T-three and now today on Hit the Bid—it's just a dream come true."

CJ's parents rushed out to give her a hug and congratulate her, as did Elliot and his parents. Now that CJ was out of the saddle and on the ground, it began to dawn on her that she was the focus of thousands of screaming people and an overwhelming media crush. She began to feel uncomfortable and a bit panicky, but she held onto Elliot's hand and tried to catch her breath. This was an important moment, and she didn't want to ruin it for Gallo, Jimmy, or any of the other people that had been so supportive over the last five months.

The normal post-race ritual of photographs took place in the winner's circle before Gallo, CJ, and their entourage went to an area of the clubhouse where the Breeders' Cup Classic trophy was presented to them on national television. At that point, print and television reporters clambered to get questions answered by the winning trainer and jockey. CJ's discomfort continued, but she persevered to answer the questions as best as she could—all the while, holding tightly to Elliot's hand. Eventually, her parents interceded and whisked her and the Monkmeyers out of the building and into a waiting limousine that took them to their hotel. They, and a small circle of friends, were to enjoy a victory dinner.

When the hordes of people moved with CJ and Gallo into the clubhouse for the presentation of the winner's trophy, Jimmy and two other grooms walked Hit the Bid off the track and down the path leading back to the stable area. One hour earlier, Hit the Bid had pranced and danced up that same path as she journeyed from the stables to the paddock. This time, another large crowd of fans watched her put on a thespian-esque performance as she walked in the opposite direction. She puffed up her chest and elevated her ears as she moved through the gauntlet of well-wishers.

Just thirty yards from the barn area, the filly started to walk slower and stopped her normal antics in front of a crowd.

"You okay, girl?" asked Jimmy. Hit the Bid seemed happy, and her eyes were bright and lively when Jimmy looked at her, so he assumed there wasn't a problem. "Yeah, we're going to get you a fresh bunch of hay, some oats and grains, and a few apples. And since you've been such a good girl, I'm going to sing a couple of the church songs that you like. As a matter of fact, I'm gonna start singin' right now!"

"Beulah Land, I'm longing for you,
And some day on thee I'll stand,
There my home shall be eternal,
Beulah Land, sweet Beulah Land."

CHAPTER EIGHTEEN

As the trainer of the horse that won the Breeder's Cup Classic, Gallo's status as a celebrity was firmly entrenched within the confines of the clubhouse at Churchill Downs. On the final day of the fall meet, he'd come to the track to pitch his services to several horse owners and to enjoy a little camaraderie with his peers in the racing industry. As he ambled about, traversing private boxes, tables in the cafés, or the clubhouse bar, he was constantly stopped by fans who wanted an autograph, a picture, or just a chance to talk about Hit the Bid and CJ Jamieson.

Since he didn't have any horses from Stone Fence Farms racing that day, it was a relaxed social event at the track that he rarely experienced. In addition, he would finish the afternoon by meeting with CJ and taking her out to dinner before she flew back to California for a few days with her parents.

CJ was riding in five events that day, including the final race on the card. By the time the ninth race was over, it was clear to Gallo that she wasn't having a great deal of success. In her first four races, she failed to finish in the money, with her best result being fifth place on a horse that crossed the tape six lengths behind the winner. But he knew that even a jockey with CJ's talent was entitled to a day when nothing went right.

Gallo decided to wait in the stable area for CJ to finish the race. He could be there when she dismounted and walk with her to the jockey room. A Churchill Downs employee gave him a ride over to the stables on a golf cart and he planted himself in front of an elevated television monitor so he could watch the competition taking place just thirty yards away on the main track.

The parade to the post for the eleven thoroughbreds was uneventful, and the horses entered the starting gate without any problems. CJ was on a four-year-old stallion named Breach Inlet and she was coming out of the fifth gate position. Gallo reviewed his program and noted that Breach Inlet was now competing in the twenty-first race of his career. The horse had never won a Grade Two or Grade One stakes race, but he had won four times over the previous three years and had numerous finishes in the money. Looking at his record over the last twelve months, it was pretty clear that his ability to be competitive was diminishing. In his four-year-old season, he only managed a third-place finish at Keeneland in the spring, and he won a claiming race against a field of horses with a much lower pedigree than his. The split times over the final furlongs of each race were less and less impressive as the horse got older. It made Gallo wonder if the stallion was having the physical issues that manifest themselves when a horse is over-raced.

Another interesting situation regarding the tenth race was the entry of two horses owned by syndicates where CJ's father was a general partner. Gallo got a chuckle out of the fact that CJ's job was to go out and beat her old man.

Gallo focused on the monitor and when the bell rang, the horses all made a clean break from the starting gate. CJ guided Breach Inlet straight down the grandstand stretch but didn't really ask him to run. Rather, she let the four horses to her left clear out of the way and then immediately took the stallion down to the rail. By the time the field had covered six furlongs and transitioned to the backstretch, Breach Inlet was in last place, seventeen lengths behind the leader. Gallo watched CJ as closely as he could on the monitor. She was riding with smooth, coordinated motions, but was definitely not encouraging the horse to accelerate or make a move to catch up with the pack. She seemed content to take her mount out on an easy breeze and not push him over the course of the race. Eventually, one of the horses owned by Crawford Jamieson's limited partnership won the race, and Breach Inlet crossed the finish line nineteen lengths behind the winner and ten lengths behind his nearest competitor.

Gallo was curious about the unusual way CJ had run the race, but Breach Inlet's trainer, who was now standing next to Gallo and looking at the same monitor, was a little more than surprised. He was *angry*.

"Do you believe this shit? Do you believe the ride I got out of this chick?" The trainer looked at Gallo and raised his voice. "What is this crap? She only rides for big guys like you? She only busts her ass in Breeders' Cup races? Her father had two horses in that race. I guess this is how she pays daddy back for winning on your horses—right, Gallo?"

Although the trainer knew who he was, Gallo had never met him before. He understood the genesis of the man's anger, but he was sure that CJ wouldn't purposefully take a dive in a race. "Let's see what she has to say when she dismounts. I'm sure CJ can explain her actions."

"Oh, I see, she screws up and you *defend* her. That was a disgraceful ride. She gets paid to compete, not to take the horse out on a Sunday jaunt. I'm going to report her ass to the stewards. She tanked this thing on purpose."

One by one, the racers entered the stable area with their muscles quivering, their blood vessels popping through their skin, and sweat dripping off their bodies. The enormous expenditure of energy consumed in the race left the animals dehydrated. They were all foaming at the mouth.

Breach Inlet was the last horse to step off the dirt track. Two grooms moved in to take control of the horse, and as soon as CJ jumped to the ground, the trainer let her have it. "What the *hell* was that all about? You didn't do a damn thing I told you! You just parked the horse on the rail and took a gentle jog around the track. Is this what you think I pay you for? What the hell is wrong with you?"

CJ seemed completely surprised by the man's aggressive language and threatening gesticulations. As the trainer continued to yell at her, she reacted by backing up and saying nothing. She looked as though she was going to cry. Gallo stepped forward in an effort to calm him down, but this action had the opposite effect.

"Hey," he said, trying to prevent his voice from raising the way it wanted to, "she doesn't react well to people yelling at her and getting in her face. Give her a second to wind down, and I'm sure she can tell us what happened out there."

"Why don't you mind your own goddamned business?" The trainer threw a roundhouse right hook into the left side of Gallo's face. The blow stunned Gallo, knocking him to the ground. As he started to get up, the angry trainer drew back his right hand to initiate another punch, but before he could release the blow, Gallo launched an uppercut into his groin. Now it was the aggressor's turn to roll in the dirt.

Several grooms and workers entered the fray and separated the two men. "I'm going to report her! I'm gonna get her license suspended. You can't do this shit and get away with it. The big-time trainers get the solid rides, and the rest of us get the bullshit. I'm just trying to make a living here, and we can't let *you* big-money guys screw with us!"

The grooms that worked for the man escorted him back towards the stall where Breach Inlet was quartered. He continued to shout at CJ and Gallo as he walked away, making several obscene gestures with his middle fingers. Gallo walked over to a stunned and tearful CJ and asked if she was all right.

"I'm okay, Mister Gallo, but he never let me explain what went wrong."

"CJ, I watched you ride this race. Anybody with any amount of knowledge about horse racing could see that you didn't make *any* effort to let the horse compete. You just dogged it around the track. If he complains to the stewards, you may very well have your license suspended."

"He's not going to put in a complaint on me, Mister Gallo."

"Why not?"

"Because when I got aboard the horse in the paddock, I told that trainer that the horse wasn't sound enough to run. The horse had no business being in this race."

Gallo's brows furrowed. "How do you know that, CJ?"

"Because the horse told me."

Gallo hung his head. "CJ, I get it. I know you can sense this stuff. But the stewards are just going to think you're blowing smoke up their asses. You could be in big trouble."

"Mister Gallo, there's another reason why he won't report me. Breach Inlet got a shot of Lasix from a vet earlier today. After the vet left, the trainer shot him up with more Lasix. This horse urinated like Niagara Falls from the time I left the paddock until I got to the starting gate. Also, they must have injected him with thyroxin. I could smell it in his urine. Not only that, but a groom told me they gave him a bi-carb milkshake this morning, and they injected phenylbutazone into each of his front knees. I'm telling you, Mister Gallo—this horse is *done*. He doesn't want to race anymore! I could have whipped him from the starting gate to the finish line, and he still wouldn't have had a snowball's chance in hell of winning. The trainer wouldn't listen to me and told me just to try and get a third-place finish out of the horse. By the time I got to the starting gate, I knew I should have refused to ride, so at that point, I just let him jog around the track and hoped that he wouldn't get hurt."

"Well, if they pulled all those stunts before they sent the horse out there, they violated a bunch of rules. They probably won't want you explaining all this to the rule-makers, especially given the fact that you told the trainer not to run the horse prior to the race."

Gallo and CJ started walking in the direction of the jockey room. "Sorry about your sport coat and pants getting all dirty. I didn't know what to do when that man hit you. I don't like violence, but I was glad you hit him in the nuts."

"How's my face look?"

"Hm, not too good. We better get some ice on it. You're starting to look like a pumpkin."

Gallo laughed as he wiped the side of his face with a handkerchief.

"CJ, have you ever had a circumstance before where you knew a horse wasn't ready to race, but you rode him anyway?"

"No, Mister Gallo. A few times last spring—and once or twice in the fall meets—I got to a horse in the paddock, and I just *knew* it wasn't ready to run. In each case, the trainers took my word for it and scratched the horse. They weren't happy, but they did it. I don't think they wanted to be confronted by a situation where the horse broke down or was injured, and it looked like they ignored the advice of their jockey. In this case, with Breach Inlet, the trainer insisted I ride him. It's an ethical thing with me, Mister Gallo. The mistake I made today is I should have just walked out and let John McCann deal with a 'failure to perform' suit from the trainer."

"So, did Breach Inlet tell you anything else besides his physical health issues?"

"As a matter of fact, he did. This horse is a real sweetheart, but he's lost his desire to run because his knees hurt and he's been a bleeder in the past. I can tell from riding him that his lung capacity isn't what it used to be. He would just like to graze in a field of sweet grass and maybe enjoy an occasional visit to the breeding barn. As stallions go, I think he'd be a fairly gentle lover."

"Oh, really?" said Gallo with a bit of skepticism in his voice.

"Yeah, Mister Gallo. He's a really good horse and he loves kids."

"He loves kids? Did he tell you that also?"

"Well, actually, I just sensed it. As we were making the parade to the post, he stopped when we passed two young boys sitting on the fence next to the entry gate. He looked at them, his ears went up, and I could tell that his heartbeat increased. He wanted to walk over to the children, and I knew that the young boys wanted to pet him, but I had to keep him moving in the parade. He's a gentle and loving horse. I think he would be great in one of these equine treatment programs where they use horses to help kids with mental issues like Downs Syndrome or autism. Look how much horses helped me!"

CJs eyes got wide as she conjured up what she thought was a great idea. "Maybe what we should do, Mister Gallo, is buy Breach Inlet from this stupid trainer and donate him to one of the non-profit organizations that conducts this type of therapy. Don't you think that's a terrific idea?"

"Yeah, but it can get a little expensive buying thoroughbreds and giving them for free to non-profit organizations. Maybe we should win a few more races first. What do you think?"

CJ smiled. "Sounds good to me. But I'm going to hold on to this idea, just like Mister Jimmy holds on to a cup of free coffee!"

CHAPTER NINETEEN

Stone Fence Farms wasn't the biggest or most prestigious breeding and training farm for thoroughbreds in Kentucky, but it was certainly one of the most beautiful. Nearly two hundred acres of rolling grasslands cut into rectangles and squares by black fences defined the fields where horses could graze, run, and play. The main house was a classic brick Georgian Colonial that welcomed visitors who traveled up a quarter-mile crushed-stone driveway from the highway. Behind the house, four large white barns with dark green trim housed sixty horses. About a half of the animals were being trained to race, with the rest enjoying retirement as breeding stallions or broodmares.

On a cool but bright December day, the farm was the location for a video crew whose mission was to shoot a breakfast cereal commercial starring CJ and Hit the Bid.

Large lights and space heaters were in position around the entrance to Hit the Bid's stall, and several cameras were aimed at the horse as she stood with her head bobbing up and down at the stall door. After fifteen attempts to get CJ and the horse to perform as planned, the director of the commercial was losing his patience and his ability to project his smarmy and patronizing personality. Either CJ would butcher the lines she was to speak, or she would say them without a smile on her face and the right inflection in her voice.

Hit the Bid added to the dysfunctional situation by refusing to eat the large bowl of cornflakes CJ was placing in front of her, or by ignoring the bowl and nudging CJ in the shoulder with her nose. Between a playful horse that didn't like cornflakes, and a young woman with marginal public speaking skills, the director realized he may have bitten off more than he could chew.

Finally, on the sixteenth take, CJ recited the lines correctly with the proper level of emotion and sincerity. She smiled throughout and raised the large bowl of cereal up to the horse's mouth. Just as Hit the Bid was about to eat the product, a powerful stream of golden liquid shot forth from her loins, causing CJ to jump out of the way. It splattered all over the light reflectors placed on either side of the stall.

"Cut! Cut! Cut! The horse screwed it up—*again*!"

The director walked up to CJ and Hit the Bid, carefully stepping around urine-soaked clumps of hay. "You're supposed to be able to talk to horses, young lady. Didn't you know she was going to pee?"

"I'm sorry, sir," said a distraught CJ. "She can pretty much pee anytime she wants."

The man turned around and looked at Jimmy Crowder. "How long is it going to take to clean this up?"

"No sweat, brother. I'll take care of this right away."

When Jimmy walked up to the thoroughbred, he smiled and looked her in the eye. "You're having fun now, aren't you, baby girl?"

Jimmy's question was followed by a loud blast of flatulent gas from the horse's backside, and the passage of four stools, each the size of a grapefruit, hitting the stall floor with an unceremonious *plop*.

The director put his hands on his hips and lowered his head in frustration. "And I thought *actors* were a pain in the ass," he muttered under his breath. Looking to his left, he spotted Ritchie Gallo, who was standing with his hand over his mouth and a concerned look on his face.

Gallo could see that things weren't going well, and he sympathized with the anguish the director was enduring as he tried to bring a horse and an inarticulate young woman into his fantasy world. He decided they had reached a point where he needed to intervene in order to bring this to completion.

"Hey there, Mister Director—why don't we take a break and let me talk to CJ for a minute?" Gallo then looked over at Jimmy Crowder. "Jimmy, get the horse some water and brush her down a little bit. Why don't you sing to her, maybe that will make her more cooperative?"

The director told everyone to take a fifteen-minute break, and CJ walked over to Ritchie. She was wearing the racing silks for Stone Fence Farms: a white shirt with thick royal blue stripes running down each arm from her collar. Another wide blue stripe encircled her chest and back. She wore white racing pants with a black belt and brand-new racing boots that came up just below her knee.

"How's it going, kid?" asked Gallo. "Are you enjoying being a movie star?"

"Not really, Mister Gallo. I don't think I'm too good at this. I'm confused by all the things this man is saying to me, and I don't think Hit the Bid likes the cereal we're giving her."

"You know, CJ, I've never worried a lot about making money with Hit the Bid. I'm more focused on her legacy as a great filly. But this commercial is a pretty lucrative way to make some money without putting her at risk. We both are being paid well. All you and the horse have to do is make the director happy."

"I don't know, Mister Gallo . . . I'm having trouble dealing with all the activity. I think I need some alone time."

When CJ made that statement, Gallo became alarmed. She hadn't mentioned "alone time" for several months. He let John McCann talk him into collaborating on this commercial because he thought she had matured to the point where she could handle an event that was very unnatural for her, but now he was second-guessing the decision.

He placed his hands on her shoulders and bent over so he could look her in the eye. In a calm and sympathetic voice, he tried to get her to focus on the task at hand. "CJ, you make a living riding on the back of a twelve-hundred-pound animal running at forty miles-per-hour surrounded by a whole gaggle of other horses running like hell in front of thousands of screaming people. Do you really think *this* is more chaotic and complicated than something you routinely accomplish on a daily basis?"

"I can't explain it, Mister Gallo. When I'm in a race, on horseback, I think with clarity. I know what I have to do to win the race, and sometimes I even know that the horse next to me is too good to beat and we're just going to lose because there's nothing I can do about it. On the track, everything just comes to me, and I know how to react to it. When I'm in a situation like today, surrounded by people I don't know, I feel like I'm on a dance floor with a strobe light above my head. Everything is herky-jerky and nothing is logically connected. My psychiatrist back in California tells me it's okay to take a time-out and collect myself. She says it will help me deal with being in the public eye."

Gallo took a breath and decided it was time for a heart-to-heart: "Listen, CJ, I really care about you. Somehow, we've formed a bond, and you mean a lot to me. In life, there are always people who will try to convince you that you're a victim, and someone else is making your life difficult for you. The reality is that no one has to be a victim if they don't want to be. I've seen you grow dramatically as a person over the last six months. Every time you've been confronted by a new challenge, you've risen to the occasion and learned how to deal with it. Maybe it's not as easy for you as it is for other people, but it doesn't mean you can't do it. You've also got a gift that few others have—a great sensitivity to these magnificent animals we work with every day—and I have to believe there is some way to redirect or develop that sensitivity towards human beings as well as horses. Look, life isn't fair and there are always serious obstacles to overcome. People who have to take a time-out whenever things get tough typically aren't very successful or happy. There's and old saying: 'When the going gets tough, the tough get going.' It's something worth thinking about."

The young lady's eyes welled up with tears. She looked down, gazing at the ground. Gallo put his hand under her chin and brought her face back to eye level. He spoke softly and smiled. "Hey, what do I always tell you about looking people in the eye? Keep your chin up and keep rolling. You're Cicely Jamieson, one of the finest riders in the world. Knocking out this stupid commercial is a piece of cake. Now go back there and generate some cosmic communication with our filly so she will cooperate and finish the job. When this is over, you have my personal commitment that I will kick this dick-head director in the ass and push him face-first into a big pile of horse crap."

CJ smiled and wiped a tear from her face. Gallo took his hands off her shoulders and stood up. "Sorry about placing my hands on you. I know that makes you uncomfortable at times."

CJ's reaction to that statement was to step forward and wrap her arms around him, squeezing him as hard as she could. Gallo was a bit surprised by this display of public affection, responding by patting her softly her on the back and bending over to kiss her on the top of her head. When they pulled back from their embrace, CJ smiled. "Don't worry, Mister Gallo. I'll make this work."

She turned and started walking back toward the cluster of cameras and lights aimed at the stall. As she walked away, Gallo shouted out one more measure of encouragement: "Get back on stage! Break a leg!"

CJ stopped and turned. "Why would I break a leg, Mister Gallo?"

"Ah, forget it, just go back and make it work."

Gallo shook his head and walked over to the large food and refreshment table that had been set out for the video crew. When he surveyed the spread, he was happy to see a tub of ice filled with light beers. *I need a drink,* he thought. When he twisted off the top to the bottle, he heard a familiar voice behind him.

"C'mon, Ritch, it can't be *that* bad—this is the easiest hundred and fifty grand you'll ever make in your life." John McCann reached over and captured a beer for himself, and the two men moved over to a stone fence to take a seat and watch the proceedings from a distance.

"I want to thank you again, John, for brokering this commercial deal for me. I never had an agent before, so I appreciate your efforts to negotiate the money and get a contract in place."

"No problem, buddy, I'm happy to do it. I'm even doing it *pro bono*; I'm not taking my normal 20 percent cut."

"I'm grateful but, knowing you, I keep waiting for the next shoe to drop. What do you have up your sleeve?"

McCann smiled and took a swig of his beer. "I'm not going to bullshit you because we are good friends, but there is something I can put in place that you really need to consider. Do you remember last August when we ran into Crawford Jamieson on the veranda at Saratoga National? He proposed a match race between Tamarlane, the stallion from Dubai, and an American horse. Everything is almost in place for this race. We're guaranteed to have a huge national television audience in the U.S. on ESPN, and they want to run it in March at Santa Anita Park. The race would reach an enormous international audience over Sky TV and Al Jazeera.

All the pieces are in place except *one*—we need a horse to race against Tamarlane. We have a tentative agreement with the owners of the Kentucky Derby winner, Find That Bird, but we really want your horse. Hit the Bid has already beaten Find That Bird in the Travers and the Breeders' Cup Classic, and the attraction of a filly and a lady jockey going against an Arabian stallion is huge. The television viewership for this race could set a record for horse racing. Sponsors are lining up to pay for thirty-second commercials before and after the race. We're talking about some big-time money here, Ritchie."

"John, you know my intention is to retire Hit the Bid. She's accomplished enough with her performances this year. She'll always be remembered as one of the great fillies in racing history."

"Ritchie, just consider this—the ownership of each horse will get a minimum of one million dollars just for showing up and competing. There will be a two-million-dollar winner-take-all pool for the horse that crosses the finish line first. How often do you have a chance to make that kind of money with one of your mounts?"

"Well, that's very enticing, but maybe it's time for Hit the Bid to retire and enjoy an active sex life with some of the most famous stallions in the business."

"Ritchie, get real. We've both been in the breeding barn. Getting humped by a hormone-driven stallion is not enjoyable sex. That horse would rather run her heart out on a racetrack than go through the trauma of breeding."

Gallo took a deep breath and another sip of his beer. He knew the filly was meant to be on the racetrack, but breeding her was an inevitable business decision every owner had to make when in possession of a mare as talented as Hit the Bid.

"Ritchie, let me ask you this. Are you still training Hit the Bid?"

"Uh, well, yeah. We're still exercising the horse."

"No, kidding? So why are you still working the horse if you're going to retire her?"

Gallo said nothing.

"Okay, I'll tell you why you're keeping her in shape. It's because you don't want it to be over. *You* don't want it to be over, *thousands* of racing fans don't want it to be over, and many thousands of *women* who don't know a mare from a filly still want to see CJ and Hit the Bid win races. In the last five months, they've become national heroes, and this is a way for her to go out on top and leave a legacy no one will forget." John sat closer, his untouched beer sweating in his palms. "You and I both know that over the distance of a mile and a quarter, she's probably the fastest horse in the world, and this is the only way to prove it. Do me a favor, just think about it for a day or two, and we'll talk it over again later. What do you say?"

Gallo again didn't respond, but he knew that McCann had a point. He couldn't imagine never seeing this extraordinary horse compete again; she had become a national figure. "Okay, I'll think about it, and we'll see how I feel in a few days."

As they walked back toward the barn, they could hear the video director shouting with joy. "That's it, that's it—that's a wrap! What a great job by the jockey, and this beautiful horse, and everyone involved." He appeared to be so glad that the torment of filming this commercial was over that the words of gratuitous admiration just kept flowing from his lips. He hugged the videographer, the lighting guys, the makeup artist, and surely to CJ's horror, lifted her off the ground with a bear hug. He then moved to the stall and grabbed Hit the Bid around the neck and gave the horse a kiss. Hit the Bid responded by snorting a large loogy all over his shirt.

CHAPTER TWENTY

G allo guided General Custer to the training track at Stone Fence Farms. He was closely followed by Hit the Bid with CJ in the saddle. Since there were no other thoroughbreds training on the one-mile dirt oval, they moved down near the rail and walked the horses side by side so they could talk about the business decisions that had just been concluded and the challenging months of racing ahead for Hit the Bid and Tackle Tim Tom .

He had just returned from New York City, where he participated in two days of negotiations and planning for a match race to be held at Santa Anita Racetrack in California. There, on March 9, Hit the Bid would race against Tamerlane. Gallo still couldn't believe it—John McCann had convinced him to delay the retirement of Hit the Bid in order to engage in one more highly publicized race that would have a worldwide audience.

Gallo was glad that the business aspects of the deal were over— now, he could concentrate on preparing his horse for the race. The publicity campaign was already in progress, and the unique situation of having a filly with a female jockey racing against a stallion and a male rider was piquing public interest. Tamerlane would be ridden by an experienced Irish jockey named Tommy Mullen, who had achieved success riding in Europe and the Middle East. The payoff to the winning jockey would be over two hundred thousand dollars. Gallo was sure this would be a real motivator for Mullen, but he also knew that CJ approached racing with her love of horses and *not* her bank account. In a match race against only one other horse, Gallo thought he had a real advantage because CJ and Hit the Bid were always in sync as they moved around a racetrack. Mullen would get his horse to the finish with his whip, but CJ would do it with her head and her heart.

For the last two weeks and right up until the match race in March, CJ would be commuting on weekends from her home in Pasadena to the farm in Kentucky. It was expensive to hire a private jet to transport her back and forth, but with so much money on the line, Gallo felt it was important to have her conduct the exercise rides on Saturdays and Sundays. During the week, CJ attended classes at Pomona College and on Friday nights, flew to Lexington to work with Hit the Bid and Tackle Tim Tom.

"I know this a real grind for you, CJ. But no one is as successful training these two thoroughbreds as you are. Once again, I really appreciate your dedication and help."

"That's okay, Mister Gallo. I work hard mid-week to study and complete my homework, and I really look forward to the weekend so I can be around the horses. By Friday afternoon, I've enjoyed all I can stand of my fellow students and professors. At that point, I can't wait to smell horse poop in Kentucky!"

Gallo laughed. "You know, I don't think I've ever asked you this, but what are you majoring in at college?"

"I'm a psychology major."

"Psychology?"

"Yeah—I'm good at understanding horses; it's *people* I need the help with."

"Well, I guess that makes sense."

They continued to walk the horses as Gallo explained the racing schedule for each horse over the next four months. "This match race with Tamerlane is obviously a big deal, but no matter what happens, I'm going to retire Hit the Bid at that point. The race against the stallion from Dubai will be her last, so we only have to get her ready for one race. Tackle Tim Tom, however, is a different situation. To get him into the Kentucky Derby, we must earn enough Derby qualifying points. He got twenty points when you won the Breeders' Cup Juveniles race last November, but I figure we need another thirty to forty points to guarantee his inclusion in the Derby, so I have him entered in the Fountain of Youth Stakes at Gulfstream on March 2. John has arranged for you to ride T-three in that race, so we will fly you down to Florida for that event. Assuming we earn points at Gulfstream by finishing in the money, we'll ship him out to California in April to run in the Santa Anita Derby. Again, if we can get some points in that race, I think he's a shoo-in for the Derby in May."

"Honestly, Mister Gallo, I think we've got a good shot at winning both races. These sprint workouts you've designed for T-three and Hit the Bid seem to be working. We've always known how fast Bid was, and this training regimen has her in the best shape of her life. But the split times we've seen lately from T-three are just spectacular."

"Well, you've got to remember that Bid is a full year older than T-three, and she's more mature physically. With the colt coming into his three-year-old season, that final element of physical maturity is kicking in, and he just gets stronger and stronger. I don't know of any horse that bursts out of the gate as quickly as he does. He can hang with anyone for the next mile, and when you turn for home, he seems to get shot out of a cannon. That's the simple tactic we're going to use in every race—you've just got to make sure he's got room to run."

"I get it, Mister Gallo, and I'm looking forward to those races. I've never been to Florida, and racing in my backyard at Santa Anita is always a real blast!"

"Okay, let's go ahead and start the workout for Hit the Bid. Take her up to a trot for one furlong and then let her breeze as fast as she can for two furlongs. She should be able to do eleven seconds per furlong, no sweat. At that point, slow her down to a trot for two furlongs and then do it all over again. We want to go through this sequence four times. You got it?"

"I got it. Let's go, Bid, time to get to work."

CJ moved the horse up to a trot for one-eighth of a mile and then let her go full throttle for two furlongs. She cooled her down for a quarter of a mile and then let her run again. Throughout, Gallo stood by and timed each sprint, yet again impressed by the athletic ability of this great filly. Her fourth sprint was almost as fast as her first. She was blessed with great speed and an unbridled desire to run.

After CJ slowed Hit the Bid down to a walk, he rode out to her on General Custer and took the reins so he had control of the racehorse. They walked together for another few minutes in order to lower the thoroughbred's heartbeat and then headed for the stable.

"That was a good workout, CJ. She's really running with consistent speed."

"Yeah, she is, but on that last sprint I sensed that she was a little reluctant to accelerate through the finish line. She was happy and strong when we completed the sprint, but she seemed to dog it a little over the final fifty meters. That's not like her. Maybe she's trying to tell me something. . . ."

"Well, the split times didn't vary by much; she certainly showed good stamina right through the entire session."

"I don't know—it just didn't feel right to me. When I touch her, I get the image of an apple. Do you know what that might mean?" Gallo stared wordlessly. "I just think you better check her over *very* carefully when we get her back to the stall."

"No problem, we'll check her out really good," he said, forcing a smile. It was better if CJ didn't know all of this made him a little nervous—not now. "Hey, look, she's starting to dance again even though there are no fans around. This horse is always performing whether she's running, walking, or standing still."

CJ smiled and patted Hit the Bid on the neck. As always, the filly seemed delighted to be heading back to the stable after a vigorous workout, but today, even Gallo noticed a little something different about the way she carried herself.

As CJ walked Hit the Bid away, he heard her say, "Are you trying to hide something for me, Bid? What are you thinking?"

CHAPTER TWENTY-ONE

A s Gallo drove into Gulfstream Park Village, he was struck once again by the extraordinary difference between this venue for thoroughbred racing and his childhood home of Saratoga Springs.

Saratoga was the perfect embodiment of its most timeless traditions: horse races, classic old homes perched along rustic streets, copses of Adirondack pine trees, and, of course, a racetrack that looked just as it did one hundred years ago.

Gulfstream, on the other hand, glistened in the Florida sunshine like a modern-day emerald city. Situated just one mile from the Atlantic Ocean, it provided a destination resort environment that included a shopping mall with an array of restaurants, world-class art galleries, a bowling alley, outdoor cafes and nightclubs, fashion boutiques, health and beauty services, and more. Anchoring this impressive infrastructure was the legendary Gulfstream Park racetrack.

Gallo had just arrived in Florida the day prior with Jimmy and Tackle Tim Tom. They were there to run the horse in the Fountain of Youth Stakes, a Grade Two race for three-year-olds that was competed at a distance of one-and-one-sixteenth miles. The race was part of the championship series on the road to the Kentucky Derby and worth fifty, twenty, ten, and five qualifying points to the top four finishers. Eleven horses were entered in the race, and all had shown promise as two-year-olds.

Today, Gallo had to make his way to the third floor of the racetrack clubhouse for a meeting with track officials and other trainers to discuss the final preparations for this important race. As Gallo exited the elevator, he was surprised to find John standing there waiting for him—and even more surprised to see him with a concerned look on his face.

"How you doin', Ritch? Let's go over here—we need to talk."

The men chose a café that looked out over the track. They were the only ones in the room, as the establishment had not yet opened for the day. Gallo was getting a strange vibe from John. "What's the story, John? You don't look so good."

John shook his head. "I just got off the phone with Crawford Jamieson. We agreed to cancel CJ's flight. She won't be coming here to Florida."

"What?" Gallo felt his heart stop in his chest. "Are you nuts? I need her here tomorrow to exercise the horse and ride him on Saturday!"

"That's the problem, Ritchie. CJ isn't going to be able to ride Tackle Tim Tom in the Fountain of Youth Stakes."

"Why the hell not?"

John took a deep breath. "When we negotiated the contract with Tamerlane's owners and all the sponsors for the match race next week at Santa Anita, we agreed that Crawford and his partners would have the option to scratch CJ as a jockey on any races or exercise rides if they felt it risked her ability to ride Hit the Bid in the match race. They have exercised that option; they don't want to take a chance on her getting hurt this Saturday when she rides T-three. They've scratched her as the jockey, and she can't exercise a horse without their permission until the day of the match race. They're just trying to protect their investment."

"Their investment? What about *my* investment? I'm trying to get a horse into the Kentucky Derby! Tackle Tim Tom can win the Derby—but I must earn points in this prep race to qualify. These guys are removing the only jockey I've found that can consistently ride this colt! Where am I going to find another jockey that can connect with the horse in two days?"

"Look, Ritch, I've got four or five world-class jockeys riding in the meet here at Gulfstream that would all love a shot at riding your colt. Getting you a replacement isn't going to be a problem. We know the colt is talented, and these are experienced guys—you can still win the Fountain of Youth."

"John, this isn't how I prepared to run this race, and no one rides him like CJ. Without her, it increases the odds that I don't get as many points as I need."

"Jeez, Ritchie, you've gotta look at this from the perspective of Tamerlane's owners and all the television networks and sponsors involved in the match race. If she falls off T-three on Saturday and can't ride the next week, the attractiveness of the match race drops *precipitously*. Viewers all around the world want to see a female jockey on a female horse kick the shit out of a couple of males. That's what they want to see! If they aren't going to see that, the biggest hook for the race evaporates. This thing is a huge event provided that a twenty-year-old woman with a history of brain damage is riding an American filly against an Arabian stallion. Anything less than that is probably going to wipe out one-third of the potential audience. Crawford Jamieson knows that whether Tamerlane wins or loses this race, the big payoff comes with an enormous global audience. He believes his horse can beat his daughter's mount, and he wants this to be as big an event as possible."

Gallo sat back in his chair and exhaled a breath of frustration. He was a planner. He believed his careful and precise training plans with his horses was the key to success and didn't like having his plans change. Tackle Tim Tom was perhaps the most talented three-year-old in racing, but he was also a stubborn horse who would only run consistently for one jockey.

And that jockey had just been yanked out of the saddle.

"John, you're CJ's agent. If I don't get points out of this race on Saturday, racing T-three in the Santa Anita Derby is mandatory. Can you *guarantee* me that CJ will be in the saddle for that race?"

"Ritchie, you know CJ as well as anybody. Right now, she's a heartbroken young lady sitting in her parents' home in Pasadena. The Santa Anita Derby is after the match race. There is no way CJ won't be riding the colt at that point. I'm sure her mother will also be delighted to see her win on their local track. The problem only exists for this Saturday and the following week. Once the match race is over, Crawford Jamieson and his partners no longer have the ability to dictate when she rides."

"Okay, I see how this is going down, but before I resign myself to the situation, I want to talk to Crawford."

"Ritch, is this really necessary?"

"Goddammit, John! Dial him up so I can talk to him!"

Reluctantly, John took out his cell phone and made a call to Crawford Jamieson. When he had him on the line, he handed the phone to Gallo.

"Hello, Mister Gallo. I guess by now you have heard the bad news. I'm sorry about this, but in discussions with the networks, the sponsors who are ponying up a ton of money, and my business partners, we just felt it best not to take any risks with CJ's health. We need her on that filly next week."

"Yeah, and I need her on the colt this Saturday. How do I explain this to my partners at Stone Fence Farms, who own Tackle Tim Tom? I'm protecting my financial ass since I own Hit the Bid, but I'm putting their best interests in jeopardy by not having CJ aboard T-three. How do you think this makes me look with the men and women who trust me to do the best I can with the horses they own or manage? You're making me look like a selfish fool."

"Mister Gallo, I'm sympathetic, but they have to know this isn't your call. It's ours. This is going to be a great television event, and we must make sure we capture all the market share we can to make it pay for everyone involved. Please keep in mind, Mister Gallo, that I own part of Tamerlane, and yet my daughter is the jockey for the competing horse. We can't have anything happen to her, so it looks like a setup. Fans and bettors need to be confident that CJ will be doing everything she can to beat my horse, including the preservation of her fitness prior to the race. In a sense, I can't lose. If my horse wins, I make a ton of money, and if Hit the Bid wins, I still make a lot of money, *and* I have a daughter who is financially independent. Either way, this has to look like it's on the up and up."

This did absolutely *nothing* to staunch Gallo's rising anger, so he took a moment to collect his thoughts before saying something he would later regret—but this only gave Crawford Jamieson an opportunity to bring another business aspect of the match race into the conversation: "I'm sure you are aware, Mister Gallo, that there is a clause in our contract which enables you to withdraw Hit the Bid if there is a serious injury or health issue with the horse prior to the match race. If you scratch the filly on this basis, we would, of course, require an expert team of veterinarians to examine the animal to validate your claim and ensure you weren't just trying to be cute and back out of the race. If you did pull a stunt like this, we would then invoke the Failure to Perform clause, requiring you to pay one million dollars as default payment. Do you have a million dollars in your bank account, Mister Gallo?"

"I see you've thought of everything, Mister Jamieson."

"That's my job. It is a business, after all, isn't it?"

"I guess it is. I'll see you next week at Santa Anita."

Gallo terminated the call on the cell phone and handed it back to John, who looked visibly shaken by everything that was unfolding. "Ritch, I'm really sorry about this. We're good friends, and I feel like I've failed you in the deal. But this is the type of stuff that happens when you have big money thrown around by a lot of powerful forces in the racing business."

Gallo nodded in agreement. "It's not your fault, John. I guess I'm still naïve when it comes to horses. I always chafe at the fact that some people are critical of what we do and accuse us of being inhumane. I know there is nothing in my heart or conduct that is bad for the horses I train, but I can see how competing at this level makes it a more cutthroat business. I'll just have to do my best for Tackle Tim Tom and get him ready for Saturday. Let's figure out which jock we want to put in the irons and get this thing rolling."

Gallo proceeded to speak with several men that were represented by McCann. He settled on a time-tested jockey named Braulio Cordero—a veteran of many stakes races, and a winner of both the Preakness and the Belmont Stakes. Gallo, Jimmy, and Cordero subsequently met to discuss race strategy, and Cordero took the horse out for a gentle one-mile gallop. Tackle Tim Tom was cooperative with the new rider in the saddle, and Gallo was becoming more optimistic about the race the next day.

On Saturday afternoon, CJ sat in the living room of her parents' home in Pasadena with their big-screen TV tuned to *Trackside Live*— the cable channel that was about to broadcast The Fountain of Youth Stakes from Gulfstream Park.

CJ felt like there was a belt around her chest. She should be there. This was *her* race—a fact made evident by Tackle Tim Tom's behavior. Already, attendants were having a problem getting him into the fifth spot in the starting gate. The colt didn't seem to have any interest in being placed in the enclosure and struggled mightily against attempts to get him there. After three tries, the gate attendants finally forced him into the chute—and a minute later, when the last horse was set in the eleventh position, the bell rang, and the gates opened.

The horses sprinted down the track. After running one-eighth of a mile, T-three was five lengths behind the leader and in sixth place.

CJ shouted at the TV, "C'mon, T-three! You should've blasted right to the front! You're dogging it. You have to get up with the leaders!"

CJ watched intently as her replacement gradually worked the horse to the front of the pack, where he was running stride for stride with two other competitors. As they entered the final turn, the black colt was six horses wide from the rail and would be covering a greater distance than the thoroughbreds to his left if he didn't come down closer to the infield.

CJ began yelling again at the jockey and horse—though she knew very well neither could possibly hear her. "Move him *inside,* Braulio, move him inside! His speed through turns is spectacular—let him run!"

To her dismay, Tackle Tim Tom ran the entire turn wide of the rail and entered the top of the stretch in the third position, following the leader by a length and the second position horse by half a length. At that point, Braulio did something that CJ would never have done— he began to use his whip to motivate the horse.

Tackle Tim Tom did not like being whipped. When CJ saw the jockey hit the colt, she knew it was all over. Rather than accelerating out of the turn, the horse just continued to run down the stretch at the same speed. Luckily, he was able to finish third by a nose and garnered ten Kentucky Derby qualifying points for a lackluster performance.

CJ turned to her father, who was sitting in an overstuffed chair to her left. "I could have won that race," she said, her voice nearly emotionless—which felt, strangely, more dangerous than if she were to cry or rage. "T-three knows he should have won, but he didn't like the way he was ridden."

"CJ, it's a *horse race,*" her father replied dismissively. "Maybe you could have won—but it's not a disaster. Gallo picked up some points for the Derby, and now we can all concentrate on Hit the Bid's match race next weekend."

When her father got up and walked out of the living room, CJ tossed the remote control at the television screen and picked up her cell phone to call Ritchie Gallo. Initially, she got his voicemail, but fifteen minutes later, he called back.

"Hey kid, how's it goin'?"

"It's going okay," she lied. "How's it going with you?"

"Well, obviously I am a little disappointed, but at least we earned ten Derby points and we're a step closer to getting T-three into the big dance."

"I'm really sorry, Mister Gallo. I should have been there on Tackle Tim Tom. I know he would have won if I was riding him. I'm really angry with my dad for doing this."

"Hey, look, it's not your fault, and you shouldn't be angry with your father. Once I cooled down, I could see that he was just serving the best interests of all the parties that have skin in the game for this match race. He's just doing what he does best—he's a businessman and, like it or not, this is a business."

"What's the next step for you?"

"Jimmy and I will fly back to Kentucky with Tackle Tim Tom tomorrow, and then on Monday we reboard the same transport plane with Hit the Bid and fly to California. I'll have her at Santa Anita getting acclimated Tuesday through Friday, and we race on Saturday. I'm sure John has briefed you on all the media activities we have during the week to publicize the race, but luckily there isn't a lot to do with Bid during this time—we just need her to run some easy miles before Saturday and make sure she's eating right."

"My dad has agreed to let me exercise her one day, but they want an exercise rider on her the other three days."

"No sweat, you can take her out on Tuesday. That will be the most demanding day of the four."

"How about T-three? What's next for him?"

"Since we only added ten points today, it's mandatory that we run him in the Santa Anita Derby on April 13, so we'll have to make another trip out to California. If he runs first or second in that race, we should be among the top twenty point earners, and he'll qualify for the Kentucky Derby." He paused for a moment, and all CJ could hear was the rustling feedback of faceless voices in the background. "I'm *really* going to need you in the chair for that race, CJ."

"Don't worry, Mister Gallo. After Hit the Bid beats the stallion from Dubai next Saturday, nothing in the world will keep me from riding T-three in the Santa Anita Derby. Nothing in the world!"

CHAPTER TWENTY-TWO

S anta Ana winds from the east blew the layer of smog that
smothers the Los Angeles basin out to sea, rewarding Southern
California residents with a warm and crystal clear day. Based
on this atmospheric clarity, racing fans attending the match race at
Santa Anita Park could sit in the stands and feel as though they could
touch the San Gabriel Mountains just a mile or two away. A perfectly
maintained dirt racetrack surrounded a green turf course and a lush
infield populated with manicured shrubbery, flower beds, and palm
trees that swayed gently in the wind.

Earlier in the week, when they arrived at the track, Ritchie wanted
Hit the Bid to be monitored twenty-four hours a day, so he had Jimmy
set up a bunkbed in the horse's stall. The groom would be with her
around the clock—her shadow and protector until they returned
to Stone Fence Farms in Kentucky. Fortunately for Jimmy, Hit the
Bid was very quiet and docile during the night, so he did manage
to get some sleep, but once awakened, she was in constant motion:
eating, nudging grooms, dancing, and enjoying the life of a superstar
racehorse.

Cameramen and photographers were a constant presence in the
stables or at trackside all week as Hit the Bid was pampered and
exercised in preparation for the race against Tamerlane. Gallo was
interviewed multiple times each day, as were Tamerlane's owners and
the stallion's jockey, Tommy Mullen. Press access to CJ had been a bit
more limited because she was still attending college classes during

the week and wasn't at the track daily. When she was there, Gallo was pleased to see how well she handled the questions thrown at her by reporters. She addressed the inquiries calmly and directly, and occasionally even managed to smile. All in all, a good performance by the same young woman who couldn't look people in the eye eight months earlier.

As Jimmy started to place clean polo wraps on her legs, Gallo could sense that Hit the Bid was getting the message that today was a race day. The trainer wasn't taking any chances—he'd make sure she didn't accidentally clip herself with a hoof or bump against something and cut her leg. The horse had been trained to compete, and Gallo could tell the filly was excited as she anticipated the race. He also knew that when CJ arrived, the fun would really start. Hit the Bid had a real affinity for the young jockey, both on and off the racetrack. Whenever CJ was in the irons, the horse and the woman were clearly having a great time as they blew past their competitors.

Gallo was delighted with the thoroughbred's sunny disposition on this important day. He was, however, a bit concerned when Jimmy told him she wasn't dancing about as was her normal habit. He figured she was just waiting for a larger audience.

The race was scheduled to begin at 3:00 p.m. Pacific Standard Time. An hour earlier, television networks all around the world began to broadcast a pre-game show that informed the public about the owners, trainers, jockeys, and the two horses entered in the contest. A detailed history of Tamerlane's success in Europe and the Middle East was presented, as well as an overview of the syndicate that owned the horse. Alternatively, a human-interest piece about CJ and her relationship with Gallo and Hit the Bid made her a sentimental favorite with the viewers, as it detailed her growth as a person as well as a jockey. Whether the producers of the show realized it or not, they were stacking the deck against the stallion—but the competition between genders was the primary draw of the program, and everyone involved knew that the filly had a good chance to win.

Thirty minutes before post time, Tamerlane and Hit the Bid were brought to the paddock to be saddled. Gallo had always thought that Hit the Bid was the most beautiful thoroughbred he had ever seen. Although big for a female, she was perfectly proportioned, had a beautiful coat, and a body built for speed. Her looks, skills, and personality made her a horse that every fan loved to support. Tamerlane, on the other hand, was the equine personification of charisma. At 17 hands in height and weighing over thirteen hundred pounds, he was even bigger than Hit the Bid or Tackle Tim Tom. A four-year-old chestnut stallion with a white blaze on his forehead, he carried himself with a measured sense of majesty that exuded confidence and the aura of a champion. The horse had already earned over four million dollars for his owners, and their plan was to run him this racing season in the States before putting him out to stud. The match race with Hit the Bid would be his introduction to American fans and the U.S. racing industry. As a trained observer of thoroughbreds, Gallo could easily see the potential Tamerlane had as a racehorse by his looks and his temperament. This race would be a real challenge for Hit the Bid.

As the two competitors were being prepared to race, CJ and Tommy Mullen made their way from the jockey room accompanied by cameras that broadcast their faces to television screens around the globe. Once they arrived in the paddock, the jockeys shook hands and moved directly to their assigned mounts.

When CJ reached Hit the Bid, she gave the horse a hug and looked into her eyes. "You ready to go, girl? You ready to win?" The filly's eyes were bright and happy; she made a little prancing move with her front legs and her ears were straight up. She was ready to race.

Before boosting CJ into the saddle, Gallo gave her his instructions, "This is pretty simple, CJ. You've only got one other horse to worry about. You're coming out of the number four chute, and

Tamerlane is out of the five, so you'll be on the rail. The track's fast so take the shortest distance to the finish line and don't waste any strides. Just run neck and neck with the stallion, and then we'll see who has it over the last furlong. If this jock, Mullen, plays a little game over the first six furlongs and holds the stallion back, go ahead and take the lead and let him try to catch you. You've got a good sense of how much gas she's got in the tank as the race progresses, so just use her energy wisely."

"I got it, Mister Gallo. I'll vary her speed based on what the stallion does. Bid seems excited. I'll have to take control so she doesn't go out and try to run sub-eleven-second splits. She usually cooperates with me, so I think we'll be okay."

Gallo smiled. "All right, kid, go out there and have fun!"

Once the jockeys were mounted, an outrider in a black helmet, red jacket, and white pants led the two horses out to the main track. CJ was wearing the white and blue stripe silks that represented Stone Fence Farm. Tommy Mullen's silks featured a complicated set of blocks and stripes colored in red, white, green, and black—the colors of the United Arab Emirates. When the horses stepped on to the track, thirty-five thousand patrons were immediately mesmerized by the beauty and grace of these two equine athletes. The fans began to applaud and whistle. Hit the Bid's immediate reaction was to start dancing and bobbing her head up and down. Tamerlane followed the filly with a calm and purposeful stride, reserving his energy for the task that lay ahead.

Since there were only two horses in the race, the jockeys could warm up their steeds on their own without the help of an attendant on a track pony. Once the outrider gave CJ the okay to proceed along the outside area of the track, she moved Hit the Bid from a walk to a trot, and eventually let the horse canter for an eighth of a mile. At that point, she turned the filly around and began to walk towards the starting gate where several attendants were waiting. As she passed

Tommy Mullen and Tamerlane, who were still moving in a clockwise direction, she could see the Arabian stallion sizing up her horse.

CJ sensed that Tamerlane wasn't your typical stallion whose instinctual attraction to a mare could divert his focus from the race. This horse understood the purpose of the contest and wanted to dominate his competitors, regardless of whether they were males or females. Tamerlane had the personality of a mustang that had the power, strength, and determination to lead a herd of wild horses across the plains of Oklahoma. He didn't just want to win races, he wanted to beat the other horses badly to prove that he was the alpha male. Fortunately, Hit the Bid was so busy entertaining the crowd and enjoying her afternoon, she didn't seem to be affected by the negative vibe emanating from her male competitor, and she happily followed a gate attendant into chute number four. A few moments later, Tamerlane was positioned into the five slot, and the race was ready to begin. The studio and trackside commentators surrendered the airwaves to the track announcer:

> *"Welcome, ladies and gentlemen, to the historical horse race everyone has been talking about for the last two months. We have a beautiful Southern California day and a fast track, so the conditions are perfect for Hit the Bid and Tamerlane, arguably the two fastest horses in the world. Both horses are in the gate, and seem to be steady and calm as they await the bell.*
>
> *"The starter has advised the riders to be ready—AND THEY'RE OFF!*
>
> *"That's Tamerlane making a clean break from the gate, but Hit the Bid got an awkward start and seems to have banged her front right leg on the side of the chute. CJ Jamieson has the filly straightened up, and after five or*

six strides, the filly is just one-half a length behind the stallion.

"Tamerlane is on the outside and moving along smoothly, but Hit the Bid has caught up with him on the inside and only trails by a head.

"These two great athletes are running stride for stride, and it's really a sight to see. But now comes the first tactical move of the race: CJ Jamieson is letting Hit the Bid run and the filly now leads Tamerlane by one-half a length. Jockey Tommy Mullen isn't willing to let Hit the Bid get too much of a lead so he's urging his horse to press the pace on the outside.

"As they complete the first turn, they've run the first quarter-mile in twenty-two seconds! That's a blazing speed you would expect from world-class horses, but can they keep this pace for another mile, or will one horse run out of gas?

"As they head down the backstretch, Hit the Bid has the lead by a head. On the outside, Tamerlane is staying right with her. They continue to run at a blistering pace, and each time Tommy Mullen urges his horse to take the lead, Hit the Bid surges and maintains the front position by a slim margin.

"They are thundering down the backstretch with Hit the Bid on the rail—unwilling to give up that half-length lead to her competitor—but Tamerlane still looks strong and continues to challenge on the outside.

"Now the filly is in front by a length, but Mullen is urging his mount to keep up with the speedy ladies that are holding their lead. They ran the first half-mile in forty-four and change. How can they maintain this speed? They'll be entering the far turn in just over a furlong; I can't believe they'll be able to keep running split-times at this rate. This race is everything we hoped it would be.

"There's less than one furlong to the far turn and . . . Wait a minute! WAIT A MINUTE! Hit the Bid is pulling up! HIT THE BID IS PULLING UP! Tamerlane continues to sprint into the turn, but Hit the Bid has broken down. Oh my God, she's broken down! Jockey CJ Jamieson has jumped to the ground and is holding the reins trying to get the filly to stop moving and stand still. The horse is limping badly and can't put any weight on her right front leg. Jeez, this is so difficult to watch— it looks like the filly snapped her lower right leg—I don't want to speculate, but it looks like a bad break. What a shame! What a shame! Hit the Bid has broken down! The crowd of thirty-five thousand fans has gone dead silent. Jamieson is still struggling to control the horse and everyone in attendance is shocked. Hit the Bid has broken down—my God, what a shame!"

CHAPTER TWENTY-THREE

CJ heard the cannon bone snap just as Tamerlane was making a move to pass on the backstretch. She knew immediately what happened and felt the jolt of pain that shot through the horse travel through her own body. She'd pulled on the reins with everything she had, and when the horse slowed down, jumped to the ground and tried to get Hit the Bid to stop moving. The animal was clearly panicked, and CJ could see the terror and pain in the horse's eyes.

"Stay still, Bid, stay still!" The jockey moved under the thoroughbred's neck and tried to immobilize her front legs, but a 105-pound young woman wasn't about to take physical control of a twelve-hundred-pound racehorse. Each time Hit the Bid put down her right front leg, the pain exploded up into her chest. The filly couldn't comprehend what had happened to her. Instinctive fear began to take over, and CJ's emotional reaction to the event wasn't providing the comfort and confidence the animal normally felt in her presence.

Thirty seconds after CJ dismounted, a motorized cart that had been trailing the racers pulled up with several attendants and a veterinarian aboard. The three men surrounded the horse and succeeded in helping CJ minimize the animal's movements. They spoke in calm voices to Hit the Bid and gradually got the horse to stay still. While the vet examined the filly's right front leg, a horse ambulance—an ambulance that pulled an enclosed trailer that was used to transport injured racehorses—arrived at the scene. There were pulleys and straps inside the enclosure that would allow a disabled horse to be moved without putting weight on its legs. While the ambulance angled into position, another electric cart reached their location carrying Ritchie Gallo, Jimmy Crowder, and Elliot Monkmeyer. Jimmy quickly moved to the front of the filly and held her upper leg so that the lower limb couldn't be placed on the ground. "It's okay, girl, it's okay. You gonna be fine—me and Ritchie are here now—you gonna be fine."

Gallo stood next to Hit the Bid and stroked her neck. He looked at his jockey. "Are you okay, CJ?"

CJ had begun to cry. "I thought there was something wrong when we were in the gate! I just felt it. Something didn't seem right. She wanted to run, but something wasn't right. She banged her leg on the gate as we took off, but she ignored the pain and kept running. She ran like *crazy*—she knew she could beat the stallion. I shouldn't have let her run. I should have stopped right away as soon as I felt that something wasn't right. I shouldn't have let her run!"

"It's okay, CJ, it will be all right. Just calm down so Hit the Bid will calm down, and we can get her back into the stables."

Gallo looked at Elliot and motioned for the young man to move CJ away from the horse. After Elliot put his arm around her and backed up a few paces, Gallo bent over to look at the leg. His heart dropped. He wasn't a vet, but he knew what he was looking at.

"I'm sorry, Mister Gallo," said the veterinarian. "It's a catastrophic compound fracture of the cannon bone right at the carpal joint. Even if we could repair it with surgery—and frankly, I don't think that's possible—we'd have to immobilize the leg for many months, which would only result in laminitis setting into the other three legs. Recovery would be very painful with little probability of success. I think it's pretty clear what we need to do."

Gallo considered debating with the vet, but he knew the man was right. He couldn't bear to authorize what was about to happen, but this magnificent champion didn't deserve to die a slow, painful death as an invalid.

He stood and put his arms around the horse's neck, placing his forehead against hers. "I'm sorry, Bid. I'm sorry. You're the greatest gift God ever gave me, and I let you down. I'm sorry, girl." He felt the tears flowing from his face and he could hear Jimmy getting choked up as he hummed a song. "Okay, Doc—can we at least get her in the ambulance and take her back to the stable so we can do this in private? I don't want to take her down on the track. She's only been a champion on a track. This isn't a place where she loses."

"Sure, Ritchie, we'll get her in and take her back to the infirmary."

Jimmy, the vet, and several track attendants gradually moved Hit the Bid into the trailer. They cinched her up so she couldn't put any weight on her right front leg. Jimmy was constantly singing—his soothing voice worked miracles as the horse remained calm despite the pain and cooperated with the men surrounding her.

"What's going to happen now, Mister Gallo?" asked CJ.

"Ah, we're going to take her back to the infirmary and make her comfortable. . . ." Gallo couldn't finish the sentence.

"You can't put her down, Mister Gallo. It was *my* fault. I shouldn't have let her run. She doesn't deserve this!"

"CJ, she has the heart of a champion. We can't make her into a science project, and that's what she'll be if we try to save her. She would have a miserable life until she dies of collateral issues. *That's* what she doesn't deserve."

"No, Mister Gallo, please don't put her down! Please, don't do this!"

C.J moved toward the horse ambulance and tried to enter the trailer where Hit the Bid was strapped in, but Elliot wouldn't let her go and pulled her back from the vehicle. She began to cry hysterically and fell to the ground. The rich brown dirt on the track soiled her silks and white pants as she lay there, weeping. The head of security for Santa Anita was now standing by with several police officers. Gallo made a request: "Can you guys please take Miss Jamieson and Mister Monkmeyer back to the jockey room where her parents can pick her up? Try to keep her away from the press, if you can."

The cops agreed to protect her and bring her back to the clubhouse. Elliot reached down and picked her up in his arms. He carried her to the police van and held her in the back seat as she wept on his shoulder.

Once the filly was secured in the horse ambulance, the vet injected her with a strong sedative that would minimize the emotional trauma she would suffer as she was transported back to the infirmary. Jimmy and Gallo stayed with her in the trailer as thousands of fans in attendance, and millions watching on television, saw the horse ambulance make its way to the stable area where everyone surmised that this amazing animal's life would soon end.

Once they had arrived at the infirmary, the President of Santa Anita Racetrack was waiting to speak with Gallo. He had already been informed as to the severity of the horse's injury and knew what the inevitable outcome would be. When Gallo stepped out of the trailer, he made a request. "Ritchie, I know how tough this is for you, and I'm sure every sports fan in the country is brokenhearted right now. She was a charismatic champion, and she deserves to be remembered. We have a plot in the infield we've been saving for the day we could bury a legendary racehorse here at Santa Anita. I can't think of a better horse to be immortalized at this great track than Hit the Bid. With your permission, we would like to place her there and put up a memorial."

Gallo exhaled and hung his head for a second to think. He would have loved to bury Hit the Bid at Stone Fence Farms, but the idea of transporting her dead body, as though she was going to the slaughterhouse, didn't feel right. Many more race fans would see a memorial at Santa Anita than at his farm in Kentucky.

175

"I appreciate that, sir, and I think this is a great place for her eternal home. You have my permission, and I thank you for this honor."

Gallo huddled with the vet and the representatives from the track. It was decided that the horse would be euthanized in the trailer—and later in the day, when everyone had left the facility, Hit the Bid would be moved to her final resting place on the infield of Santa Anita Park and buried.

Gallo and Jimmy held the heavily sedated horse's head in their arms until she was completely still. At that point, the veterinarian injected a large dose of barbiturates into an artery, which ended her life in just a matter of minutes. When her heart stopped, the two men hugged one another and rested their hands one more time on this beautiful and very special champion. Gallo remembered a line from a play he read in high school. He repeated it as he stroked her mane for the last time: "Good night, sweet princess, and flights of angels sing thee to thy rest."

Several hours later, when the grandstands and the clubhouse were empty, the horse ambulance was driven to the track infield where a backhoe operator dug a large grave in the middle of an acre of green grass.

Gallo had spent most of the time since the accident being interviewed by the media who wanted to know what happened on the track and how the decision was made to euthanize the horse. He was reasonably successful at containing his emotions, but it was clear to everyone present that this loss was taking a toll on him. Mercifully, the members of the press didn't require too much of his time and were satisfied to get a detailed description from the track vet as to the magnitude of the injury and the method used to put the horse down.

Jimmy declined to join Gallo and a contingent of track officials who went along to witness the burial of Hit the Bid. The groom apparently couldn't bear to see her lowered in the ground, and Gallo couldn't blame him, but he felt obligated to be there, since he was her owner and trainer. The body was wrapped in a clean tarp, and Hit the Bid was placed in her grave with the saddle and bridles she had been wearing when she broke down. Gallo also placed a set of jockey silks reflecting the colors of Stone Fence Farms in the grave. He said a silent prayer, then walked back across the track towards the stables, not wanting to see a backhoe intern the horse for eternity.

Gallo made his way to an office within the backstretch complex, where he left his briefcase and a gym bag carrying some work clothes. It was after sunset, and it was becoming darker by the minute, as he left the office and headed to the parking lot where his car was located. As if drawn by a magnet, he walked down the concourse in the stable where Hit the Bid was stationed for the last week. When he approached her stall, he could see the upper-half of the door was open and there was a light on inside. He could hear someone singing. It was no surprise to find Jimmy sitting in the makeshift bunk he had slept in for the previous few nights.

"What are you doing here, Jimmy? We can certainly afford a hotel room for you tonight."

"Nah, I think I'm going to sleep right here. It's my last chance to be near her." Jimmy was holding a bottle of bourbon in his hand. He raised the bottle in Gallo's direction. "You want a taste, boss?"

Gallo entered the stall and sat on the bunk next to his friend. He grabbed the bottle, put it to his lips, and tossed down a big swig of the brown liquid. "Doggone, Jimmy, this bourbon is terrible. You're a Kentucky man now—you shouldn't be drinking this garbage."

"Hey man, I ain't no owner or trainer. I only make groom money. Besides, this stuff is just fine for my needs tonight. I'm going to get really drunk, go to sleep, and have one hell of a hangover tomorrow. After that, I'll be ready to move on. Ready to move on with T-three and the other fine horses we got at Stone Fence. But right now, I just want to remember and grieve."

Gallo took another hit from the bottle and handed it back to Jimmy. "Yeah, she was a heck of a horse. It was such a gift to be around her and watch her run. Just think of the effect she had on people all over this country. People we never met, and we'll never know. But they turned on their televisions or came to the track just to see her dance and win. Yeah, she was a hell of a horse, and I got to be her trainer and owner. Pretty special—*really* special."

Both men sat there quietly for several long moments until Jimmy broke the silence. "You know, here I am, sixty-one years old—and I never been married or had a kid or made a ton of money—but I've had this great life around these great horses. And then, at this stage of my life, Hit the Bid comes along. For the last four years, I have been going into her stall every morning, and she's always so stinkin' glad to see me. I'm singing and humming and brushing her down, and she's just enjoying the whole situation. Then, if I turn around and bend over, she bumps me in the ass with her nose and knocks me head over tea kettle! I'm telling you, that doggone filly would do that every time. She just thought that was so damned funny. I'd always act like I was angry, and I would scold her like she was a child. But, in reality, I thought it was damned funny, too. I'll miss seeing her run, but more than anything, I'll miss seeing her early in the morning, at the beginning of the day. At that time every day, she was just *my* horse, you know what I'm sayin'? For just thirty minutes every morning, it was just me and her. I got more out of the time than she did. Just me and her."

Both men sat quietly in the bunk, weighed down by sorrow and sadness. They each thought about happier times spent with Hit the Bid, but the weight of the sadness became more profound.

"I'm heading back to the hotel, Jimmy," Gallo said at last. "You sure you want to stay here tonight?"

"Yeah, boss, this is where I belong tonight. You can come by and pick me up in the morning. I'll be ready to go then—I'll be ready to do my job as best I can. I may feel lousy, but I'll still be ready to work."

"Okay, Jimmy." Gallo slapped Jimmy on the knee and stood up to leave. As he walked down the concourse away from the stall, he could hear Jimmy singing:

> *"A rainy night in Georgia,*
> *a rainy night in Georgia,*
> *I believe it's raining all over the world."*

CHAPTER TWENTY-FOUR

Crawford Jamieson walked from the kitchen to the back patio of his house. He was immediately gratified by the splendid view of the mountains just north of Pasadena. The view was the primary reason he purchased this beautiful and palatial home. Nonetheless, his feelings of happiness were diminished when he looked into the faces of his wife and Dr. Janet Stephens, who had been treating his daughter. They were sitting in chairs next to the pool awaiting his arrival.

The doctor was there to discuss CJ's condition and the young woman's reaction to the tragic death of Hit the Bid.

"Well, Mister and Missus Jamieson," she began by adjusting her glasses and folding her hands in her lap. "I've known CJ ever since her accident as a young child, and I've been delighted with the progress she has made over the last year. Unfortunately, the event at Santa Anita three and a half weeks ago has had a profoundly negative impact on her. We've had four lengthy sessions together since then and, to be quite frank, things aren't going very well. Her behavior and mental stability continue to degrade.

She has become more and more detached from other people, clearly evidenced by her decision to drop out of school. She's told me that she has flashbacks and nightmares about the incident on the track with the racehorse. She does everything she can to avoid reminding herself of the incident. If you look in her bedroom, every reference to a horse, or her work with horses, has been removed.

Every trophy, every ribbon, every photograph is gone and is now dumped at the back of her closet. She's having trouble sleeping and lacks motivation; she just sits around in her room all day. When I do speak with her, she shows flashes of anger, and she always seems like she's on edge. I'm sure you've noticed these same symptoms since you're with her all the time."

Crawford nodded his head, relieved to find his wife doing the same—confirming that every behavior mentioned was also evident to them as parents.

"It's pretty clear to me that she's progressing through the natural stages of grief and loss, and the result is a severe level of situational depression."

Crawford couldn't find anything to say. Channing couldn't either, evidently. What *was* there to say? Their daughter was different—special. There was no way of knowing how, exactly, she'd respond to this great loss.

The only thing they could do was sit quietly in their chairs, wishing things had been different.

"Unfortunately, it's not uncommon to see this condition with individuals dealing with the aftermath of a traumatic brain injury. The world is chaotic and crazy for a young person who is developing normally, but for someone suffering from brain trauma?" Dr. Stephens paused for dramatic effect, eyes unblinking behind her glasses. "Well, it can be super overwhelming and confusing, even for a highly functioning trauma survivor like CJ. The collateral problem here is that she's also experiencing a regression of her skills to communicate and live like a normal person. The tremendous strides she's made since she started out as a jockey last spring seem to have regressed. I'm sure you see signs of this every day."

"You're right about that," said his wife—at last. At least *one* of them had something to say, something to contribute. All Crawford could do was clench his teeth. "She had a boyfriend named Elliot—he's her first, and she was just *crazy* about this young guy. Since Hit the Bid's death, she hasn't spoken to him. He calls every day. I know he's heartbroken, but CJ won't come to the phone. It's the same situation with Ritchie, the horse's trainer—she had a great rapport with this man, and even though he routinely calls the house to see how she's doing, I can't get her on the phone to talk with him." Channing paused, tears welling up in her eyes—and yet her voice didn't waver. "All her life, she had difficulty building relationships with other people, and yet she was able to build a tight bond with both men. Now it's *gone*," she added, chin quivering. "Just like she never knew or cared for either of them."

The psychiatrist looked at Crawford. "What other regressive types of behaviors have you witnessed, Mister Jamieson?"

Crawford took a deep breath. He now had the same look of concern on his face that his wife and the therapist exhibited. "She doesn't talk to me. She doesn't talk to me *at all*. Since the day of the accident, she hasn't looked directly at me or spoken a word. She's just completely shut me out."

"I'm sorry, Mister Jamieson. This must be so painful for both of you, especially given the tremendous improvement she's made over the previous year. Just a month ago, she was a national celebrity—and now she's a recluse, burdened by a tragedy that was out of her control. I know this is difficult, but we can't quit. She's demonstrated the ability to live a productive and successful life. We just have to find a way to get her through this."

"So, what do we do now?" asked Channing. "How do we rescue her from this psychological quicksand that's pulling her down?"

"I think we need to engage in a counseling technique referred to as Trauma-Focused Cognitive Behavioral Therapy."

"Oh, great," said Crawford. "More psychiatric gibberish. What the heck does that mean, Doc? How does this stuff help my daughter?"

"Trauma-Focused Cognitive Behavioral Therapy is a treatment designed to reduce negative emotional and behavioral responses by a person who has suffered a significant traumatic event. The treatment addresses upsetting beliefs related to trauma and provides a supportive environment in which the person is encouraged to talk about their experience and confront the resulting behavioral issues head-on. This would involve a weekly meeting with CJ, the two of you, and myself. We would set goals regarding what we want to address each week and try to move through these behavioral issues in a very structured way."

Crawford sat back in his chair and shook his head in frustration. "It sounds like more of this 'I'm okay, you're okay' baloney that never gets anywhere. Is this really going to do anything to move the needle?"

"Crawford, what the hell else are we going to do?" asked Channing. Immediately, he knew he'd crossed a line. "Are we just supposed to let her rot in that room? Maybe this is just what we all need: a chance to honestly address this horrific event that knocked her off-kilter. We need to move forward toward being a family again, a family that rejoices in the achievements of our daughter and enjoys being together. We've seen that she has the capability to be an engaging, happy, productive person who can communicate well with other people if she must. Just letting her slide into the gloom doesn't make any sense."

"You know," said the psychiatrist, "this isn't going to work unless we all buy into it. That includes the both of you and CJ. I think the first step is to bring her down here and get her agreement to engage in a process that will allow her to confront her issues. She's a smart young lady. Hopefully, she will understand that this can help her."

"I agree that we need to move out on this," said Channing. "I'll go upstairs and bring her down. In the meantime, you and my husband can discuss how to pitch this idea to her. I can't bear to see her continue to slide into the darkness. We have to get ahead of this now."

Channing entered the house and within ten minutes, returned with CJ—who didn't smile and had a very unemotional look on her face, but cooperated and sat at a round table where all four participants to the meeting could easily look at one another.

The therapist began to explain to CJ the progressive approach she thought would be productive in allowing her to confront her trauma and find a way to deal with it. She described how her parents would be there every step of the way to support her and help her recover the confidence and social behaviors she had displayed so effectively prior to the accident on the track. "Each member of the Jamieson family has to be there for the others. You know your parents are there for you—are you there for them? You can make your life better by helping to improve their lives as well. Do you really want to live the rest of your life in a perpetual session of 'alone time' just sitting in your room?"

The term "alone time" created a spark of awareness in CJ. For the first time since Hit the Bid broke down on a racetrack, someone said something that triggered the memory of an insightful moment in her life. For a heartbeat, she shook loose the memory of Bid's buckled leg, and the desperate look in the filly's eyes as the horse tried to comprehend what had happened to her. That look haunted CJ because there was nothing she could do to fix it, and in fact, the jockey felt as though the accident was her fault. While this memory still plagued her like a knife in her chest, the words "alone time" prompted her to remember a December day in Kentucky when she was challenged to do something that was very difficult for her. She recalled the feeling of a good friend's hands on her shoulders and the sight of a playful horse knocking over bowls of cereal.

She glanced around the table at the three others seated there, including her father. "You know, Mister Gallo once told me that people who need alone time whenever things get tough are typically people who are not successful or happy. I guess my situation right now qualifies as a tough time. Maybe I need to get going."

The psychiatrist traded quizzical looks with Crawford and Channing. They had no idea what she was talking about.

"I'm willing to try this discussion approach . . . but only if Mister Gallo is present."

That comment produced a flash of anger in Crawford Jamieson. He hung his head and closed his eyes. He had never failed at anything in his life, but his inability to enhance and guide the life of his daughter frustrated him and taxed his patience.

Channing could see her husband was upset, but CJ's comment indicated that the door to recovery was at least cracked open an inch or two. She addressed her daughter. "CJ, Ritchie Gallo doesn't live here in California, and this process may take several weeks. We can't rightly expect him to participate in this. This is about *our* family. We can't expect someone outside our family to be committed to something like this."

"Today is Monday," CJ said, dropping her gaze. "This Saturday is the Santa Anita Derby. If Mister Gallo, Mister Jimmy, and Tackle Tim Tom aren't here today, I'm sure they will be here by tomorrow. Why can't he meet with us this week?"

"No!" barked Crawford. "This isn't about Gallo, this is about us. *I'm* your father. It's my responsibility to take care of you and make you better. It's my responsibility to get this family back to normal again. We can do this if we stick together. We don't need an outsider to fix this problem. We will fix it ourselves!"

He stood, then, and looked at the three women seated at the table. "You can schedule our first session for this *kumbaya* marathon this week or early next week—but one way or another, we're going to address this with the people at this table, and *that's it*. Now CJ, I want you to go upstairs and get dressed. You, your mom, and I are going out to dinner as a family, okay? So please get changed."

CJ cast her gaze down at her shoes. "I don't really want to go out to dinner."

"I don't care whether you want to go out or not—you're going to do it. Now go upstairs and get changed!"

CJ rose, made her way into the house, and walked up the stairs toward her bedroom.

Channing snapped at her husband: "Crawford, I don't think treating her like she's one of your employees at the bank is going to be very helpful! You may be driving her further away from us."

"Look, I'm going to cooperate with whatever you two want to do, and I am there 100 percent for our daughter, but we have to *expect* something of her. She just admitted herself that she understands self-pitying people don't get anywhere. We've got to expect something of her if this is going to work. She expected something out of every one of those horses she rode to victory. This isn't an alien concept to her. We have to be willing to use the stick as well as the carrot."

He turned and walked back into the house while Channing escorted the doctor to her car.

"Go ahead and schedule our first session when it fits your calendar. I'm sure Crawford will be there."

The psychiatrist gave Channing a hopeful smile and put her arm around her shoulder. "Don't get too emotional, Mrs. Jamieson. Your husband doesn't have a great attitude about this process, but he made a good point about expecting some effort on her part to make this work. CJ has already experienced what it's like to live on this side of the looking glass. That's a big advantage in this case. We'll bring her back, don't worry."

When the doctor left, Channing went into the house and found Crawford imbibing a stiff drink in the dining room.

"You know," he said, not bothering to look up, "this is all *your* fault. You know that, don't you, Channing?"

"My fault? What do you mean by that?"

"You talked me into allowing this jockey thing and it was a huge mistake. We should have concentrated on her psychological counseling and her schoolwork. She could have blossomed into a nice young lady who would meet and marry a good guy and live a reasonably normal life."

"Crawford, how can you say that? Before we engaged her with

horses, she was on her way to being a basket case. But as recently as a month ago, her accomplishments made her a national figure, and she developed very normal relationships with the people that surround her. The fact that she is rejecting horses right now scares the hell out of me. The connection with these animals enabled her to grow as a person. It's allowed her to escape the jumbled mess that existed inside her cranium and become a woman who can enjoy and live in the world around her. For sure, there are risks in horse racing, but you can't deny the emotional gratification she got from it."

"Well, I'll give this behavioral therapy garbage a shot, but if this doesn't work quickly, we need to find some national expert that can treat her and get some results. Thoroughbreds are a business. They're not some ride at Disneyland that suddenly turns the kitchen maid into Cinderella. We need to find something rational that works."

"Crawford, I don't know what your problem is. You've never been able to connect with her, and now that you see her having success and blossoming as an individual, it's almost like you feel you've been cheated out of something."

"How could I connect with her? Since the day she had the accident, you've been between her and me every moment of every day. She's the crusade of your life; I'm just a side show!"

"That's not fair, Crawford. I always tried to get you engaged but you were too busy running a bank and building businesses. You could have been in the middle of this if you really wanted to be."

Crawford slammed his glass on the table and turned away. "I've got to go out and meet a colleague for dinner."

"I thought we were going to dinner with CJ?"

"I forgot about this appointment I have. I'll see you later."

Channing watched her husband pull out of the driveway and drive down the street. She knew where he was going.

187

CHAPTER TWENTY-FIVE

Gallo's recent success as a trainer provided an income that enabled him to stay at fine hotels and eat at the best restaurants. However, in the days before the Santa Anita Derby, he and Jimmy toughed it out at eighty-six bucks a night in a budget motel across the street from the track. This location allowed them to walk to work at the crack of dawn to prepare Tackle Tim Tom for the Santa Anita Derby.

As they ambled toward the stables on the morning of the race, Jimmy engaged in his daily habit of grousing about the need to work in Los Angeles. After five minutes of the groom's monologue, Ritchie had had enough. "Jimmy, what are you bitching about? The weather here is perfect. Not too cold, not too hot, it's perfect all the time, which makes planning our training routine pretty easy."

"That's what I'm saying, boss. It's always the same! I like a little rain, a little snow, some falling leaves, and some Kentucky bluegrass. Something to challenge me every day when I get up."

"Right, you don't think our job is challenging enough as it is?"

"Hey, variety is the spice of life, which brings me to the food around here. If I eat any more tacos or burritos, I'm gonna start speaking Mexican."

"Jimmy, Mexicans speak Spanish."

"Whatever—there's too many people, too many cars, and too many Mexican restaurants around here. I'm dying for some bourbon-basted barbecue ribs."

Gallo just smiled and resigned himself to another few minutes of Jimmy's complaints. Once they got to T-three, Jimmy would be all business, completing a highly orchestrated set of tasks prior to the race this afternoon.

"C'mon, Jimmy, let's get our coffees over here at the break truck."

"Are you buyin'?"

"Of course, I'm buying. Ever since CJ disappeared, I do all the buying."

"Yeah, I miss that girl," said Jimmy. "I miss getting free coffee and lunch every day. Sometimes when she was around after the races, I even got her to pay for dinner. I don't miss her dumb questions or her annoying habit of getting in the way, but I sure miss the free food."

Gallo smiled to himself. He knew Jimmy missed CJ just as much as he missed Hit the Bid. Things were different now, and they were all trying to cope with the change. Since the match race disaster, Gallo had been embroiled in numerous administrative issues—from insurance claims on Hit the Bid's death, to efforts by Crawford Jamieson and other race sponsors to forego any payments to him based on the failure of his horse to finish the race. The trainer was so saddened by the death of the filly, he instructed John McCann to capitulate on all the contentious issues so he could put the episode behind them. Despite the grief he still felt for Hit the Bid, Gallo was determined to rebound emotionally by achieving success on the track with his three-year-old colt.

Once they had secured their coffees and reached the barn where Tackle Tim Tom was stabled, they began to carry out their race-day schedule. The horse was fed a light breakfast of hay and a small amount of grains. After he'd eaten, Gallo mounted General Custer and accompanied T-three out to the track for a light workout with a local exercise rider in the saddle. The horse walked a half-mile and then jogged four furlongs just to get loosened up and ready to run at top speed later in the day.

After Gallo brought T-three back to the stable, Jimmy hosed him down, dried him off, and brushed his coat until the black colt shined like a Cadillac limousine.

At just before 10:00 a.m., a track veterinarian employed by the State Racing Commission arrived to conduct the inspection and examination given to every horse that would run that day. The vet's job was to determine that each horse was sound enough to race. When Tackle Tim Tom was taken out of the stall, the vet first confirmed his identity by checking his lip tattoo and matching the number against the official registration records. He then had Jimmy lead T-three on a fast walk in an area just in front of the stable. After that, he ran his hands up and down the horse's legs, feeling for any heat or swelling of the joints, tendons, or soft-tissue structures. He flexed the thoroughbred's legs at the knee, looking for any inflammation or an indication that the horse may be feeling pain, and then he examined the horse's nose for any trace of blood.

Gallo understood that the pre-race exams were necessary to protect the health of the horses and the riders, but they certainly weren't infallible. The micro-cracks in Hit the Bid's cannon bone, and her exacerbation of that defect when she struck the side of the gate at the start of the match race, were not circumstances that could be preordained by this type of cursory examination. These were the risks of horse racing and the tragedies that accompany the sport.

While Gallo and Jimmy carried on with their normal game day ritual, just nine miles away, Crawford Jamieson was hustling his wife along so they wouldn't be late for a luncheon in the clubhouse at Santa Anita. This gathering would be attended by most of the owners of the horses racing that day. In addition, sponsors for the various races would be there glad-handing and entertaining the affluent class of people that finance the sport. Although the Santa Anita Derby was the marquee event, seven other stakes races would also be run, guaranteeing a quality field for each race.

As her husband entered the garage to start up the car, Channing walked upstairs and knocked on CJ's bedroom door. When she entered, she found her daughter sitting at a desk reading a book. "CJ, are you sure you don't want to come with us to see the races? Tackle Tim Tom would really want you there cheering for him. He's one of your favorites."

CJ looked up and shook her head. "I'm not ready yet, mom. I feel sad. I don't want to keep slipping away, but I'm not sure how to come back."

Channing stepped forward and reached down to hug her daughter. CJ didn't recoil, but rather put her arms around her mother and shared an embrace. She bent down and kissed her daughter's forehead. "We are here for you because we love you with all our hearts. Just keep trying, okay?"

"Okay, mom—have fun. If I need you, I have my cell."

Once her parents had left the house, CJ continued to read for another hour until she became bored with a plotline that was evolving too slowly for her to remain engaged. She paced about her room for quite a while, trying to figure out why she had lost her ability to function like an average person in society. Then, when she remembered Hit the Bid, she immediately regressed into a mindset of sadness and regret. She slumped into a chair and wept until she was exhausted by the flow of tears and drained by the physical outpouring of emotion. At that point, she sat there in silence, contemplating her surroundings. Her eyes came to rest on the door to her walk-in closet. She knew that on the other side of that door, on the floor under a rack of dresses, was the documented history of the best part of her life.

She rose, entered the small room, and sat cross-legged in front of a pile of pictures, trophies, and awards. Reaching out to a photograph in a frame, she looked at a seven-year-old girl holding a blue ribbon and standing in front of a pony. She smiled as she thought about the picture: *That little guy's name was Oscar. I got him to jump over a bunch of small fences, and we won first prize. He was so cute. That was fun.*

CJ continued to rummage through the items she had cast on the floor several weeks earlier until she came to another picture that resonated with her. It was a photo taken in the winner's circle at Saratoga after she won the American Oaks on Hit the Bid. In the staged photo, Jimmy was holding Bid's reins while she and Mister Gallo held a large trophy in their arms. But Gallo only had one hand on the trophy—he had his other arm draped over her shoulders, like a good friend or a proud papa. Jimmy had the typical sardonic look on his face that he wore like a badge of honor. But she and Gallo were displaying big smiles—smiles of *happiness.* She realized that this picture recorded the first time since her childhood accident that she allowed a man other than her father to touch her—and that touch had made her happy. *Why wouldn't I want it to be like that all the time?*

CJ went downstairs to the living room, where she turned on the big screen television and brought up the cable channel that would broadcast The Santa Anita Derby. She watched two races that went off prior to the Derby and allowed herself to be engaged in both contests. She knew a few of the jockeys in each race and felt a degree of regret for not being there.

Finally, the pre-race broadcast for the main event came on, and there, in the middle of the television screen, was Tackle Tim Tom— the magnificent and muscular three-year-old colt with a mind of his own and the skill set of a champion. All he needed was a rider who understood how to use those skills in order to win a race. CJ wondered if Braulio Cordero had learned anything about the colt since finishing third in the Fountain of Youth Stakes at Gulfstream.

As post time approached, the six entries were guided down to the starting gate. Just as T-three had shown little interest in entering the gate in Florida, his current location in sunny Southern California didn't make him any more cooperative. It took the attendants two minutes and four tries to get the horse into the fourth slot, undoubtedly annoying the other five jockeys trying to keep their horses calm and focused prior to the start of the race. Once the bell went off, and the gates opened, it was déjà vu all over again. CJ knew that one of the colt's greatest strengths was his ability to clear the gate and get a fast start. On this day, he broke out clean but slow, immediately putting himself in the last position. *Oh man,* thought CJ. *He should have gone right to the front. There're only six horses in the race. Getting to the top should have been a piece of cake!*

The race progressed, and Tackle Tim Tom remained in sixth place until the horses entered the far turn where he was seven lengths back from the leader. At that point, Braulio did something smart—he took T-three down to the rail and let him run. CJ had never ridden a horse that ran turns with the power, precision, and discipline of Tackle Tim Tom. He surged to second place as the pack came to the top of the stretch. When he transitioned from the turn to the straightaway, the horse changed leads on his own without guidance from the jockey. CJ smiled, thinking that he had this race in the bag. Unfortunately, jockeys are creatures of habit just like everyone else, and Cordero began to use his whip to motivate the horse.

Tackle Tim Tom did not like being whipped.

The horse maintained the same pace to the finish, losing the contest by less than a length. CJ tossed the remote at the television screen in disgust.

———————

Watching from a trackside location, Gallo breathed a sigh of relief when Tackle Tim Tom crossed the finish line in second place. Gallo knew the strong-willed colt should have won the race, but at least he ran well enough to capture forty Kentucky Derby qualifying points. Based on his win last fall at The Breeders' Cup and the third-place finish in the Fountain of Youth Stakes at Gulfstream, the horse had amassed seventy qualifying points—enough to guarantee a spot in the Kentucky Derby, just three weeks into the future.

Gallo rushed to the paddock, where he found Jimmy cooling the colt down and slowly providing him with water. He checked T-three's legs for inflammation and his nose for blood. There didn't appear to be any problems, so he and Jimmy began the walk back to the stables where Tackle Tim Tom would be fed, hosed down, and allowed to rest.

As they walked, Gallo talked to the horse. "I don't know what your problem is, T-three. You could have easily won that race. From the top of the stretch, you barely busted your ass. All you had to do was step it up one notch and you had a win. What is it with you? You don't like being whipped? You don't like Hispanic jockeys? Do you miss Hit the Bid? I mean, what the hell is your problem?"

The horse said nothing, of course, and they continued to walk the path towards the stables.

"Listen, big guy, you gotta understand something. We may never see CJ again. She may never come back. Hey—Jimmy and I miss her just as much as you do, but the reality is that she may never be coming back. You have to learn how to win without her!"

Gallo was an experienced horseman, but he didn't have the savant skill for understanding these animals that CJ Jamieson had. CJ could feel an emotional connection with Tackle Tim Tom when she rode him that enabled the horse to have fun and be free. She knew that he loved to run, but he didn't share the same fearful instincts that most horses had. Her emotional and physical empathy for the horse resulted in his determination to please her. His response to intimidation was to fight back. When CJ Jamieson was in the irons, he was fighting back against the other horses in the race. When Braulio Cordero was his rider, he was fighting back against the jockey.

Jimmy looked at Gallo. "I guess he don't got nothin' to say, boss."

Gallo patted Tackle Tim Tom on the neck. "Nope, I guess not."

CHAPTER TWENTY-SIX

Crawford and Channing enjoyed cocktails in a reserved section of the clubhouse with nearly one hundred horse owners and race sponsors. Channing observed her husband's emotions transform from nervous to ecstatic after watching a colt owned by one of his limited partnerships win the Santa Anita Derby by half a length. The thoroughbred's name was Davis Rules, and he went off as a slight favorite over Tackle Tim Tom. Winning the Santa Anita Derby guaranteed Davis Rules a slot in the Kentucky Derby, and another chance to race against Ritchie Gallo's colt from Stone Fence Farms. Channing suspected that CJ's participation in the race could have generated a different result, and she surmised that her husband was thankful that CJ was sitting at home watching the event on television. In her mind, it was a sure thing that the colt would succeed if CJ was in the irons, but unfortunately, that wasn't the case.

As she observed her husband work the crowd of well-heeled and successful people, she admired his skill at swimming in the pond with the big fish. Crawford was handsome, smart, and personable. He looked straight into the eyes of everyone with whom he spoke, and made each person feel as though he was a good and trusted friend. Crawford viewed people the way he viewed assets on a balance sheet—if they had value, he was a loyal and solid associate willing to nurture and build a collaborative relationship. If the asset no longer had value or became a liability, a good businessman knew when it was time to cut losses. Crawford made no bones about taking action like that quickly and efficiently.

Like him or hate him, there was no question that Crawford Jamieson was a brilliant businessman. Sometimes his business efforts were a bit obsessive, which led him to rub some people the wrong way, but he always wanted to be successful and he wanted to succeed by doing things right. Whether or not he was doing the right thing rarely fit into the economic equation.

Channing could never figure out exactly why he and CJ were unable to duplicate the connection she had with their daughter. During CJ's childhood, her father would occasionally retreat from his business persona and try to enjoy time spent with her—but he never seemed to actively follow through on those efforts. It was as though he feared failure or being rejected by a child that was not always easy to understand. Decisions at the bank that consistently resulted in success were decisions he enjoyed making—decisions on how to interact with a daughter who was obsessed with horses and wasn't on the same page with the rest of the world apparently didn't come to him easily. It wasn't that Crawford was a bad person—he was just bad at dealing with things he couldn't guide to a successful resolution. The failure to connect with his child was probably the only major failure in her husband's life. She knew it bothered him, which made the discussion she was about to have with him even more difficult.

When Crawford finished telling a witty joke to several ladies who were clearly charmed by his attention, Channing took him by the elbow and apologized for whisking him away. She guided her husband to a porch looking out on the track and told him her plan. "We've scheduled our first therapy session with CJ for tomorrow. I've arranged to have the session in a conference room here at the track."

"Here? Why's that? Why not do it at our home or at the doctor's office?"

"Because I'm going to ask Ritchie Gallo to attend."

"What? Goddammit, Channing, I told you that this is about our family! This isn't about anyone else. We've got to do this together."

Channing took a deep breath and began to explain her thoughts to her husband. "Crawford, please understand something. I am so grateful for the hard work you've put in over the years to take care of CJ and me. You've been an exceptional provider, and I know that in your own way, you love CJ. But we are at a point now where I'm afraid that all the progress we've made over the last fifteen years, and *especially* over the last twelve months, will go down the drain based on the tragedy she's experienced. For some reason, she thinks Gallo's participation in this therapy process is a positive step. How can we ignore a chance that she may be right? Maybe her bond with him will help pull her back to reality. Why wouldn't we explore every path available in order to help her? I just think we must do whatever it takes to improve the odds that she makes a recovery. You understand the concept of playing the odds. You're in the racing business. We want the odds in our favor, don't we?"

Crawford turned and looked out over the track as he sighed with frustration. "So, what are you going to do? Go down to the stables and beg this guy to help us out?"

"Well, I wouldn't put it that way, exactly—but yes, I'm going down to ask his help, and I think he will go for it because he has a great affection for CJ. She means a lot to him, and I know he wants her to have a good life."

"Okay, I'll wait for you here. I'm not going down there with you."

"I understand. I know this is tough for you, but please be patient and give this a chance to work."

Crawford's response was abrupt. "Fine. I'll be waiting here."

Channing left the clubhouse and walked to the stable area of the track. Because of her husband's business connections, she had an identification badge that allowed access to the stabling area. When she got to Tackle Tim Tom's stall, she found Jimmy and Gallo attending to the thoroughbred.

A shocked Gallo stood up when he saw her. "Hey, Channing, how are you? How's our girl?"

"Well, that's what I wanted to discuss with you. Is there someplace we can talk?"

"Sure, I have access to an office down at the end of the barn—follow me."

Channing and Gallo walked past six stalls housing thoroughbreds and stepped into a small room outfitted with a desk, phone, and chairs. Channing began to explain the reason for her visit. "Do you recall the morning last July in Saratoga when CJ approached you and asked for an opportunity to ride your horses?"

"I remember it well. I thought she was a very strange young lady. She wouldn't look us in the eye, and she had this very dispassionate way of talking. She didn't seem to be enthused about anything, just kind of floating through life. That all changed when she got in the saddle with T-three, but when she wasn't on horseback?" He smiled, as though reliving the memory. "She was a *very* different kid."

Channing smiled but didn't quite feel it—and maybe she wouldn't, not until her daughter was back on track. "What you don't know about that morning is that I encouraged her to go see you and ask for an opportunity to work with you."

"Really? Well, I'm glad you did. I've become great friends with her, and she's definitely contributed to my success as a trainer by working with some of my horses. Jimmy and I miss her, and we hope she'll come back and start racing again. But why did you want her to meet *me*? I mean, we hadn't seen each other in over twenty-one years, and you've obviously had a very rewarding life during that period, despite dealing with CJ's disability. Why, after all this time, did you want to reconnect with me through your daughter?"

"Because I wanted her to meet the man who could have been her father."

"Could have been her father? What does that mean?"

"Ritchie, our love affair took place over the course of two summers. In between those summer vacations, while I lived in New York, I met and dated Crawford. I liked Crawford very much. He was kind, smart, handsome, intelligent, and a gentleman—the kind of guy every girl wants to marry. But my heart was always with you. After my father insisted I leave Saratoga and break off my relationship with you, he encouraged Crawford to ask me out again. I think my dad saw this as an opportunity to merge two blue-blood families in a way that would ensure the financial security of his daughter and any grandchildren he may be lucky enough to have. At that point, Crawford tried valiantly to get me to fall in love with him. He was a wonderful suitor who did everything he could to make me happy. Based on his commitments to me and the pressure I was getting from my family, I agreed to marry a man I wasn't sure I truly loved. One month after the wedding, I found that I was pregnant, and I eventually gave birth to CJ. The morning after her delivery I had an epiphany—I realized that I was still in love with a man in Saratoga Springs, not the man holding my hand while I lay in a hospital bed."

They sat silently for a second and looked at one another with a sense of regret.

"I wanted to leave, but I couldn't do it. I couldn't be that disloyal to a person who had made such a huge commitment in his life to me. How could I shame my family? How could I shame Crawford? I didn't know how *you* would react. I decided I would be a loyal wife and mother, and try to make the best life I could for my daughter."

Gallo exhaled and placed his head in his hands. "I'm sorry you got pushed into a marriage where you had some concerns about your relationship with your husband, but it looks like you've done a great job of being a loyal wife and terrific mom. I still don't understand why you wanted me to meet her. Why bring us together?"

"Because I had a hunch, Ritchie, and my hunch turned out to be right. Like I told you before, after her accident, CJ struggled to develop a relationship with Crawford like the one she has with me. I always suspected that she couldn't connect with him because somehow, she sensed that I didn't really love Crawford the way a wife should love her husband and that my heart was elsewhere. Maybe she's able to read me the way she can read horses, or it may be that despite her mental disability, we are so very much alike. I fell in love with a guy named Ritchie Gallo, and I figured there was a good chance she would fall in love with you also.

I always felt that she only needed to break down one more mental barrier in order to reach her full potential as a person. She needed to have a connection with a mother and a father figure. The afternoon after she met you, I was delighted. She said things to me I had never heard from her before. She said she liked you even though you yelled at her. She felt that you were an honorable and kind man who would be nice to her and help her to be a jockey. She trusted you right away. Believe me, she never said anything like that before in her life about someone she's just met."

"You said she liked Jimmy that first day also."

"Yes, but she liked Jimmy after she met you. This whole process of connecting with other people began *after* she met *you*—other jockeys, other trainers, horse owners, track workers, and fans. Heck, she even managed to develop a romantic relationship with a young man. I never thought that would happen. You enabled her to break down that last barrier. Something emotional or spiritual between you two helped her continue her escape from a world that was limited by a brain injury."

Gallo sat silently for a few moments, thinking about what Channing had just said. "You know, it's crazy—but from the first moment I met CJ, I felt that there was something between us. My feelings are similar to yours. I think I have the mental and emotional connection with her that she has with horses. Sometimes, she'd follow me around the stables and I could feel her desire to be with me and talk to me. Sometimes her unusual antics and probing questions would drive me nuts, but it never turned me off. It just made me want to know her better. I was always proud of her. Not just because she was becoming an accomplished rider, but because of her willingness and efforts to grow as an individual. I believe that she can sense that. Even if I don't have genetic ties to her, I feel like she is a gift in my life that makes up for the other things that haven't gone so well. There is something between me and CJ that binds us together."

Gallo reached out and took Channing's hand. "You said you still loved me when CJ was born and that your love for your husband wasn't perfect. How do you feel now?"

"I suspect I feel the same way about you that you feel for me, but nothing has changed since then. First and foremost, I'm a wife and a mother, completely loyal to my family. Crawford and I are struggling right now, but when we were initially married, he was totally committed to me and our life together. I'm the one who has short-changed him. Why shouldn't he be a bit disgruntled when he feels that his wife has never given him the unconditional and total love he deserves?"

She withdrew her hand back from Gallo's. "Crawford is my partner and CJ's father. Our job is to do all we can to give our child the life she deserves. Right now, CJ is in a difficult place and we are doing everything we can to bring her back into the life she built over the last year. We could use your help in making that happen, Ritchie. I'd be so grateful if you would be willing to help us out."

"I'd do anything for that kid, Channing. I'll do anything for her."

Channing smiled. "Thanks, Ritchie. You're still the big-hearted boy everyone likes on the backstretch. I'm so happy you're a part of CJ's life."

CHAPTER TWENTY-SEVEN

The Jamieson family, Dr. Stephens, and Ritchie Gallo sat around a table, sharing a mutual sense of discomfort. The psychiatrist was doing her best to relax everyone and prepare them for the therapy session they were about to conduct, but her smile, soothing voice, and personable eye contact weren't enough to decrease the level of anxiety in the room.

CJ wasn't very demonstrative when she first saw Gallo, even though they hadn't seen each other in nearly a month. She was very quiet and responded to most of the therapist's questions with monosyllabic answers. Nonetheless, the doctor persevered with enthusiasm, explaining the format of the therapy and defining terms like stress management, cognitive coping, and re-creation of the trauma narrative.

Crawford's internal thoughts led him to believe that this was a waste of time, and he didn't like having Gallo there, but externally, he projected a positive attitude. Channing, always the supportive mom, smiled and cooperated with the therapist as best she could. Ritchie just sat there with a puzzled look on his face. It was off to a rocky start.

"CJ, I would like you to talk about your life and your activities last year. You know, the time you spent riding at Santa Anita, Saratoga, and Churchill Downs. How did your behavior change from the spring through the fall? How did you change your thinking during that time?"

CJ shrugged and said nothing.

The therapist tried again. "Let's address your time here at Santa Anita last year. You were a brand-new apprentice jockey, and you won four or five races. How did that change you?"

"Well, it really didn't change me that much. I mean, it confirmed to me that I had this ability to communicate with horses, and I could use that skill as a jockey to help horses win races. Before that, I'd only been an exercise rider—and I knew it was useful in training horses, but I didn't know for sure that I could translate the skill successfully to the racecourse. It made me feel good to win and I liked the fact that it made the horses feel good."

"Did riding and winning help you to deal with people?"

"Not really. It was kind of like when I went to high school. I got good grades, but I spent four years looking at the floor as I walked the halls and staring at pages in books in order to learn. I didn't really have any friends or close relationships, other than my mom, and once I got into racing at Santa Anita, it was about the same."

"Okay, so let's fast forward to Saratoga. Your parents allowed you to have your own apartment and live on your own. What happened there? How did things change for you?"

A hint of a smile came to the young woman's face, and she briefly glanced across the table at Gallo. "I met Mister Gallo. Something changed."

"Ah, so you two became friends right away? Was he nice to you?"

"No, he was always yelling at me and making fun of me. I don't usually understand it when people make fun of me, but I knew he was doing it all the time."

". . . and you were okay with that?"

Again, a hint of a smile came to CJ's face. "Yeah, I actually liked it. I understood that it meant he cared about me. Mister Gallo is demanding of everybody who works with him, but everyone at the farm or the track respects him and thinks he's a good boss. He treated me like he treats everyone else. He treated me the same, not like a girl with brain damage. I liked that."

The therapist addressed her next question to Gallo. "What did you think about Cicely when you first met her?"

Gallo answered without thinking. "I thought she was really weird." He quickly glanced at Channing and then backed off the remark. "Well, I mean, she was very shy and quiet, not the personality you expect of someone who rides racehorses."

"Did you see something special in this young woman?"

"Not right away, not until she walked into the stall with Tackle Tim Tom. This is a horse who can be a real pain in the neck, but he immediately responded to her commands and touch with total cooperation. Then, once she was on his back, she was a drastically different person. She showed great confidence in the saddle and was aware of everything around her: the horse, the track, the ability to move the horse around the track at different speeds, *everything*. She had complete control of the colt, and she was as happy and positive as a person can be when she was in the irons. I've watched great riders and jockeys all my life. Never seen one better than her. She's a unique talent."

"That's high praise coming from someone like you," said Channing.

"Well, she could ride from day one. The thing that made the last nine months so great for me was seeing her develop as a person." Gallo looked directly at CJ. "I've been really proud of you CJ—really proud of the person you have become."

CJ raised her hands to her face and began to cry. Channing immediately went around the table to comfort her daughter, and Gallo backtracked: "Oh, man, I'm sorry for saying that, Doc! I guess I'm not supposed to say stuff like that in this therapy session. I'm not clear on the rules. I'm sorry, kid, I didn't mean to upset you."

Channing calmed CJ down and brushed her hair back from her

eyes. She smiled at her daughter, kissed her face, and was pleased to get a reluctant smile in return at the same time she wiped away the tears.

Gallo made another effort to resurrect the session. "Look, would it be okay if CJ and I just took a walk for a few minutes? I'm not going to be able to participate in future meetings, so I'd just like a chance to talk to her a little bit before I have to say goodbye."

Crawford appeared reluctant to give his approval, but after a quick exchange of looks with his wife, he gave his consent. "Okay, you guys take a walk and we'll wait here for you to come back."

"What do you say, CJ? Can you give me a few minutes?"

CJ nodded, stood, and walked out of the office with Gallo. They left the corporate offices at Santa Anita and headed toward the stables. Gallo felt at ease being alone with CJ and was relieved to escape the middle of a psychiatric scrum that seemed to have little purpose and few empirical goals.

"Sorry to make you cry back there. I just expressed what I felt. I don't really know what to say to you to make it all better, but I can tell you for sure that I really miss having you around."

"Now that you're here, I realize how much I miss you, Mister Gallo."

"Yeah, it's been tough. Without you around, I pay for everything Jimmy eats and drinks. It costs me a ton of dough."

CJ laughed out loud. "Is he still whimpering about how he was financially abused at Saratoga?"

"For sure. But it's just his way of expressing how much he misses having you around. Jimmy's an odd duck, but he knows horses, and he's also damned good at identifying people who have character. He valued your friendship, CJ."

"I miss him too," she said softly.

As they ambled along, Gallo decided he would take a shot at his own version of backstretch psychology. "Did I ever tell you about the owner I worked for a number of years ago who was a philosophy professor at Stanford University?"

CJ shook her head, so he proceeded with his story. "This owner had been a big-time high-tech entrepreneur in Silicon Valley who decided to cash in his chips and do what he really wanted to do, which was to study philosophy. But he also loved to bet on the ponies so he took some of his mega-millions and bought a couple of thoroughbreds, which he hired me to train. The first horse he assigned to me was named Epictetus. I thought that was a weird name for a horse, so I asked him how he came upon that name. Turns out that Epictetus was a philosopher in ancient Greece that taught the concepts of stoicism—basically some line of bull that philosophy majors in college like to study. Anyway, I decided to do a little research on this Greek guy, and a few of his ideas stuck with me. In one of his famous quotes, he said, *'No man is free who is not master of himself.'* For some reason, that saying illuminated a lightbulb in my head. We normally think of freedom as a situation where you escape a master, kinda like in slavery. But in reality, individual freedom comes to a person who masters *themselves*. You know, like a person who has the discipline to sacrifice things in order to train for something that's important to them. Or maybe like a guy or girl that has the power to make themselves think positively about what they are trying to accomplish. Someone who doesn't allow circumstances to control them but uses circumstances to their advantage. I always thought that was a good philosophy to follow as I lived my life."

CJ gave Gallo a look of disbelief. "I never realized there was a profound and scholarly side to your thinking, Mister Gallo. I figured you only thought about horses."

"Yeah, well my thinking on this isn't very broad or deep, but I do try to be philosophical from time to time."

Gallo could tell that CJ wasn't sure where he was going with this discussion, but he knew he had her attention. "Was Epictetus a good horse?" she asked.

"Nah, he couldn't clear the gate without banging his knees, ran sideways through the turns, and had no gas down the stretch. Other than that, he was a helluva racer."

CJ laughed again.

"Now, the next horse this Stanford philosophy professor brings me is a gelding named Marcus Aurelius. He bought the horse as a two-year-old for 125,000 dollars. The horse ran in the money in his first four races, and we thought he would have some upside as a three-year-old. Hell, as a gelding, we could run him for years if he stayed healthy. Once again, I'm puzzled by the horse's name so I do a little research and find that Marcus Aurelius was one of the emperors of Rome and was also a stoic philosopher. He was influenced by the work of Epictetus and he wrote something that I've always used as a guide in my own life. He said that very little is needed to make a happy life. It is all within yourself. It's all in your way of thinking. That's a very powerful statement, don't you think?"

"I suppose," said CJ.

Undaunted, he continued: "You know, once upon a time I fell in love with a woman and then I lost her. I was heartbroken for years, and that emotional loss was always a dark rain cloud that hung over my head. But when I started understanding this stoicism baloney, it made a difference in my life. I became a better trainer when I committed myself to personal freedom by mastering the things I thought and did. I was really happy as a result of positive and happy thinking. To this day, I still hold love in my heart for that lady, but my life is enriched by my willingness to let myself be free, to let myself be happy. With my mind, I choose to be free and I choose to be happy."

CJ turned and looked Gallo in the eye. "I always looked outside myself to find happiness, but I could never figure out how to attain it. It always seemed that my problem was understanding what was going on around me. I never thought a lot about creating happiness inside my head. I guess I will never be free, Mister Gallo. I don't have the ability to master myself."

"But CJ, that's not true. When you're in the saddle, you have enormous power over yourself and the spectacular athletes that you ride. You told me yourself that you think with clarity on the track. Life goes clicking by you at forty miles per hour in the middle of tons of horseflesh. Despite that, you control your circumstances like no other person I've ever seen. You've got to concentrate on bringing that skill from the racetrack to the broader measure of your life. You can make yourself happy by how you think, how you control yourself. You can never control outside events like the death of Hit the Bid, but you have the power to control your mind. Understand that and you will find the strength to get on with your life."

The trainer and the jockey walked along in silence. CJ tried to think about what Gallo had just said and wondered how she could generate the power over her mind that would allow her to be free. When Ritchie stopped walking, CJ realized that they were standing in front of a stall. She could see the outline of a horse standing at the back of the enclosure.

"Why are we here?"

"Well, I thought you might want to see an old friend one more time."

In the shadows at the back of the stall, Tackle Tim Tom raised his head to look at the people that came to visit him. He walked forward and stuck his head through the open half of the stall door. He looked at Gallo and then focused on CJ.

CJ knew the connection wasn't there. Not anymore. Tackle Tim Tom couldn't sense what was in her mind or what she was thinking. He was emoting as best he could, but nothing was coming from her, and she wasn't sure how to bond with the horse the way she used to.

CJ turned toward Gallo. "I killed Hit the Bid, Mister Gallo. It was my fault. I don't want to hurt T-three or any other horse. These animals are what brought me to life in this world and made me happy. But now, my fear of disappointing them or hurting them makes me want to keep them at a distance. I've spent most of my life living at a distance from everything around me. I guess that's where I'm going again.'"

Gallo placed his hand on CJ's shoulder. She didn't pull back from his touch. "Listen, CJ, Hit the Bid could have suffered that fatal injury frolicking on twenty acres of Kentucky bluegrass back at Stone Fence Farms. Thoroughbreds aren't so different from people. They achieve extraordinary things running on fragile legs. People achieve extraordinary things running on fragile hearts. The beauty, grace, and power of a racehorse can tragically disappear in an instant. The things that make them so wonderful are also the cause of their downfall. It's the same with humans like you and me. We want our life, our liberty, and our freedom to pursue the things that bring value to our lives. That desire can be our downfall as well as a source of our success. When you love someone with all your heart, and that person doesn't love you back, you pay a terrible price for investing that powerful emotion in one person. But it doesn't mean you should stop trying to love other people. If you don't win a race you were supposed to win, you don't stop racing because you disappointed yourself or other people. If someone that you love dies, it doesn't mean *you* have to die. Hit the Bid ended her life doing something she loved with her best friend in the saddle. She took her last breath in the arms of two men who loved her dearly. Compare that to all the people or horses or other animals that pass away all alone without someone who loves them to say goodbye. When you think about it, she went out in a way we would all like our lives to end: doing what makes us happy, surrounded by people we love. The margin between fulfilling your dreams in life and tragedy is very slim, CJ. But unless you're willing to risk tragedy, your dreams can never come true."

CJ stepped forward and caressed T-three's face. "I understand what you're saying, Mister Gallo. I just need to figure out how to master myself so I can be free—so I can learn how to think in a way that will give me a happy life."

"Why don't you step inside the stall with Tackle Tim Tom? Maybe he can help you."

CJ raised the latch on the door and walked in with the colt. She moved toward the back of the enclosure, and the horse turned to face her. Gallo sat down in a chair just a few yards away. He couldn't see the young woman or the horse, but he could hear CJ speaking softly to her friend. The one-sided discussion continued for some time and then there was silence. For several minutes, he didn't hear her talking or the horse making any noise. Gallo stood and moved to a spot where he could look into the stall. He smiled as he recalled seeing this same scene ten months earlier when a shy, emotionless, and detached twenty-year-old brought a rambunctious young stallion under her control.

She was doing it again.

CHAPTER TWENTY-EIGHT

J immy bolted upright when the alarm clock went off at five in the morning. It took him a moment to realize he was sleeping on the couch in the living room of his apartment located above a maintenance building at Stone Fence Farms. Still dressed in his pajamas, he waddled over to the bathroom only to find the door closed. "Miss CJ, are you in there again? I thought we had a deal—I get in there first in the morning, and then you get the bathroom when I'm done. How many times we got to go over these rules?"

"Sorry, Jimmy," CJ yelled from inside. "I had to go peeps, so since I was up anyway, I just started getting cleaned up. I'll be done in just a moment."

"Dang! I don't know why you couldn't live with Ritchie Gallo for these two weeks. Ritchie's got a big old house just a mile or two away. Instead, you gotta live here in my apartment and drive me crazy."

"I told you before," shouted CJ. "I want to be as close as possible to T-three before I ride him in the Derby next weekend. It's more fun for me to live with you, just thirty yards away from the barn. This is the closest I can get without living in his stall."

"Well, I sure do wish you were sleeping in that stall!" Jimmy headed over to the kitchen, where he fired up the coffee maker in order to make enough java to fill three large aluminum travel mugs. One with three sugars for himself, one with a big dollop of cream for CJ, and a third, just black, for Gallo.

After getting the coffee started, he walked past his bedroom.

The bed was made, and the room was as neat and clean as one could possibly make it. *That just don't seem normal,* thought Jimmy. *I can't wait 'til the Derby's over so I can get my messy bedroom back.*

Jimmy picked up his work clothes, which CJ had washed and folded, and stood outside the bathroom door impatiently tapping his toe until the jockey bounced out, looking clean, happy, and beautiful. "See that, Mister Jimmy? I didn't take long. Now it's all yours."

"Oh—well, thank you very much, little lady, for letting me use my *own* bathroom, even though I am now exactly five minutes behind schedule. I guess you big-time jockeys don't pay any attention to being on time, what with everyone telling you how wonderful you are to be winning races and all. But I'm a doggone groom. I got to be on time—people are counting on me to do my job!"

Jimmy continued to mutter under his breath as he disappeared into the bathroom and shut the door. After sharing an apartment for a week with Jimmy, CJ had reached a point where she enjoyed these contentious exchanges. She finally figured out when he was sarcastic and when he was straight with her. The sarcasm always centered on his frustration at ceding her the bedroom and having her live in his apartment. But from time to time, he looked at her with a smile and said something nice. He enjoyed having her around, and she knew it. This allowed her the liberty of tweaking him occasionally, resulting in another of his tirades feigning anger and indignation.

"You know, Jimmy, everything you need to achieve happiness in life is between your ears." She was yelling in the direction of the closed bathroom door. "Happiness comes when you have the power in your mind to choose a life of happiness. You should think about that, Mister Jimmy."

"Oh yeah, sure, that's all I need to be happy. I'm just goin' to *think* myself into a state of giddiness. When you're a celebrity white girl makin' half-a-million dollars a year riding horses and being on the cover of *Sports Illustrated*, it ain't hard to be happy. But, in my case, all I got to do is think about it! Yeah, that's going to make me really happy—really, *really* happy!"

Eventually, Jimmy finished his morning ritual and moved to the kitchen, where he poured the freshly brewed coffee into three aluminum containers. He was anxious to go downstairs and get the workday started but CJ wouldn't leave until she cleaned the bathroom. "Miss CJ, we spend all day walking through horse turds—why on earth are you so nuts about cleaning everything else you touch?"

"Just remember, Jimmy, cleanliness is next to godliness."

"Now, I don't need no young lady lecturing me on godliness. I sing at church every Sunday and raise a joyful noise to the Lord. Can *you* sing, Miss CJ?"

"Not a note," she said with a smile. "C'mon, Mister Jimmy, let's go to work."

As they walked down the stairs from Jimmy's apartment, they could see several sets of headlights moving up the crushed stone driveway from the main road. Pickup trucks carrying farm employees were arriving one by one. When Ritchie Gallo arrived, he parked his truck next to the largest white barn, where his office was located. He waved to CJ and Jimmy, knowing they would immediately provide him with the cup of coffee he desperately needed at that early hour. "Here you go, boss. Black coffee, just the way you like it."

"Thanks, Jimmy, but I think we're going to need CJ to make another cup of coffee this morning for a guest."

Gallo turned and pointed at a man exiting the passenger side of his pickup truck. Elliot Monkmeyer got out and walked over to the trio of coffee drinkers.

"Hey there, Mister Monkmeyer, how y'all doing?"

"I'm doing great, Jimmy. Great to see you again."

"I got a lot to do, so I'll be on my way." Jimmy tactfully moved off in the direction of the barn.

"Yeah, I got a lot going on also," said Gallo. "I'll be in my office if anybody needs me."

When Gallo walked away, CJ was left alone with a young man who had thought about her constantly for the last month and a half. "Hi, CJ. You look really beautiful this morning."

"Thanks, Elliot, you look beautiful also."

"How about it—can you help me out with that cup of coffee?"

"Sure, let's go up to Jimmy's apartment."

They returned to the kitchen, where CJ proceeded to make an additional cup of coffee. They made small talk but didn't say anything profound to one another. Neither of them really knew what to say. Elliot wasn't the most confident guy in the world when it came to dealing with the opposite sex, and he certainly didn't know how to reestablish a relationship with a woman who had suffered emotional trauma. However, the past few weeks had proven to him that CJ's presence in his life was light-years better than living without her. He could cope with her unusual behavior driven by a traumatic brain injury, but he couldn't deal with her absence.

Elliot tried to break the ice. "Mister Gallo says you're doing really well these days, CJ. He says you're doing a great job helping him prepare T-three for the Derby and that you seem to be really happy."

CJ handed Elliot the cup of coffee, and they sat at the kitchen table. "What are you doing here, Elliot?"

"Well, it's Derby Week here in Louisville, and Mister Gallo invited me to come out and be his guest for the week. How can I turn down a chance to hang out with the trainer of the horse that's probably going to win the Kentucky Derby?"

"So . . . that's the *only* reason you are here?"

Elliot exhaled a sad breath and shook his head. "CJ, you know that's not the only reason. When you ran away from me after the match race and wouldn't talk to me for the last seven weeks, I just didn't know what to do. I knew you were going through a tough time and I wanted to help, but I didn't know what I did wrong. I didn't know how you could suddenly dislike me so much after we had built what I thought was a strong and trusting relationship. I just wanted a chance to talk to you again and apologize for whatever it is that I did. I would never hurt you, CJ. I just wanted to be helpful."

CJ stood up and walked around the table. She sat in Elliot's lap and put her arms around his neck. "Elliot, I'm the one who owes you an apology, not the other way around. When Hit the Bid died, I didn't know how to deal with it. The only choice in my head seemed to be a retreat to the world I have lived in since I was a child. But that world didn't include the most important thing in my life—my love of horses. Without that obsession, it was hard for me to love my mom, to love my friends, to love a guy who had been so wonderful to me and opened my eyes to so many beautiful things that surround us. I just kind of moved into this place where I was nothing and I didn't care about anything. I just wanted to be alone."

"What changed? What brought you back?"

"After the Santa Anita Derby, Mister Gallo met with me and my parents. When I went off alone with him, I felt a tug. It's hard to describe, really, but it seemed like I was in this blurry place filled with *nothing*—and I felt a tug towards a colorful place filled with *something*. Just being with Mister Gallo took me from nothing to something, and then I saw Tackle Tim Tom again. When I first was alone with the horse, it broke my heart. He felt just like you. He thought he had done something wrong, and that's why I hadn't been there to train him or ride him in those important races. When I held his head in my hands and we touched our foreheads together, it was like I was six years old. That's when I touched my first horse. Something flipped in my brain, in my heart, in my soul. I knew right then I had to try and master myself. I had to find the power to make myself happy from within, rather than trying to derive happiness from the things around me."

CJ gently stroked Elliot's face and brushed his hair back off his forehead. His glasses had slipped down his nose, and she smiled as she adjusted them to the correct position.

"Elliot, you look different. Did you lose weight?"

"Yeah. It's crazy what you will do when you're pining for a woman. I started taking long runs, hitting the gym, I quit drinking, and wouldn't eat bad stuff. I lost over forty pounds."

CJ wrapped her arm farther around his neck and put her face very close to his. "You're looking pretty hot, Elliot. Now that you're a handsome colt, do you really want a filly like me? I'm doing my best to control my life and make myself happy, but there's no guarantee I won't get flipped off the rails again in the future. There are so many potential tragedies in life; I don't know if I can handle them all. Don't you deserve someone more normal than that?"

"It's not about *deserving* someone. It's about *needing* someone. I know I need you. I need you in my life, and I'm willing to do everything I can to be there for you in the future."

CJ softly kissed the young man and then touched his lips with her fingers. "I'm sorry, Elliot, that I didn't reach out to you sooner. I thought you may not want anything to do with this crazy lady and feared that you would reject me. That was a terrible mistake on my part. I knew you were a man with a great heart and great character. I need that strong heart and that great character so I can become a better person. I need you, too, Elliot."

They passionately kissed again, and CJ hugged him as hard as she could. When she pulled back from the embrace, Elliot smiled at her. "So . . . You really think I'm hot?"

CHAPTER TWENTY-NINE

O n the Tuesday morning prior to the first Saturday in May, Gallo entered the main track at Churchill Downs astride General Custer. As the horse progressed from the backside area to the dirt oval, Gallo could clearly see the twin spires atop the grandstand: an iconic symbol of the track and the Kentucky Derby. Trailing several lengths behind, CJ and Tackle Tim Tom surveyed the landscape that surrounded them. The trainer, the jockey, and the two horses were experiencing a surreal moment. This vast stadium filled with empty seats was quiet and solitary as the two riders walked their mounts over the soft brown surface. In his mind's eye, Gallo envisioned the thoroughbreds that had competed here, thundering for home before a crowd that exceeded one hundred and fifty thousand fans. Since 1875, the winners of this race had become household names, often remembered and glorified for decades after their victory. Whirlaway, Secretariat, Seattle Slew, Affirmed, and Barbaro were examples of thoroughbreds who would survive in the memory of sports fans, based on their exemplary performances in the run for the roses.

"I know we've worked this track before, CJ—but there's just something special about being here during Derby Week."

"I agree, Mister Gallo. I've raced and won here when there were fifty thousand patrons in the stands, but this Saturday, that number will be three times as large. I'm getting goosebumps just thinking about it."

One year earlier, Gallo had been at Churchill Downs racing Hit the Bid in the Kentucky Oaks, a sister race to the Derby run on Friday. That was the biggest win in Gallo's life at that point, but the gravity of winning the Derby with T-three was something he only dreamed about. Now the reality of that task was at hand, and he took a few moments to soak it all in before giving CJ his instructions for exercising the talented black colt. "This is the last day we'll let him breeze before the race on Saturday. We'll be taking it easy on him for the next three days. Keep an eye on the heart rate monitor, because I don't want to exceed the benchmarks we discussed. Let him walk for a quarter-mile and then take him up to a trot, but keep his rate at 130 beats per minute. After a two-furlong trot, let him breeze for two more furlongs and then slow him down to a gentle canter, no more than 160 beats. You got it?"

"I got it, Mister Gallo. Let's go T-three, time to get to work."

As CJ rode off with the colt, Gallo began to ponder all the variables that come into play when running a horse in the Kentucky Derby. For the twenty three-year-old thoroughbreds entered in the race, some circumstances are fixed, and some are influenced by luck. Each horse will carry the same weight—126 pounds—and run the same one-and-a-quarter mile distance. But the luck of the draw became paramount that Tuesday morning when the race stewards would randomly assign the post positions. Gallo had carefully analyzed the history of this famous race and knew that the influence of the post position on the race's outcome was far from arbitrary.

Because of the large field of twenty colts, the Derby had to use two starting gates. The main gate holds fourteen horses, and the attached auxiliary gate holds six more competitors. The location in a gate where a horse is positioned can have a substantial impact on racing strategy and, potentially, on the race's outcome. Logic dictates that the inside posts are favorable since running near the rail is the shortest way around the track. But Gallo knew that was only true in races with fields of ten horses or less. In the Kentucky Derby, there are twenty racehorses leaping from the gate and rushing to secure position before the field heads into the first turn. Significant bumping and jostling take place as the field compresses to the inside of the track. Therefore, the horses on the inside are going to get the worst of it, which could discourage them or negatively impact their positioning.

Gallo figured that horses starting from the outside slots are usually subject to less bumping, but if they don't make it across the track before the first turn, they're left wide. In the Kentucky Derby, the turns account for more than 40 percent of the one-and-a-quarter mile race. Gallo calculated that a horse that ran both turns six horses wide of the rail, would end up running a distance fifty yards longer than racers that stayed closer to the infield. In this race, it was paramount to find a balance between far enough inside to save ground, and far enough outside to provide a buffer for the horse when the real running started. *The home stretch.*

Conventional wisdom among handicappers for the Derby states that the best starting position is in the middle of the gate, numbers five through fifteen. Gallo's preference was the outside of the main gate—post fourteen—or inside the auxiliary gate—post fifteen—for the extra space they afford. Tackle Tim Tom's ability to break from the gate fast and clean would allow CJ to avoid the bumper-car environment at the start and maneuver the horse into a rail position on the first turn. In Gallo's opinion, there wasn't another horse in the race that ran the turns like T-three. If he came out of the first turn near the front, he had a good shot at winning the race.

Based on the mathematical analysis or just superstition, Gallo knew he didn't want gate seventeen. No horse had ever won the Kentucky Derby from that position. For most trainers and jockeys, slot number seventeen was the kiss of death.

Another factor that had a traditional impact on the Kentucky

Derby was the weather. May is the wettest month of the year in Kentucky, and many Derbies had been plagued by a slow and sloppy track. Fortunately, this year, Mother Nature and Lady Luck were being kind to the racegoers as the forecast for the balance of the week was cool and dry temperatures with daily highs in the low seventies. Gallo was relieved to discount weather as a factor in the race.

He rode General Custer around to the finish line located at the spot where the grandstand abuts the clubhouse. From there, he could look back across the track at the high-definition video board constructed along the outside of the backstretch. At that moment, technicians located in the communications room at the top of the clubhouse were testing the video system, and, to Gallo's delight, were focusing their camera on CJ and T-three as they circled the track. CJ gave the colt the green light to run a quarter-mile at top speed as they were entering the far turn. The camera operator zoomed in for a close-up of the rider and the jockey, and their images were displayed in the center of a video screen that was 171 feet wide and 90 feet high. The trainer was transfixed by the sight of the two talented athletes moving with grace, power, speed, and precision around the turn and on the way to the homestretch. "It's like poetry in motion, General Custer. Poetry written by a higher power. Good stuff!"

An eighth of a mile before the finish line, CJ stood up in the saddle and gently tugged on the reins, giving T-three the message that she wanted him to slow down. Breaking into a gentle canter and then to a trot, she guided the horse back to the opening on the backstretch that led to the stables. Gallo and General Custer caught up with them and walked to the building that housed the stalls for their horses. Jimmy was waiting with a hose and a bucket so he could give T-three a shower after removing the saddle and saddle cloth.

CJ jumped down from the saddle into the groom's arms. "Miss CJ, your father is waiting for you by T-three's stall. He's been here for about twenty minutes."

CJ waved to her dad and walked over to where he was seated. "Hey, what are you doing here?"

"Good morning, CJ. I got in last night, so I thought I'd come by and see how things were going for you. Your mom will be in tomorrow. We've got a couple of horses running on Thursday and in the Oaks on Friday, so I have a lot of business partners to deal with this week. Hopefully, by Saturday, your mother and I can relax and enjoy watching you run in the Derby against my horse, Davis Rules."

CJ smiled at her father but said nothing. She sensed that he was making an unusual effort to connect with her, but the emotional channel she had with her father was still blurry. It lacked the clarity with which she was able to communicate with Gallo and Jimmy.

"Hey, how about we go to lunch together? There's a really good deli on 4th Street I've wanted to try. We can just walk over and get something to eat."

"Okay," said CJ. "Just give me a minute to clean up, and we can head out."

When she disappeared into the lady's room, Gallo approached Crawford to say hello. He still felt uneasy when he was with him. Crawford's efforts to screw him financially after the match race tragedy left a real sense of distrust with Gallo. It was out of respect for CJ that he was willing to speak to her father in a civil manner. "Nice to see you again, Crawford. Are you here to enjoy Derby week?"

"Well, for me, it is kind of a workweek. We have a couple horses running between now and Saturday, and obviously, I'm excited to see the rematch between Davis Rules and Tackle Tim Tom. Our colt is in good shape, Mister Gallo. I hope you have T-three ready to go."

"I think we'll hold our own," said Gallo, trying not to sound too combative.

There was an uncomfortable pause for a few moments until Crawford reluctantly mentioned something to Gallo that he thought needed to be stated: "I know we've had our disagreements in the past,

Ritchie, but I feel I should thank you for your help a few weeks ago. I don't know what you did or said, but your presence really helped my daughter to get over her depression. Channing is very grateful."

"Ah, I don't know that I really did anything important. She just decided to take control of her mind, her heart, and her circumstance and move on with life. You gotta give her credit—when she has to rise above it all, she gets it done."

CJ returned to the stall where the men were standing. She was somewhat surprised that they were talking in an amiable fashion. She indicated that she was ready to go, so they made their way across the street to a restaurant populated by a few customers eating a late breakfast or an early lunch. CJ ordered a scoop of chicken salad on a bed of lettuce. Her dad ordered a robust breakfast of eggs, bacon, hash browns, and toast. They began to talk as they waited for the food to be served. "So, how has it been living out here in Kentucky for the last week?"

"I really enjoyed being at Stone Fence. I think I drove Mister Jimmy crazy by taking over his apartment. He seems happy that each of us has our own hotel room, now that we're here in Louisville. He can be a cantankerous old coot, but I really like him, and I think he likes me."

"Yeah, it's obvious you have a strong relationship with him and with Gallo. You're a tight group of friends. I guess that's important to you, isn't it?"

CJ just nodded and smiled. She wasn't sure what to say.

"You know, CJ, your mom and I were so happy and relieved two weeks ago when you bounced back from the depressed state you were in. Your mother was terrified that we were going to lose you again, and then somehow, you came back with flying colors. I guess we must be thankful for Ritchie and Tackle Tim Tom. They seem to be the two most important entities in your life. If those relationships are necessary to keep you happy and productive, I'm glad you have them."

Her father had never said anything to her in the past sanctioning the relationships she had developed over the last year. She wondered if he was really about to make a sincere effort to connect with her. Perhaps she would try to meet him halfway: "You've been a good father. You deserve a better daughter than me. You deserve a daughter that can be there for you when you're going through a tough time, or when you need emotional support, instead of someone like me who is bouncing around in her own little world."

"Ah, I wouldn't worry about that, CJ—we'll make it work." Crawford didn't really want to get into a serious emotional discussion; he had more important things to run by his daughter. "You know, this weekend it looks like Davis Rules and Tackle Tim Tom will be the favorites in the Derby. It's sort of like the match race in March. I get to win in either case. If Davis Rules wins, I make a lot of money for me and my partners, and if Tackle Tim Tom wins, I get to say I'm the father of the jockey who won the Kentucky Derby. Pretty good deal for me, huh?"

"Sure, but to be honest, I don't think of it that way. My only focus is on winning with T-three."

"I get that. It's your job, and you must be a professional. But . . . you know, if you're coming off the far turn and you don't think you have enough horse to win, getting in someone else's way could be helpful if my horse has a shot."

"Why would I do that? We've all got to run a clean race."

"Come on, CJ," her father scoffed. "You know as well as I do that the jocks occasionally play some games out there."

"Yeah, maybe in a ten-thousand-dollar claiming race, but not in the Kentucky Derby!"

"Hey, look, you go out there and do your best. Just something to keep in mind, you know what I'm saying?"

"Yes, I know what you are saying."

While CJ and her father discussed the Derby over lunch, Gallo went to a meeting at the steward's offices. Along with nineteen other trainers, he sat and waited for the Kentucky Derby gate assignments. They announced the assignments in numerical order and handed each trainer a colored saddle cloth containing the number associated with the gate position. When slots number fourteen and fifteen were allocated, and Gallo still didn't have a saddle cloth in his hand, he began to get worried. Position sixteen went to Davis Rules, the horse that beat Tackle Tim Tom by half a length at the Santa Anita Derby and was owned by a Jamieson syndicate. At that point, the four trainers in the room without an assignment all looked at the floor and hoped their straw wasn't about to be drawn.

A Steward read the next position aloud, "Position number seventeen—Tackle Tim Tom, Stone Fence Farms, Ritchie Gallo, trainer."

CHAPTER THIRTY

To any casual observer who visits Kentucky, the city of Louisville appears to be a normal mid-sized American metropolis. With a population of just over 600,000 citizens, it hosts a triple-A baseball team, a soccer team, and a thriving arts scene for those who enjoy theater, classical music, opera, or ballet. Located on the Ohio River and sitting at the crossroads of three interstate highways, Louisville is a key hub in the national shipping and logistics system. Other major contributors to the local economy are the healthcare system and a manufacturing base that produces products as diverse as bourbon and baseball bats.

Then, beginning in early April, the city begins to focus its collective consciousness on one single event: the Kentucky Derby. The weather gets warmer, and cottage industries that depend on the annual horserace bloom right along with the flowers and buds on the trees. Fireworks displays, an air show, a marathon race, a steamboat race, a hot air balloon race, a parade, waterfront concerts, and countless parties and galas take place in the heady days leading up to the first Saturday in May. This colloquial holiday season culminates at 5:50 Central Time, when the gates open and twenty thoroughbreds sprint forth in a run for the roses. Billed as "The Greatest Two Minutes in Sports," it's a massive undertaking that impacts every aspect of life in this city for nearly a month.

Crawford and Channing Jamieson had been to the Derby numerous times, but this one was extraordinary due to the participation of their daughter and a horse owned by a Jamieson syndicate. They left their hotel on West Main Street with the intention of reaching Churchill Downs by the time the first race of the day went off. Once they arrived at the venue, they made their way to "The Mansion" on the sixth floor of the clubhouse. This was the most exclusive location at the track—a restaurant and bar reserved for the wealthy, the famous, and the well-connected. As Crawford transitioned into his networking mode, Channing moved to a porch overlooking the stadium and took the time to enjoy the visible traditions that take place at the Kentucky Derby. Looking down at the crowd in the clubhouse, the unique and flamboyant fashions on display brought a smile to her face. Bright colors, flashy suits, stunning dresses and elaborate hats on the ladies, all contributed to the ambiance and style of this iconic event where everyone wants to see and be seen.

Across the track on the infield, she observed the crowd in that location burgeoning to over seventy thousand fans. Unlike the genteel and sophisticated salon where she was standing, the infield would explode with a party-hearty environment often described as "spring break on crack." The antics that went on in the infield were legendary.

Invisible to the throngs filing into the grandstands, the clubhouse and the infield, activity on the backstretch was business as usual for the trainers, grooms, and track attendants. A full slate of races was being run prior to the Kentucky Derby, so most of the workers on the backside were completing the same tasks they would normally face on any other race day. Gallo had two horses from Stone Fence Farms entered in races that Saturday in addition to T-three's entry in the Derby. The work he and his grooms carried out to prepare and deliver the horses to the paddock allowed him to get his mind off the big race and enjoy what would otherwise be a slow and tense afternoon. When he and Jimmy finished the post-race efforts associated with his first two competitors of the day, he looked at his watch and realized that it was almost time for the "walkover."

On Derby Day, owners and trainers walk with their horse from where the stables are located to the paddock tucked behind the clubhouse. At the Kentucky Derby, there are few perks more coveted than the "walkover." Beaming owners and their guests revel in the exclusive privilege of accompanying their thoroughbred on this quarter-of-a-mile parade before one hundred and fifty thousand screaming fans. When Gallo and Jimmy led Tackle Tim Tom through the backstretch gap onto the track, they were accompanied by the three owners of Stone Fence Farms, along with John and Elliot. Since this was the first time the Stone Fence crew had ever participated in a Derby, the six men and one woman tried to take it all in, but the enormity of the event was somewhat overwhelming. There were twenty horses in the race, but on this day, they were accompanied by over 200 people.

"This is nuts!" said Jimmy. "Half these folks are drunk and the other half don't know the front end of a colt from the back end of a filly. All this is gonna do is make the horses nervous."

Gallo laughed. "Jimmy, just for once, stop complaining and try to live in the moment. We may never get back here again."

The procession wound around the Clubhouse Turn and then swung left through the tunnel below the Clubhouse to the paddock. Once there, the horses and grooms continued to walk around an elliptical walking ring bordered with thick arrangements of red roses. Twenty saddling stalls were situated on the north side of the ellipse, and a fenced-in gallery populated by several thousand fans formed the south side of the area. Gallo and his contingent of friends and business partners walked into the number seventeen saddling shed and waited for CJ to arrive. The jockeys finally filed into the paddock after having an official photograph taken of the twenty riders.

Gallo smiled when CJ hugged him, right after she gave Elliot a kiss. He reintroduced her to the folks from Stone Fence and she did her best to make small talk and appear calm. He could tell she was a bit nervous because she understood the enormity of the Derby within the world of thoroughbred racing. He surmised that she also remembered what happened in her last race, and was consciously erasing any negative thoughts about Hit the Bid's tragedy from her mind. Gallo said nothing of the superstition associated with starting in gate number seventeen.

Jimmy brought Tackle Tim Tom into the stall, and Gallo helped him set the bridals, reins, and saddle. Gallo put his arm around the jockey and gave her his instructions. "We talked this through before, CJ. You're coming out of seventeen, so you're way the heck out in space. We know he can come out of the chute clean and hot, so take him out as fast as you can and get about halfway down to the rail by the end of the first furlong. Over the next furlong, work your way down to the rail. If you can get on the rail at the turn, let him run. We want to come into the backstretch with no more than one or two horses ahead of him. At that point, just stay with the leaders until the far turn. Once you're in the far turn, let him do what he does best: run like hell on the rail. You should be in the lead or near the lead when you transition to the homestretch. From then on, it's time for T-three to prove he's a champion. Just get him to the wire first!"

"I got it, Mister Gallo." CJ made a point of looking him in the eyes when she added, "We're going to win this one for Hit the Bid."

The call of "Riders Up!" came from a Steward in the paddock. The jockeys jumped into the saddles, and grooms began leading the horses on one more walk around the ellipse before turning back into the tunnel under the clubhouse. As Gallo watched CJ ride away on Tackle Tim Tom, it felt very different from the previous times he had seen her participate in the parade to the post. This time he felt as though it was *his* daughter on the horse, not just a close friend. He felt proud and happy, but also somewhat scared. His love for her was more profound, more existential than in the past. *Dear Lord, please keep her safe*, was the last thought in his head as she entered the tunnel.

When the front hoof of the first racehorse touched the racetrack, the University of Kentucky Marching Band began to play "My Old Kentucky Home." Over one hundred and fifty thousand fans, ranging from the completely inebriated to the solidly sober, began to sing the words in unison as the parade of colts made their way on to the track. Because CJ was seventeenth in line, the song was almost over by the time Jimmy finished leading T-three onto the track surface. Before he handed the reins over to an escort pony-rider, he looked up at the jockey. "You can do this, Miss CJ," he said, voice barely audible over the roar of the crowd. "You're the best rider in this race, and you got the best colt in the country. You be safe. Just bring him home first and get those roses."

"I will, Mister Jimmy," said CJ with a smile, the thunder in her heart as loud as the world around her—a world she had avoided for so long. "I'll see you in the winner's circle."

CHAPTER THIRTY-ONE

Unlike his behavior at the Fountain of Youth Stakes or the Santa Anita Derby, Tackle Tim Tom walked straight into the seventeenth chute of the starting gate of the Kentucky Derby without any hesitation. He and his jockey were locked in. They were there to win, and the horse acted as though he was ready to get on with it. From the moment they stepped onto the track, CJ talked continuously to T-three. She never looked at or thought about the enormous crowd, and she paid no attention to the other horses. She just ran the anticipated race repeatedly in her mind and explained it in detail to her mount. T-three knew what was coming.

As the last horse settled into the twentieth post position, the starter advised the riders to be ready, and moments later—*the gates opened.*

For CJ, the crowd's boisterous cheering faded to a dull roar, her sole focus now on doing what she's always done best. As predicted, T-three got the clean and fast start, and fifteen strides into the race was already a full length ahead of the three racers to his right. Davis Rules, the thoroughbred that shot out of the sixteenth position, also got an excellent start and was only half a length behind, preventing CJ from moving T-three left, towards the infield. It wasn't until they had run one furlong that T-three was able to get past the number sixteen horse so that she could navigate toward the lead group.

When the front-runner hit the quarter-mile point, he had covered the distance at a very fast pace of twenty-two-and-one-tenth seconds.

Still traversing the straightaway, CJ found herself seven lengths behind the leader and trailing twelve horses situated between her and the infield. Ten strides later, the pack began to enter the clubhouse turn, and it was clear to her that she wouldn't be able to access the rail during the turn, so she had no choice but to continue on a route that was four horses wide of where she'd planned to be. Halfway through the turn, T-three was only six lengths back but trailing eleven of his competitors. CJ thought about asking him to step it up and take the lead as they transitioned to the backstretch, but her mental clock was telling her that they were running split times well below twelve seconds per furlong. All the colts were fast and strong. CJ had to save his energy for the homestretch. They ran the first half-mile in forty-five-and-four-tenths seconds.

After the pack completed the clubhouse turn and proceeded along the backstretch, CJ was able to make up ground on the lead horse without pushing T-three into high gear. The horse's strides were smooth and powerful. She could tell he was having fun and wanted to accelerate, but she held him at cruise speed. "Run smooth, big guy. . . . Run smooth. We'll get 'em at the turn."

Despite the roars of over one hundred and fifty thousand people and the muffled thunder of twenty horses running on a dirt track, CJ felt like she was operating in a vacuum, and she sensed that her mount was experiencing the same sensation. She didn't hear the crowd or the other horses. She just felt their bodies and their minds working together as though they were one. When great athletes have a superior day playing their sport, they often describe the sensation as "being in the zone." That was the sense that CJ had as she approached the far turn, and she imagined Tackle Tim Tom felt the same way—*in the zone*. Despite the enormous consumption of energy taking place in their bodies, the race felt effortless.

By the time the entire field entered the far turn, CJ had successfully moved her mount to a position two horses wide of the rail. When she went to pass the horse to her left and get T-three down near the infield, a horse in front got in her way. Almost simultaneously, Davis Rules came up on her right side, and when she bent her head under her right armpit to look behind, she was surprised to find a fourth horse directly at her six o'clock position.

Tackle Tim Tom was boxed in.

Throughout the turn, this formation of five horses ran in lockstep, approximately four lengths behind the leader. CJ couldn't move her mount left or right, nor could she accelerate due to the horse directly ahead. Even a desperate move to slow down and shift to the outside was precluded by a colt with his nose up T-three's backside. She was locked in with less than a sixteenth-of-a-mile until the transition to the homestretch.

CJ remained patient and talked to her horse. "Hang in there, hang in there, somebody's gonna move, just hang in there!"

Some horses are better at running turns than others. Few racers had Tackle Tim Tom's ability to hold a tight line in a turn that was generating eight times its body weight on spindly legs. Several strides before the beginning of the backstretch, where each horse would switch from a left lead to a right, the horse in front of T-three made the switch too early and faded a few feet to his right. Instantly, CJ tapped her horse's hindquarters with the whip in her right hand and increased a leftward pressure on the rein with the other hand. She shouted a command: "Go now, T-three, go now!"

It was like flooring the gas pedal on a race car. Tackle Tim Tom blew past the horse to his left and continued past the horse that had been in front of him. As they transitioned to the homestretch, she had the black colt on the rail and three lengths behind the leader. Now it was time to prove he was a champion. CJ knew the horse wanted it. She didn't have to ask him to run; she just let him go. No whipping, no screaming of commands, just a hand ride to the finish line. The grandstands and clubhouse exploded when Tackle Tim Tom overtook the leader and accelerated to the finish line with a winning time of two minutes and two-fifths seconds, just one second slower than the record set by Secretariat forty-six years earlier.

Tackle Tim Tom and CJ won the Kentucky Derby. Crawford Jamieson's horse, Davis Rules, finished second.

CHAPTER THIRTY-TWO

As CJ sat astride Tackle Tim Tom in the winner's circle of Churchill Downs, she began to refocus her mind from the disciplined concentration required by the race, to the process of dealing with the sea of humanity encircling her. A garland of five hundred red roses was tossed over Tackle Tim Tom's shoulders, an accouterment the horse clearly didn't appreciate, but Jimmy got the colt to stand still long enough to take the obligatory photos with the jockey, trainer, owners, and race sponsors.

Once CJ dismounted, the ceremony moved to the small stage at the back of the winner's circle. There, on national television, a solid gold trophy was presented to the owners of Stone Fence Farms, and a television commentator asked the same banal questions typically posed to owners and jockeys over the last fifty years.

CJ handled herself professionally during this session and answered an unexpected but direct question regarding her struggle with traumatic brain injury. "When I was very young, I was ashamed of the fact that I didn't think or act like other children, but I'm no longer ashamed of myself, and I believe the accident I suffered as a child does not define who I am. In fact, it is that injury that gave me the ability to communicate so well with horses and fueled my love for riding and racing. No one should feel sorry for me; I have great people surrounding me, and I continue to accomplish things that are important to me each and every day of my life."

Channing choked up when her daughter handled the disarming

question with poise and confidence. Gallo felt the same emotional connection to this young woman who had now changed his life. He wished he'd known her for the last twenty years rather than the last ten months. Crawford was still chafing at the fact that Davis Rules finished second. If T-three hadn't escaped the boxed-in position on the far turn, his horse would have won.

When the television segment of the program was over, the participants in the awards ceremony adjourned to the Mansion on the sixth floor of the clubhouse for a post-race reception. Ritchie and his business partners attended the event along with John McCann, Crawford Jamieson, and the Monkmeyers. Channing Jamieson accompanied her daughter to the jockey locker room so CJ could take a shower and change into a dress. Once that was done, CJ returned to the reception and was treated like a rock star. Her beauty was obvious, but her shy and restrained manner was endearing. Everyone in the room wanted to meet and speak with her, so she made a conscious effort to greet every person with a smile and a handshake, all the while keeping a firm grip on Elliot Monkmeyer's right arm.

Gallo marveled as he watched her deal with a situation that she couldn't have navigated ten months earlier. He wanted to tell her how much it meant to him to win the Kentucky Derby with her help, but he thought he would wait until later in the evening when they could be alone.

Crawford put on a happy face, but his dream of winning the Kentucky Derby had been dashed by his own daughter. Yet another failure in his relationship with his only child.

As the party wore on, Gallo downed a couple of mint juleps. He didn't particularly like the drink, but given the culture and traditions surrounding the Derby, he felt obligated to imbibe this iconic cocktail. As he was making his way around the room, shaking hands and receiving congratulations, he could feel the vibration of his cell phone in his pocket. He was going to ignore it, but when he looked at the screen, he could see that it was Jimmy trying to reach him. He stepped out on to a porch to escape the noise in the reception and answered the call.

"Hey, Jimmy, what's up?"

"I think you should come down to the stable boss. The vet's here, and we may have a little problem with T-three."

"What? What's the problem?"

"Don't panic, it ain't life or death, but I think you better gather the folks from Stone Fence and get down here."

Gallo immediately rounded up his business partners and started to leave the Mansion. As he walked to the door, CJ tugged on his arm. "Where are you going, Mister Gallo? Is there something wrong?"

"I don't think it's anything big, CJ—but the vet's looking at T-three, and Jimmy thinks there may be a problem."

"I'm coming with you," said CJ as she dragged Elliot out of the door by the hand.

The crew made its way to the stall where Tackle Tim Tom was located, and the veterinarian that treated the horse briefed them on the situation. "When Jimmy was bringing the horse back to the stall, he noticed that the colt was favoring his left front leg. We quickly examined the leg and did an ultrasound. The good news is that there doesn't appear to be any issues with his bones or carpal joints—structurally, his leg looks fine. But you can see right here that he has a tendon that's obviously swollen. There's blood or fluid moving into the tissue because it's either strained or has a minor tear. We couldn't see a tear on the ultrasound, but that doesn't mean it doesn't exist. The colt doesn't have any history of tendinitis, so it may be that during the race, he took an awkward step or an unexpected blow that damaged the tendon or ligament in this area of his leg. We can see the swelling, he's a bit lame, and I'm sure he's feeling some pain."

Gallo ran his hand over the bowed tendon and could feel the heat generated by an additional volume of blood on the tissue. "What do we do now, Doc?"

"Well, I don't think this is a career-ending injury, provided you're diligent in treating it. The first course of action is to cold hose or ice the injury several times a day. For the next few weeks, we'll give him a dose of a non-steroidal anti-inflammatory drug to relieve the pain and stave off more inflammation. When it's not iced, you want to wrap the area with a support bandage to minimize swelling and stabilize the limb. At a minimum, he needs thirty days of stall rest. At that point, you can hand-walk him around and then have him checked by your vet at the farm."

"Assuming he's walking okay at that point, when can we start training again?"

"Look, Ritchie, I'm going to be honest with you—if you really care about this horse, you won't put him back into a full training regimen for eight to twelve months. Tendon and ligament injuries can be frustrating in horses because they don't heal with normal tendon and ligament tissue. The tissue that replaces normal type-one collagen is different. The replacement tissue is neither as strong nor as elastic. Therefore, recovery can take a long time."

"I guess that means the end of his three-year-old racing campaign."

The vet shrugged. "Hey, he just won the Kentucky Derby. He's worth more in the breeding barn than on the racecourse."

"You may be right, but I'll sure miss seeing him run. Thanks, Doc."

The jubilation of winning the biggest race of the year was quickly dampened by the injury to the colt. Everyone in the stall gathered around T-three and stroked his neck, back, and hindquarters. Normally Jimmy didn't want anyone's help when he was servicing a horse, but the groom was sensitive to the sadness hanging in the air, and each visitor took a turn brushing him down. Jimmy brought in a large, deep bucket filled with ice water and placed T-three's left front leg in the vessel.

"What do you think, Ritch?" asked one of the owners.

"Well, he's your horse, so the ultimate decision is up to you, but I agree with the vet. If we take our time and he heals properly, we can race him as a four-year-old and win some big races. If he doesn't heal well, he gets to be a lover rather than a fighter. Either way, it's a hell of a lot better than what happened to Hit the Bid."

All three of the owners agreed with Gallo. Tackle Tim Tom was a talented thoroughbred who could still win Grade One races if he was healthy, but no one wanted to risk a career-ending injury to the horse. They loved the colt and were mindful of the fact that a great breeding stallion would bring a substantial amount of future revenue to Stone Fence Farms. His three-year-old season was over, and the next season was in doubt.

As everyone moped about the stall, Elliot Monkmeyer spoke up. "What a shame we won't get a chance to see T-three win the Triple Crown. The Preakness is only two weeks away, but he won't even be walking around by that time." Elliot reached out and stroked the horse between the ears and then broke out a big smile. "T-three didn't like having a garland of red roses draped all over him, so I don't think a blanket of Black-Eyed Susans would make him any happier."

"Maybe not," said CJ. "But I was looking forward to racing in the Preakness. It's still one of the most popular races."

Gallo leaned against the stall wall and folded his arms over his chest. "I wouldn't jump to any unwarranted conclusions there, Miss CJ. I think you'll still be riding in the Preakness."

All six people and one horse shot Gallo a quizzical look. "How so, Mister Gallo?"

Gallo smiled. "Backboard."

CHAPTER THIRTY-THREE

G allo and CJ stared at the speaker phone in the middle of Gallo's desk until an operator advised them that all ten of Backboard's owners were now logged into the conference call. Gallo immediately launched into his pitch: "It's great to speak to all of you, and I'm happy to give you an update on the email I sent each of you yesterday. Let's start by reviewing our racing history with Backboard."

"You folks bought the horse at the beginning of his two-year-old season for sixty grand and we had a great start when he won his maiden race. From then on, we could never get him back into the winner's circle until we matched him up with CJ. She rode him to three victories at Saratoga, Churchill Downs, and Santa Anita. As a result of those races, he earned a total of thirty Kentucky Derby qualifying points."

"I'm sure you guys remember a conference call we had back then, when I was trying to decide if we should nominate Backboard to run in the Triple Crown races. We'd run the horse four times in five months, and I wanted to give him about two months to recover. In addition, he had never run more than one-and-one-sixteenth miles, so I wasn't sure he was ready to go a mile-and-a-quarter in the Derby. All his training was aimed at sprints, not races that required more endurance. So, we put the Derby idea on the backburner and entered him, along with Tackle Tim Tom, in the Fountain of Youth Stakes down at Gulfstream. Obviously, CJ didn't participate in that race.

Tackle Tim Tom finished a disappointing third, but Backboard was right there finishing fourth. That got him another five points, for a total of thirty-five. Once again, I reached out and advised you guys that we had an outside shot of making it into the Derby. We sent in six thousand dollars as a late nomination fee, hoping that we'd make the cut. Unfortunately, when the final determination was made in April, the last qualifier for the Derby got in with thirty-eight points, leaving us three points short."

No one on the call raised a question or made a comment, so Gallo continued. "So, why is this all so important? It's important because seven horses that ran in the Kentucky Derby, including Tackle Tim Tom, are not scheduled to run in the Preakness. The limit on the number of horses running in the Preakness is fourteen, which means there's one open spot. Guess who's next in line?"

Over the speakerphone, Gallo could hear voices expressing excitement at this burst of good news.

"Ritchie, how much is this going to cost us?" asked one of the men.

"The entry fee is fifteen thousand, and the starting fee is also fifteen thousand. If we scratch the horse prior to the race, you lose the entry fee. I know thirty grand is a lot of coin, but based on Backboard's previous winnings, you still have over a hundred and fifty thousand in your escrow account with us. If he doesn't finish in the money, the whole thirty thousand goes up in smoke. But how often do you get a chance to run a horse in the Preakness Stakes?"

There was chatter on the line as the shareholders talked among themselves, and then one of the men posed a question to Gallo. "Ritchie, we need you to be straight with us. Does Backboard have a chance at winning the Preakness?"

"Look, guys, I would never recommend we run the horse unless I thought he could be competitive. I've changed his exercise routine since the Fountain of Youth, and we're starting to see that change pay off. This horse has always been a speedster—it was his endurance that was questionable. Lately, his stamina seems to be improving, and I think he can go a greater distance. Keep in mind that the Preakness is a shorter race than the Derby. The horses will run one-and-three-sixteenth miles as opposed to one-and-a-quarter. Also, the turns at Pimlico aren't as broad as Churchill Downs. There's more straight-away, so a good sprinter really has a chance to run. If we were talking about the Belmont at a mile-and-a-half, I would be more hesitant to run him. But at a mile-and-three-sixteens, I think he's got a shot."

The consultative chatter picked up again on the conference call, leading to a few seconds of silence and another question: "We'd like Miss Jamieson's opinion on this move."

Gallo looked at CJ and motioned for her to address the speakerphone. "First, I would like to say that I really respect you gentlemen as owners because I know how deeply you love this horse. I love him, too, and he's one of my all-time favorites. Secondly, I agree with Mister Gallo's assessment of Backboard's ability. I don't have the time to be his exercise rider every day, but I do ride him at least once a week, and I can tell his endurance is much better. I'm not concerned about racing him at a longer distance. The other thing I think you need to understand is an intangible. Backboard knows the purpose of the race is to win. Not all horses get that. Instinctively, they are herd animals; running along as part of a herd comes naturally. But while only a few of these thoroughbreds get it, Backboard *knows* why he's on the racetrack. That's a big advantage we have over most horses."

CJ continued with her train of thought: "We're going to be in a horse race. Nothing is guaranteed, and lots of bad things can happen on the track. You can get bumped at the start, boxed in, forced to run too wide, or the horse can just be having a bad day. But if I get a good clean ride on this horse, I know he can win."

A little more chatter was heard on the box, and then the man designated as the spokesman for the group made it official. "Ritchie, we are all really excited about this, and we appreciate the great job you've done with this horse. We will be making airline and hotel reservations for Baltimore as soon as we get off this call. We can't wait to see our colt run in the Preakness."

CJ turned toward Gallo and gave him a fist bump.

"There is one other thing we all wanted to say. Miss Jamieson, we are so happy you are back from the tragedy that occurred in March. We can't tell you how much we've enjoyed seeing you compete on Backboard. We're just a bunch of working stiffs—not rich guys who can afford expensive racehorses and jets. But we love thoroughbred racing, and you've made our dreams come true. We're so proud of the fact that you are our jockey . . . and our friend."

Gallo could see tears welling up in CJ's eyes. He pointed at the speakerphone, indicating he wanted her to say something. She managed to get out a short, stilted sentence. "Thank you for being so nice to me."

Gallo brought the phone call to an end and looked at his jockey. "I hope you just learned an important lesson there, CJ."

"I did, Mister Gallo. As a matter of fact, I've been learning a lot of lessons about people ever since I reconnected with you and T-three at Santa Anita. All my life, I rode horses because I had to do it for me. It was always all about me. I never realized that what I do could be so important to someone else. I've always known that winning is important; everyone wants to win. I guess I just never understood that what I did could bring an emotional or spiritual reward to other people. But now I get it. I barely know these men, and yet they consider me to be a friend. Two months ago, that would have surprised me, but today I understand what friendship means. The next time we are around these guys, I intend to get to know them even better. I used to hate meeting new people, but now I look forward to seeing their wives and children, and learning about their jobs. I want to be a real friend."

Gallo smiled. *Small steps in the right direction,* he thought.

Gallo began organizing paperwork he would overnight to Pimlico Racetrack in order to enter Backboard into the Preakness Stakes. He made a quick call to the bank that serviced Stone Fence Farms to arrange for the entry fee, and when he got off the phone, he realized that CJ was still lingering around the office. "Aren't you supposed to connect with Jimmy and exercise Backboard?"

"Yes, I am, but not for another few minutes. I thought I'd just hang out with you and see if I can help get things ready for the race."

"Really?" Gallo placed the papers in his hand on the desk and looked at the jockey. "CJ, is there something you want to discuss with me?"

CJ sat down in a chair next to the desk. "Mister Gallo, if a father really loved his daughter and wanted to do what was best for her, wouldn't he always be completely truthful and honest with her?"

"Sure, that's kind of self-evident, isn't it?"

CJ sat back in her chair and looked at the ceiling. "It's not as straightforward as that, Mister Gallo. I've got a problem with my dad. Do you remember the race in December when I didn't push the horse because the trainer drugged him up, and the horse wasn't sound enough to run?"

"Sure, I remember it. Nothing came of it because the bonehead trainer didn't want you to rat him out on the drug abuse."

"Right—well, it turns out that the bonehead trainer confronted my father and accused me of underperforming on Breach Inlet because I was trying to help my dad's horse win the race."

"C'mon, nobody's going to believe that."

"Well, evidently, my dad did. A few days before the Derby, when he took me to lunch, he implied that he wanted me to help Davis Rules win if I couldn't get to the wire first on T-three."

"What!? You're kidding me. Are you sure you've got this right, CJ?"

"Yeah, I knew exactly what he was alluding to. I didn't want to mention this to you, but it's really bugging me, and I'm not sure what to do about it." The young woman shook her head and looked off in the distance. "If he really loved me, why would he ask me to consider something like that? Does he have so little respect for me, he thinks I would pull an unethical stunt like that? Does he think the damage from my brain injury prevents me from knowing right from wrong? Right after the Derby, when we were all on the winner's stand getting the trophy, I could tell he was angry. He didn't congratulate me or tell me he was proud of me. He was just brooding over the fact that I'd just beaten Davis Rules on T-three. Why would a father do that to a daughter?"

The trainer and the jockey sat in silence for a few moments as they both pondered the question on the table. "I don't know why your dad would do that, CJ. He's a super competitive businessman who keeps score on everything he does. It's the thing that keeps him motivated. It's no excuse, but it's just the way he is."

"Mister Gallo, I love horses. You know that. If I'm in a race, I do everything I can to let the horse be free and run. I don't care if it's an eight-thousand-dollar claimer or a world-class thoroughbred like Hit the Bid. As long as the horse wants to run, I let it run. If a horse isn't sound, I won't get aboard. It's just that simple."

Gallo could see that this conflict with her father was seriously impacting CJ. She had made such an impressive bounce back from her bout with depression, he didn't want another emotional speed bump to throw her off balance. "Listen, kid, you've got a wonderful mother who always has your back. I think you need to seek her counsel and figure out how the two of you can straighten out your father. I'm happy to give you advice, CJ, but this is something you need to address directly with your parents."

"Yeah, I think I should address this sooner rather than later because I don't want to get into a debate with my father over the Preakness. I need to run that race clean and focused." CJ stood and began to move towards the door. "You know, it's funny, but as I continue to grow as a person and overcome the obstacles that roll around in my brain, I find one kind of problem being replaced by another. I sometimes use the analogy that I'm moving from the dark into the light. Unfortunately, bright light makes everything more visible. I'm learning that life is complicated. Things I never recognized or saw before now have to be dealt with for me to progress."

"Welcome to the real world."

CJ laughed. "I better get going, or Jimmy will be giving me another lecture about showing up on time in the real world." When she got to the door, she turned and looked at Gallo. "Do you ever wish you had children, Mister Gallo? Do you miss having a son or a daughter?"

Gallo smiled. "Well, to be honest, I do feel like I have a daughter now. You've been a great deal for me. I didn't have to change your poopy diapers, and I still get to benefit from your special skills. Hey, this parent stuff is a piece of cake!"

CJ grinned and shook her head. "I'm getting better at figuring out when you're serious and when you're giving me a bad time. I think I'll take that last comment as a back-handed compliment."

"Good assumption, kid. You're the best."

"See you later, Mister Gallo." As CJ walked out the door, Gallo had a final thought: *And when I see your father again, that son-of-a-bitch is going to have some explaining to do.*

CHAPTER THIRTY-FOUR

John McCann and Ritchie Gallo walked out of La Scala Restaurant in the Little Italy section of Baltimore and began the short walk back to the Four Seasons Hotel.

"Now tell me that wasn't one of the best Italian meals you ever had?" said McCann.

"Well, I've had some great Italian food at the mom-and-pop places in upstate New York—but you're right. That was a *terrific* meal. Not cheap, but great food."

It was still an hour before sunset when they reached the hotel lobby, so they decided to take the elevator to the restaurant on the top floor for a nightcap and a panoramic look at the Baltimore Harbor. Entering the bar on the twenty-ninth floor, Gallo was impressed by the elaborate lighting and design of this exquisite restaurant, as well as the enormous picture windows providing a breathtaking view of the harbor and the city.

"Wow, this is a really cool place," said Gallo. "Everyone is so well dressed, and the dining room is spectacular."

"That's not the only thing spectacular up here; wait until you see the price of our drinks."

The men found two empty stools at a polished oak bar set before a matrix of backlit shelves that held nearly five hundred bottles of liquor and spirits. John ordered a scotch, but Gallo stayed with the red wine he had been drinking earlier at dinner.

"I hope your day was as productive as mine, Ritch."

"Yeah, there were several lengthy meetings today here in the hotel. It seems like they're trying to do a professional job getting organized for the race, which is only eight days away. You gotta wonder how long Pimlico is going to be able to host the Preakness. It just doesn't seem like the economics work too well with a venue as old and underused as this one."

"I hear you, Ritch, but from my perspective, I don't really care where it's run. The Preakness ain't going away, and I managed to get four of the jockeys I represent into the race, in addition to CJ on Backboard."

"Like I've said before, John, you're a real humanitarian."

"I know you're flying back to Louisville tomorrow morning. When will you bring Backboard to Pimlico?"

"We'll take a tractor trailer from Stone Fence Farms to the track next Tuesday. That gives us a few days to get the horse comfortable on the dirt and the shape of the turns."

McCann excused himself and wandered off to the men's room. Just after he left, the empty chair to Gallo's right was taken by a young woman who traded a smile with him when she sat down. After she ordered a drink, Gallo took a big sip of wine to get a little shot of alcoholic courage, and he asked the lady a question: "You're too attractive to be here by yourself, so I'm assuming you are waiting for a boyfriend or a husband to show up."

"No, not really," she said. "I accompanied a friend of mine who is meeting a guy for dinner. I felt like a third wheel at the table, so I decided to wait here at the bar until they are done eating."

"Ah, well, I'm pleased to have your company, if only for a few minutes."

There was an awkward silence for several moments, and then the lady asked a surprising question. "Are you Ritchie Gallo—the trainer?"

"Uh, actually, I am. I'm shocked to be recognized in a place like this. It's usually some degenerate gambler that sees me on the street and curses at me because he lost money on one of my horses."

She laughed at his comment. The woman had it all going for her—a beautiful face, a lovely smile, long brown hair, and a little black dress that highlighted shapely legs attached to a fit body.

"Are you a racing fan?" asked Gallo.

"I have to be. I work in the public relations office of the Maryland State Racing Commission, so right now I'm very busy getting ready for the Preakness, and I know that you have a horse in the race."

"Oh, I get it. I didn't think my celebrity was so broad-based that a beautiful woman in an upscale bar would recognize me, but that's the way it goes."

They continued to chat and learn a little about each other. Her name was Mary Ann Thompson. She was a Baltimore native who graduated from Johns Hopkins University.

"So, tell me Mary Ann—does the friend you accompanied here also work for the Commission?"

"She does. She's an attorney, so she gets into a lot of the regulatory and legislative issues the Commission's involved with. The guy she's dating tonight is a big-time thoroughbred owner. She's a little bit secretive about this guy, so I'm not really sure what's going on."

"What's his name? Maybe I know him."

"I think his first name is Crawford. I don't remember the last name."

"Crawford? Is it Crawford Jamieson?"

"Yeah, that might be it. They're sitting right over there in the corner." She pointed in the direction of the dining room.

Gallo looked closely at the diners sitting next to the large windows looking out on the city. He saw an attractive woman smiling and carrying on an animated discussion with a well-dressed and perfectly coiffed man wearing a Rolex.

As Gallo stood up, John returned to his seat at the bar. "Johnny," he said, unable to take his eyes off Crawford across the way, "do me a favor and entertain this beautiful young lady for a few minutes. Her name is Mary Ann. I see someone I need to talk to."

He walked straight into the dining room to the location where the couple was eating their meal. He was now angry with Jamieson on several fronts, so he gave little thought to conducting a tactful confrontation.

"Ritchie? Ritchie Gallo. What are you doing here?" asked Crawford when Gallo loomed over the table.

"I had a few planning meetings today with the folks from the Preakness. I'm heading back to Kentucky tomorrow." Gallo looked at the woman. "Hi, how are you? I'm Ritchie Gallo."

Before she could answer, Crawford spoke up. "Uh, this is Linda. She works for me in the syndication business. We're just going over some business issues."

"Really? Gosh, for some reason she looks like a lawyer to me. Anyway, I know this is awkward, but could you spare me a couple of minutes? There's something I believe we need to discuss."

Crawford was clearly angered by Gallo's interference with his evening. He made no attempt to be conciliatory. "Is this really necessary, Mister Gallo? I'm kind of busy, and I can't imagine we have anything that important to talk about."

"Yeah, it is necessary, and I think you'll recognize its importance very quickly."

Crawford excused himself and walked with Gallo to a small atrium where the entrances to the restrooms were located.

"What's this all about, Gallo?"

"First of all, it's none of my business how you spend your spare time, but I think we both know this lady you're with isn't an employee of yours, so don't give me that bullshit."

"You're right, Gallo." Jamieson spit the words out through

clenched teeth. "It is none of your business—so if you don't mind, I will get back to my dinner."

"Hold on, Crawford—there's something between us that *is* my business. You see, in about eight days, a young jockey who has become my closest friend will risk her life on a racetrack under a dark cloud. A dark cloud created by an irresponsible father who insulted her integrity and used his position as a parent to encourage her complicity in an unethical act. How the hell could you do that? How could you treat her with such disrespect?"

"Once again, Mister Gallo, you're treading on thin ice. My communication and relationship with my daughter is privileged. We allowed you to get involved in CJ's counselling session last month, but in general you have no right to be in the middle of my family affairs."

"Normally, I would agree with you. But in this case, I can't stand by and let an enormous ego hurt someone I've come to respect and care for. In the past, I've defended you in discussions with CJ, but this stunt where you asked her to throw a race is total *bullshit*. I'm not going to let you screw this kid up. She's too special for that."

"You're not going to let me take care of my *own child*?" Jamieson was shouting. "Who the hell do you think you are? I know what you're after, Gallo. You're after my family. You've managed to take complete control of CJ, and now you want my wife. I've seen the way you look at my wife, Gallo, and I don't like it. What I ought to do right now is punch you in the mouth and beat you to a pulp."

"I got sucker-punched a couple of months ago by a trainer who's a hell of a lot tougher than you. If you want to do it right here, right now, I'm ready! We can duke it out right here in front of the damned lady's room!"

As both men tensed up and made a small move toward one another, John entered the atrium and addressed Jamieson in a friendly voice. "Hey, Crawford, how you doin'? I didn't know you were here."

Neither man said anything, and John quickly sensed that something was amiss. "What's going on here? Are you guys okay?"

Gallo and Jamieson unclenched their fists and stepped back. "Everything is okay, John. Everything is just *hunky-dory*—right, Gallo?"

Crawford turned to walk away, but stopped after two steps and turned to address Gallo. "After next Saturday, after the Preakness, you will never see my daughter or my wife again. Do you understand that, Gallo? If you come near either one of them, I will have you killed."

Gallo and John stood there, completely dumbfounded, as Jamieson roared back into the dining room.

"Jesus, Ritch—five minutes ago, you introduce me to a gorgeous young woman, and just now, someone threatens to kill you. You move from one end of the social spectrum to the other with the speed of light."

"This guy, Jamieson, is turning out to be a real prick. He's turning his back on two spectacular women and taking them for granted. I guess it's not really my business, and I shouldn't get in the middle of this, but it's tough to watch. I'm emotionally involved because of my relationship with CJ."

"How about your emotions regarding her mother?"

Gallo looked askance at John. "I've seen how you look at her, Ritch. I don't know what the background is on you two, but I don't have to be a psychologist to figure out that you're into this lady."

Gallo put his hands in his pockets and nodded towards the bar. "Let's go finish our drinks and get out of here."

"Okay, you don't want to talk about it—that's fine. But let me tell you something. In about a week, you will face one of the biggest tests of your career. Focus on the race and your job. Take control of your life and your thoughts for the next eight days and worry about this other stuff later."

Gallo smiled. "Thanks for the advice, Epictetus."

CHAPTER THIRTY-FIVE

She sat in the darkness awaiting the arrival of her husband from the airport. Upstairs, her daughter was asleep after a busy day in Kentucky and a hurried flight by private jet back to Los Angeles. CJ wanted to come home for a discussion with her mother before returning to the east coast for the Preakness. That discussion had been emotional and candid. Both women recommitted their love for one another and shed tears over the situation at hand. When CJ asked her mom how to proceed, Channing's answer was short and direct: "Leave it to me."

Sitting in an over-stuffed chair in the living room, her mind was racing as she anticipated the contentious communication she would have with Crawford when he got home. The anger in her chest simmered like bubbling lava just below the floor of a volcanic crater. She understood this would be a life-changing event, but she finally accepted a logical conclusion that she had assumed but ignored for several years.

It was useless to second-guess herself after twenty-one years of marriage, but the divide that now separated her and her husband had become insurmountably broad. Initially, Crawford had been loyal and loving to her and CJ. He set the table for a beautiful and fulfilling life together. Unfortunately, Channing never really came to that table from an emotional perspective. After CJ's accident, Crawford realized that she would never show up with the unconditional love he wanted, so he also abandoned his chair. The result was a beautifully set table with no one there to enjoy its bounty.

Despite her anger, Channing actually felt sorry for Crawford. She tried to be a loyal wife and life partner, but she understood that her emotional shortcomings occasionally drove him into the arms of another woman. He was a man—that stuff happens. His obsessions with success and fulfilling his passions drove his actions. But the break in confidence he precipitated with CJ was inexcusable. CJ was an innocent bystander in the marriage of convenience created by her parents. Even if Channing and Crawford were unable to pull it off, total love and support was owed to their daughter from both parties. Crawford violated that unwritten law. There was no point in returning to the uneasy alliance that pretended to be solid and real. She had no interest in making the trek toward Crawford's side of the great divide. Instead, she thought more and more every day about Ritchie Gallo.

Her heart began to race when she heard the garage door open and the sound of Crawford parking his car. He fumbled with his keys but eventually unlocked the door to the kitchen and entered the house. After a quick look at the contents of the refrigerator, he made his way into the darkened portion of his home. When he flicked on the living room light, he was startled by Channing's presence. "Jesus, what are you doing sitting here in the dark? It's after midnight."

"I'm waiting for you."

The cold tone of her voice was uncharacteristic of Channing Jamieson. She knew he would sense that something was seriously wrong.

"CJ is home. She flew in today to speak with me. We had a long talk—a long talk about her father and his lack of respect for his daughter."

"Ah, jeez, Channing. She must have misunderstood something I said or did. You know she doesn't get things straight a lot of times. It's just a misunderstanding."

253

"There's no misunderstanding. She knew exactly what you were asking her to do. She isn't as clueless as she used to be, and she has a solid moral compass. You asked her to do something unethical. What a shameless act on your part—an act that has ruined your relationship with her forever."

"Ah, crap, I'm tired. I don't have time for this discussion."

"You don't have time for anything now, Crawford. Your time is up."

In the past, whenever they argued, Channing always deferred to him at some point. This time, he knew it was different. Insisting that Ritchie Gallo participate in CJ's counselling session just one month ago had opened the door, and tonight she was walking through it.

"So, that's it?"

"Yes, Crawford, that's it. I'm sorry—sorry for a lot of things. It isn't just you, I understand that. But there's no use in continuing the charade. We're both young. We have a lot of life to live and enjoy. Our daughter is an adult now. She can make it on her own, and so can we."

Crawford exhaled. In a way, he was relieved. "Okay. I'll talk to our lawyers tomorrow. Don't worry, I'll be fair and reasonable."

Channing scoffed. "It's a business decision for you. I'm sure you will do what's in your best interest, whatever that might be."

Crawford stood and started to leave the room, but then stopped to say one more thing to Channing. "I really screwed up, didn't I?" He was beginning to really regret his comment to CJ before the Derby. It occurred to him that he had just lost his wife and his daughter.

"Yes, you screwed up. She's more valuable than the profit and loss statement at your bank. You forgot that."

"Maybe someday in the future I can make it right."

"I hope so."

Crawford drove into the night searching for a hotel room. Channing sat in her living room and wept.

CHAPTER THIRTY-SIX

G allo and Jimmy walked Tackle Tim Tom and General Custer down the ramp of a horse-trailer into the back-stretch section of Pimlico racetrack. They were directed to a stable that was specifically set aside for participants in the Preakness Stakes. Jimmy placed about ten pounds of oaten hay in their feed troughs, along with plenty of water and a bucket of mixed grains.

While Jimmy tended to the horses, Gallo took a few moments for a nostalgic walk out on the track to have a look around. He hadn't worked at Pimlico in fifteen years and was a bit dismayed to see that the condition of the venue had deteriorated over time. The stables were run-down, and the clubhouse and grandstand sections definitely needed an update and a makeover. The facility hadn't aged gracefully, and there were ongoing discussions between the owners and local politicians regarding its longevity as a site for the Preakness Stakes.

Even though the amount of racing conducted at Pimlico had been reduced to a single meet in the month of May consisting of twelve race days, the running of the Preakness Stakes, the second jewel in the Triple Crown, was still a major event. It would be broadcast on national television, and a crowd of over 100,000 people was antic-ipated. Just as the Kentucky Derby was a huge cultural happening for Louisville, the Preakness was a traditional holiday for Baltimore that brought tourists, big money, and a weekend of excitement that energized the citizens of the city.

Gallo turned and started the walk back to the stable area when he was confronted by someone who caused him to stop in his tracks. "Channing? What are you doing here?"

"Hey, Ritchie—I was hoping to catch you before you met up with CJ today. Let's take a walk. I want to talk to you."

Gallo accompanied Channing into the empty grandstand on the backstretch of the track. They sat all alone in the large bleacher area, and immediately, Gallo could tell something wasn't right with Channing—her eyes were puffy, as though after a night of sobbing. "Over the weekend, CJ flew back to Los Angeles so she could have a private discussion with me about her father. The talk was about some of the things he'd said to her regarding the Derby. CJ told me she had the same discussion with you a little over a week ago, and you're aware of what happened."

Gallo nodded, afraid of saying too much. Instead, he remained quiet.

"I confronted Crawford about his poor judgement. Our discussion was very brief. I think we both knew we had reached a point where our marriage was no longer tenable. I think he was actually *relieved* when he left the house that evening," she noted with a flighty, mirthless laugh. Shaking her head, she added, "At any rate, I'm on my way to being an ex-wife."

"I'm sorry, Channing. I know you really tried to make it work for CJ's benefit. I'm sure everything will turn out okay for you. What are you going to do now?"

"I'm going to start over. I'm hoping Crawford will be reasonable on the divorce settlement. I don't deserve, or want, half of what he has. He grew the business, not me. I just want to begin to do the things I was unable to do over the last twenty-one years. I especially want to go back to Wellesley and finish college. I'm only thirty credits away from a degree."

"Hey, good for you. You'll be the oldest senior in your graduating class, but you'll also be the most beautiful."

"Yeah, well, after I earn that degree, I have a promise to fulfill." Channing's eyes rested on his for a moment, and he felt his pulse spike. "A promise I made to a young man many years ago, and this time I won't screw it up. I'll ask that young guy to forgive me and to make a bet on me. You see, I am still very much in love with this fellow."

Gallo smiled. "Is that going to be a win, place, or show bet?"

"Oh, no. This is a big-time race. We're only betting on the win."

"Hey, I think I can say with confidence that the not-so-young man will bet his heart and soul on the win. I've never been so confident about a race in my life."

Gallo took her hand, brought it so his lips, and gently kissed it.

"I have a lot to go through and endure over the next few months with Crawford. It will be difficult for you and me to rebuild our relationship in a public setting. But I don't want to lose you again, Ritch. Can you be patient for a while longer?"

"Absolutely. You need to get your head screwed on straight and begin to do the things that are important to you. When you're ready, I'm here."

They stood, held hands, and began to walk back toward the stables. "How is CJ handling this?"

"She understands what's going on. I urged her to make an effort in the future to reconcile with her father. I don't know if Crawford has learned enough from this incident to get his priorities straight, but hopefully he'll figure it out."

"Did you tell CJ about you and me? About our history and your intent to reconnect with me?"

"I did. She was ecstatic. She's fallen in love with you, just like I did."

"I hate to say this, but your husband is a loser. I don't care if he beats me in the Preakness this Saturday. If I have you and CJ in my life, I've won the biggest race you can win."

Channing smiled and touched his face, but Gallo's reference to the Preakness reminded her of something she wanted to tell him.

"I don't know if you've heard, but several horses have already been scratched from the race. It gave Crawford an opportunity to introduce a coupled entry."

"An entry? Who's the second horse in the entry besides Davis Rules?"

"Jet Lab."

"Jet Lab? Jet Lab's a rabbit." Gallo and Channing both began to laugh. "So, your husband and his trainer think they've figured out a strategy to beat Backboard. It's too late, Channing. I'm standing here holding your hand. I've already won."

CHAPTER THIRTY-SEVEN

G allo walked Channing to her car and returned to the barn where his horses were located. He was delighted to see CJ standing there with John McCann. CJ had arrived at Pimlico with her mother a day earlier so she could exercise two horses she would ride during the meet. Gallo encouraged John to engage her in several races prior to the Preakness in order to gain experience running on this track. CJ had never competed at Pimlico, but John had little trouble setting her up to run in the Black-Eyed Susan Stakes on Friday and the Maryland Sprint Stakes on Saturday.

"How's it going, kid?" asked Gallo.

"It's going well, Mister Gallo. Mister McCann got me on a couple of good mounts, so by the time Backboard and I start in the Preakness, I should have a good feel for racing on this track."

"Yeah, I heard you got a nice filly for the Black-Eyed Susan."

"I did. She ran third in the Kentucky Oaks two weeks ago, but I think we can be really competitive this week. She's not Hit the Bid, but she's still a talented horse, and I like riding her."

Gallo shrugged. "A filly like Hit the Bid only comes along once in a generation, but we still have to forge ahead, right?"

"Right, Mister Gallo. I'm thinking positive all the time. I'm making myself happy." CJ looked over at Jimmy. "You should try that, Mister Jimmy—you just think positive thoughts and make yourself happy."

Jimmy shook his head in disgust and disappeared into the stall, muttering under his breath.

Gallo, John, and CJ laughed, and then Gallo got down to business. "These horses spent ten hours today in the back of a truck. We need to take them out and get them moving. I'll jump on the General, and you hop on Backboard. We'll walk them for two furlongs and then let them canter for a mile. Tomorrow morning, we go back to the normal race week routine for Backboard."

Jimmy had already saddled both horses and brought them out of the stalls. He handed the reins of each horse to Gallo and CJ, who began the short walk to the track.

John called out to them as they walked away. "I'll see you guys at dinner tonight at the Mount Washington Tavern. The reservation is for seven o'clock."

"Sounds great! We'll see you then."

They continued to walk the horses toward the gap in the fence that allowed access to the track when something caught CJ's eye. Leaning against the open gate was a man, a woman, and a child. The adults wore blue work-shirts typically worn by track employees. Their jeans were soiled with dirt, their work boots splattered with mud. They were looking directly at CJ and smiling. The woman made a timid wave as though trying to get the jockey's attention, but they stayed back against the fence and made no effort to confront Gallo, CJ, and the horses. As CJ focused her gaze away from the parents and toward the child, she saw something that piqued her curiosity.

"Mister Gallo, can you hang on to Backboard for a second? I want to talk to those people over there."

Gallo held the reins for both horses as CJ walked over to the trio. She smiled and said hello.

"You're Miss Jamieson, the jockey, aren't you?" asked the woman.

CJ nodded and looked down at the boy who appeared to be about five years old. When she and Gallo approached, it was the stare from the boy's large and beautiful brown eyes that caught her attention. She knew there was something different about him.

"Is this your son?" she asked.

"Yes, his name is Roberto . . . Roberto Santana."

CJ knelt down so she could look closely at the boy. She could tell he wanted to look at her but he was shy. His eyes continued to flicker back and forth from the horses to her face. His thoughts seemed to bounce around inside his head, just as hers did when she was five years old. His father reached down and touched his son on the shoulder. "Roberto, say hello to the lady. She is a jockey. Say hello to her."

The child slowly focused his gaze on CJ, and said hello.

His mother spoke up. "We saw you on television at the Kentucky Derby. They said you are recovering from a terrible brain injury. Is that true?"

CJ smiled at the lady. "Yes . . . Yes, that is true. When I was young, I had a lot of trouble dealing with the world around me. I'm sensing that your son has the same problem. At his age, I wasn't so different from the way he is now."

"He fell off a bike and was almost run over by a car. We don't have a lot of money, so we have to take him to the local clinic, but I don't think they know much about dealing with a brain injury. We have a woman who is a friend of ours and watches him every day. She is great with him. She reads to him and tries to help him to speak. He doesn't say much, but I think he understands everything."

"We wanted him to meet you, because . . . you know, maybe he can be like you and overcome this," his father chimed in. "We worry about him. We want him to be able to work and have a good life. People around the track say you have a special ability to talk to horses."

"Well, sometimes," said CJ. She smiled at the boy again. "He's a beautiful child. Hey, I like your black hair." She slowly reached out to the child. "Is it okay if I touch your hair?"

He stopped looking about and remained still. CJ ran her hand through his hair, smoothing it down. "There you go; now you look very handsome."

"He must like you Miss Jamieson." Said the woman. "He doesn't usually let anyone touch him but us."

CJ stood and addressed the couple. "I'll bet he likes horses, doesn't he?"

"Sí, he loves to look at horses. We walk him around here all the time so he can see them."

"Stay right here. I think we should give him a chance to meet a great horse." CJ turned and walked back to where Gallo was standing. "I'm going to take Backboard over to meet this little boy."

"Are you sure that's wise, CJ? What if the horse steps on the kid?"

"Don't worry, Mister Gallo," she said with a smile. "Backboard and I are on the same page on this one."

CJ led the gelding over to the gate where the family was standing. As she approached, the child became very still. When the horse stopped about ten feet from him, he stared, wide-eyed and silent, at the thoroughbred. CJ tossed Backboard's reins over his neck, releasing the horse from her control. She moved to the side and looked at Roberto. "Do you want to meet my horse? He is really friendly and gentle. Don't be afraid."

The boy's father took his hand off his shoulder, and the child took four tentative steps toward Backboard, but stopped a few feet in front of him. Roberto looked intently at CJ. He was torn. He wanted to go to the horse but wasn't sure what was going on around him. He was intrigued by the friendly woman who accompanied the horse, and he could sense that she liked him and wanted to be helpful; he just wasn't sure how to proceed.

Once again, CJ bent down to the child's level and spoke to him. "This could be a big moment in your life, a moment you don't want to pass up. My friend Backboard may be able to help you, and I know your touch and affection will help him. Go ahead. Say hello."

Slowly the child started toward the horse. Just a few feet away, he moved to his right as if to approach the animal from an angle. Backboard anticipated the move and turned his head to the left so that he could focus both eyes on the child. When the horse made that gesture, Roberto immediately stopped and stepped directly back in front of the horse. He moved closer until he was looking straight up at the gelding towering over him. They looked at each other for several seconds until Backboard lowered his head. Roberto reached up and softly patted the horse just above his nose. A smile came to the boy's face, and he reached up with both hands, caressing the sides of Backboard's face. The next move startled the boy's parents but came as no surprise to CJ. Backboard moved a little closer and, again, lowered his head so the boy could place his forehead against his.

Roberto's reaction to his contact with Backboard was uniquely human. Something was different.

When Backboard raised his head and Roberto stepped back from the horse, CJ put her arm around the child. "You have the power now. You must learn how to use it. Backboard gave you the power to have control over yourself. To make yourself happy. You have a chance now to move out of the shadows. Don't give up, okay?"

She took the boy by the hand and brought him back to his parents. "You want to give him as much access as you can to horses. You may find that the more time he spends with these animals, the easier it will be to teach him the behavioral skills that will allow him to be a reasonably normal kid. Horses changed my life for the better; perhaps they can do it for him also."

The Santana family looked at CJ in disbelief. There was no way of telling what had happened, if anything—but something was different. Their son seemed happy and more focused than usual.

"Roberto, can I have a hug before I go?" The boy reached out and hugged CJ around the neck. He then walked up to Backboard and hugged his left front leg.

CJ pulled a wallet from the back pocket of her jeans and removed a fifty-dollar bill. She handed it to Mrs. Santana. "This Saturday, bet fifty bucks to win on Backboard. We'll do our best to make it pay off."

CJ took Backboard's reins in hand and walked back toward the entrance to the track. When she stopped, Gallo gave her a boost into the saddle before mounting General Custer. They both waved at the family standing by the gate as they stepped on to the track. "What the hell just happened back there, CJ?"

"You know, Mister Gallo, I'm not really sure. But whatever it was, it felt great for me—and most importantly, it felt great for that little boy. That's probably the first time in my life I stood toe-to-toe with someone and helped them out, just by being myself. I feel like I made a difference in his life. It may not be a major change in his life, but I think I helped him. It really made me feel good, just like winning a race. Maybe I'm like that abused horse, Breach Inlet. I think I really like kids!"

CHAPTER THIRTY-EIGHT

The pre-game show for the Preakness Stakes began its national broadcast at 5:30 p.m. that Saturday, approximately an hour and forty-five minutes before the start of the race. The show hosts and commentators provided a historical review of the Preakness Stakes and Pimlico Racetrack. In addition, they filled the airwaves with creative video vignettes about the horses, their owners, jockeys, and trainers.

Eventually, the two most seasoned commentators focused on the specific elements of interest about this race. "You know, Becky, I think the key factors that will determine the winner of the Preakness this year will be the size of the field and the fact that a certain horse is not here to compete."

"I agree, Dave. It's a bit unusual, but four horses have been scratched from the race in the last forty-eight hours, and an entry has been added, decreasing the number of starters from fourteen to eleven. This will definitely give several horses in the field a higher probability of winning, as the jostling for position through the turns won't be as physical. I think the smaller field gives a little more advantage to the speed horses."

"Yeah, I think that's right, Becky, and you have to realize that the eight-hundred-pound gorilla in the room is the absence of Tackle Tim Tom, who is being replaced by Backboard, another horse trained by Ritchie Gallo."

"No doubt about it, Dave. Backboard has proven over the last six months that he can be competitive when he has CJ Jamieson in the saddle. The really unique situation here is the addition of a horse in the race owned by a Crawford Jamieson syndicate. Mister Jamieson is CJ's father, and he now has a pair of horses competing as a coupled entry: Jet Lab and Davis Rules."

"This has to be a strategic move by Crawford Jamieson and his trainer," said Dave. "Jet Lab is a first-rate sprinter. In a race like this, the mission of the sprinter is to act like a rabbit and pull the field along at a very fast pace. When the field gets tired, Jet Lab's stable-mate, Davis Rules, will try to take over and win the race by running off the pace. This is a tactic that's been in thoroughbred racing for decades. Sometimes it works, and sometimes it fails miserably."

"I know that CJ will be a sentimental favorite with a lot of folks in this crowd of nearly 100,000 people, but it doesn't appear that the bettors are willing to load up on the gelding. He's still at ten-to-one on the odds board. The clear favorite at this point is Davis Rules, and his coupled entry, Jet Lab."

As the television audience learned more and more about the Preakness and its competitors, Gallo and Jimmy went through their normal pre-race tasks with Backboard. He had a light exercise routine in the morning, his meals were carefully planned and measured out over the course of the day, and he was examined by a veterinarian from the Maryland Racing Commission. Jimmy delivered all the tack that would be used in the race to the valet assigned to CJ. CJ would hold the equipment in her arms when being weighed prior to the race. Once Jimmy got back to the stables, he brushed and groomed the chestnut-colored horse so he would look his best. As usual, Jimmy sang and talked to the gelding. "Too bad you ain't got no nuts any-more, Backboard. I'm making you look so pretty, those fillies will be dying to get you into the breeding barn."

Just four stalls away from Jimmy and Backboard, Crawford Jamieson huddled with his trainer and a groom as they prepared

Davis Rules and Jet Lab for the race. The trainer handed a small electronic device the size of a cigarette lighter to the groom, and Crawford handed the groom two one-hundred-dollar bills. The groom made his way to the fenced area outside of the jockey locker room. The valet who would dress Davis Rules' jockey came out to meet the man and accepted one of the bills and the device. He reentered the locker room and slipped the gadget into a small pocket on the inside of the flak jacket the jockey would wear under his racing silks.

The jockey had already been briefed on its use, and was told by Crawford Jamieson to deploy the electric shock device if Davis Rules needed additional motivation to run as they came down the stretch.

Crawford was *determined* to win this race. Winning one jewel in the Triple Crown would be a huge boost to his thoroughbred business. He told the jockeys for both his horses that if Davis Rules came in first, he would kick in an extra twenty-five thousand for each rider. They just had to make the rabbit strategy work, and if necessary, use the shocking device to get Davis Rules to the wire.

When the word came down that the competitors in the Preakness should now be walked to the saddling area, the owners, trainers, and grooms assembled next to their horses. They were lined up according to their starting gate number and began the parade to the infield. Unlike the Kentucky Derby, or most other races, the thoroughbreds in the Preakness are saddled in the infield just across the track from the grandstands and clubhouse. This allowed thousands of fans in the stadium to watch the horses being prepared for the contest and to see the jockeys climb on board.

For this race, Backboard had the largest entourage accompany him to the saddling site. Ten owners and their wives walked beside the horse along with Gallo, Jimmy, and Elliot. The men in the ownership syndicate had already knocked down about a half-keg of beer, so they were a very happy group. Gallo tried to concentrate on his horse and the race, but he couldn't help but smile as he watched these guys enjoy the time of their lives. It was fun working with people who got so much out of the sport and the culture surrounding it.

Eventually, the jockeys ventured across the track and entered the infield where the horses waited. Due to her celebrity status, CJ was the target of most of the cameras, microphones, and questions from the press who were now running amuck in the saddling area.

Mary Tierney, the trackside television reporter, heard through her earpiece that she was now live on the air. Mary quickly moved up next to CJ to begin her brief interview. "CJ, you've ridden two second-place finishes so far this week at Pimlico. Are you ready for the Preakness?"

"Yes, I am. I think it will be fun."

"Your gelding has never run this distance before. Do you think he has a good shot at winning?"

"I definitely do, he's been training really well, and he has a great heart."

"CJ, your father has two horses in this race running as an entry. It looks like they will use Jet Lab to set a fast pace and then catapult Davis Rules from the back of the pack. How do you feel about racing against your father, and how will you deal with this tactic?"

"I don't really have anything to say about my father. We'll just see how the pace is for the first couple of furlongs. Backboard's got a lot of speed and his endurance is really good."

Tierney was curious about that answer. "Is there some contention between you and your father, at least as far as this race goes?"

"Sorry, Mary, I've got to move along and get ready to go. Enjoy the Preakness."

CJ made her way into the cluster of people surrounding Backboard. She hugged Elliot, Gallo, and Jimmy, and then began to shake hands and speak with the owners and their wives. As Gallo watched her, there was something different about her behavior. Although her ability to deal with strangers had improved over the last year, today she was taking that skill to a whole new level. She was personable, artic-ulate, enthusiastic, and genuinely interested in learning more about the folks with whom she was conversing.

When Gallo realized they only had two minutes until the call of "Riders Up," he snatched CJ from the center of the social circle surrounding her and pulled her to the other side of the horse where they were separated from everyone else. "You've done a great job schmoozing the owners, CJ, but I think we need to talk about the race for a minute."

"Sorry, Mister Gallo. I was having fun talking with everyone, but I know it's time to concentrate on the race."

"Right—let's just remember what we discussed earlier. The entry, Jet Lab, is going to try to push the pace for the first mile of the race. The horse has a lot of speed and no one will want to give him too much of a lead in case they can't catch him by the time he gets to the wire. His racing partner, Davis Rules, will conserve energy and will sit back in the pack. We know Davis Rules can run. He almost beat Tackle Tim Tom in the Derby, so he's strong and he's game. Your challenge on Backboard is not to lose touch with the leader, but when you see Davis Rules make his move, you've gotta be able to stay with him. This type of race doesn't play to Backboard's strengths. You have to pace him for most of the race and be patient, but when we need him to sprint, he's got to prove he's still got enough fire in the belly to win."

"Should I try to stay tight on the rail through the turns?"

"Absolutely. We don't want to waste any strides with Backboard. He doesn't have T-three's power running on the rail, and he doesn't have Bid's athletic ability—but the horse knows how to win, and he can really sprint when he's on a straight line. You have to come into the stretch without any horses directly in front of you and with a direct line to the finish."

"I understand. We're ready to go." CJ stepped forward and wrapped her arms around the trainer. She squeezed as hard as she could. "Mister Gallo, you've made such a difference in my life, you're like a second father to me. I love you, Mister Gallo."

Even though the timing of that statement wasn't optimal, hearing those words gave him a sense of happiness that he had never experienced before. He wished they were alone so he could express the love he held in his heart for her, but unfortunately 100,000 local fans and a national television audience awaited the arrival of CJ Jamieson and Backboard.

"Look CJ, I just want you to get on that horse and have fun. Go out there with Backboard and give it the best you have. I'm so proud of you. I can't even put it into words. Be safe, and we'll talk more after the race. Are you ready?"

"You got it, Mister Gallo."

The jockey gave her horse a hug around the neck and then accepted a boost into the saddle from Jimmy. A trumpeter blew the "Call to the Post," and the procession of horses began to walk from the infield to the track. When the front hoof of the first horse stepped on the dirt, the United States Naval Academy Glee Club began to sing *"Maryland, My Maryland,"* accompanied by tens of thousands of fans populating the clubhouse, grandstands, and infield. Backboard was the second-to-last horse to step on to the track. As Jimmy handed the reins to an escort rider, he looked up at CJ and smiled. "Just like the Derby, Miss CJ. You're the best rider, and this gelding is game. Be safe and bring him home first."

"No sweat, Mister Jimmy, I'll see you in the winner's circle—you just keep thinking those happy thoughts!"

Jimmy watched Backboard and CJ proceed in the parade to the post before he crossed the track to an area on the outside rail where the grooms could wait while the race was in progress. As he walked, the groom that serviced Davis Rules called out to him. "Hey, Jimmy!

You want to make a little wager between you and me on this race? I got a hundred bucks says my horse beats yours."

"Where the hell did you get a hundred bucks, big mouth?"

"From the owner. I did him a little special, you know what I'm sayin'?"

"A little special? What the hell does that mean?"

"C'mon man. You want to make that bet, or not?"

"Kiss my ass! I ain't betting with no low-life like you."

When Jimmy reached the section at the rail reserved for the grooms and horse attendants, he recognized a sportswriter seated just behind the area. "Hey, Mister Malikovsky, you wouldn't have an extra set of binoculars with you, would you?"

"Sure, Jimmy, you can use these. Just give them back after the race."

Jimmy was going to watch this contest very closely.

CHAPTER THIRTY-NINE

G uided by the escort pony and its rider, CJ let Backboard move from a walk to a trot and then a canter for about one-eighth of a mile. At that point, they turned to a counter-clockwise direction on the track and moved down to the starting gate. Two attendants took control of her horse and hustled him into the tenth gate position. There was one horse to their right in slot number eleven, but CJ was most concerned about the runners to her left. Jet Lab was in the ninth gate, and Davis Rules was starting from the eight-hole. "Riders Ready!" crackled through the speaker above her head. Backboard heard it also. He knew what was coming.

When the bell went off and the gates opened, Backboard made a clean and swift break to start the race. Jet Lab also broke quickly, and after the field had run one furlong, Jet Lab and Backboard were leading. At that point, both horses faded to their left toward the in-field. When they entered the first turn, CJ and Backboard were two lengths behind Jet Lab, who continued to accelerate and create space between himself and the other horses in the field. CJ figured they ran the first two furlongs in about twenty-two seconds, so she was content to let her horse run comfortably. Backboard's strides were smooth and powerful. She knew he hadn't yet hit high gear, and she still had a ton of horse under her as they moved down the backstretch.

Several other jockeys pushed their mounts to keep up with the rabbit. They passed Backboard as the field moved down the back-stretch, and with one-sixteenth of a mile to go before traversing the far turn, CJ found herself in fourth place and eight lengths behind the leader. She could feel Backboard's competitive nature as he tried to accelerate. She kept some pressure on the reins and talked to the gelding. "Not yet, big guy, not yet. Be smooth, don't let that rabbit suck us in. The big run is still coming!"

The field entered the far turn with Jet Lab pressing the pace and a gap of several lengths developing between the leader and the other ten racers. CJ kept looking back under her right armpit trying to locate Davis Rules, but she couldn't see him clearly. There were still several horses between her and the odds-on favorite, so she figured the stallion's jockey was still biding his time at the back of the pack. Her gelding was running the turn efficiently, just two horses wide of the infield. She decided to stay on this line through the turn, figuring that she wouldn't have any horses in front of her when they made the transition to the straightaway. Half-way through the turn, she let up a bit on the reins and let Backboard accelerate through a gap created by horses to her left and right. She could tell that Jet Lab's ability to separate himself from the field was waning. They had run the first three quarters of a mile in one minute and ten seconds—a very fast time—and the rabbit was beginning to tire. This is where Davis Rules would make his run.

As they approached the top of the stretch with less than a quarter of a mile to go, CJ's head was bobbing up and down as she tried to locate Davis Rules. When Backboard changed leads as he entered the backstretch, she was shocked to find that she only had to look left to spot her chief competitor. Davis Rules' jockey was using a tactic that CJ had used many times with Tackle Tim Tom: he was letting his horse fly on the rail, the shortest distance around the track.

It was time to let Backboard show the bettors in the stands that any money placed on him was a good investment. CJ let the horse kick it up in order to accelerate alongside Davis Rules. The two horses thundered along in lock step. They passed Jet Lab, with Davis Rules on the rail, and Backboard to the right of the fading rabbit. Once again, CJ could feel the thoroughbred's desire to run and to win. She lowered herself in the saddle to be more aerodynamic and then relaxed. From this point, Backboard knew what he wanted to do, and she was just along for the ride. As they continued to break for home, CJ could feel the power in his strides, and she could tell his lungs were clear. Gallo's training routine was paying off; the horse had the stamina to accelerate down the stretch.

With one furlong to go, the cacophony of sound emanating from the grandstands was motivating the two leaders to give it everything they had. It was at this point that CJ realized she had the upper hand. Davis Rules ran just two weeks earlier in the Kentucky Derby. The brief recovery time was taking a toll on the horse. His jockey went to the whip to try and get his mount to turn it up one more notch. CJ's motivating tool was mental, not physical. She concentrated on reinforcing the confidence Backboard was feeling and let her mount know she was having fun.

The jockey in the saddle with Davis Rules could feel the colt starting to fade. The horse cocked his head slightly to the left, a clear indication he was tiring. In the starting gate, the rider had removed the electric shock device from his flak jacket and gripped it in his left hand. He prodded the horse twice in the side of the neck, sending painful electric bolts into the horse's nervous system. The result was one last burst of speed—but it was too little, too late.

The final strides to the finish line were arduous for a tired and whipped Davis Rules, but Backboard closed like a tornado on its way to a trailer park. He completed the race one stride ahead of his primary challenger in one minute and fifty-four seconds flat.

CJ Jamieson and Backboard the gelding won the Preakness Stakes.

When she crossed the finish line, CJ stood up in the stirrups and raised her fist into the air. She was a happy lady—happy with the race, happy with her life, and happy with her plans for the future. In one week, she would be twenty-one years old. She was a woman now, not a kid with special needs who required special care. She would always struggle to some degree with the aftermath of her brain injury, but she had reached the place where most of the blanks had been filled in. She knew who Cicely Jamieson was. She knew the person behind the pretty face in the mirror. She knew how to breeze on the inside rail.

While CJ enjoyed her moment of clarity, Jimmy seethed with anger near the finish line. Through binoculars, he watched every step and every movement made by Davis Rules and the horse's jockey. His well-trained eyes saw and understood what had happened and he wasn't about to let it pass. A great horse like Davis Rules didn't deserve to be treated like that.

CHAPTER FORTY

When the presentation of the Preakness Stakes trophy was concluded and the television cameras were off, Gallo rushed from the clubhouse to the backstretch. He wanted to catch up with Jimmy and make sure everything was good with Backboard.

As he approached the section where the Preakness competitors were stationed, he could see Jimmy carrying on an animated discussion with Crawford Jamieson and two other men. The argument got louder and louder, until one of the men standing next to Jamieson stepped forward and punched Jimmy in the face. As Jimmy fell to the ground, Gallo sprinted toward the group and tackled the worker who had struck Jimmy. At that point, Jimmy stood and started swinging, triggering an attack on Gallo by Crawford and his other associate.

None of the five men were trained fighters, so the wild swings and poorly aimed hay-makers had far less physical effect than anticipated. Nonetheless, an elbow, a fist, or a kick from a foot occasionally connected with a face, gut, or torso, causing a grunt or an outcry of pain. Grooms and attendants working in the area gravitated toward the fight but made no effort to intercede. They just stood around, enjoying the scrum.

The punching and shoving continued until a blue and white flash burst into the midst of the melee. "Stop it! Stop it!" shouted CJ as she pushed Gallo and Jimmy in one direction and the other three men towards the barn. She was still dressed in her silks, but her hair had come loose and was flailing as she tried to manhandle five men who were all much larger than her.

As each combatant realized he was being accosted by a young woman, he stopped fighting and conceded his position to the battling female. CJ got Gallo and Jimmy to move about ten feet from her father and his two colleagues. The men were all breathing heavily and staring down their opponents, but the fight had stopped.

CJ glowered at Gallo and Jimmy. "Backboard just won the Preakness, and he deserves some love and attention from his trainer and his groom! Instead, you're out here fighting like little boys in the playground. Go take care of Backboard!"

The trainer and the groom looked at each other with a sense of bewilderment. CJ had never given them a direct order with that tone in her voice. As uncharacteristic as this situation was, they could see she wasn't screwing around, so they obeyed her by backing up several steps and then moving off toward Backboard's stall.

CJ turned around to face the other three men and folded her arms over her chest. "Gentlemen, if you don't mind, I'd like to have a private word with my father."

Crawford's employees looked at their boss, who was staring at the ground, and concluded that this was a good time to clear the area.

CJ gave the men who had observed the fight a dirty look, and they quickly began to disperse.

She focused on her father.

"What was that all about?"

"Your buddy, the groom, accused us of cheating in the race."

CJ turned and looked in the direction of Jimmy and Gallo as they progressed toward Backboard's stall. Jimmy was walking backwards and staring at CJ. He took his index finger and jabbed the side of his neck two times before resuming his walk with Gallo.

"So, did you cheat?"

"Why would you ask me that?"

"Why wouldn't I ask that question? Don't you remember the discussion we had prior to the Derby?"

"I think you misunderstood me, CJ."

"I didn't misunderstand you. Quite the opposite. *You* misunderstood *me*. You underestimated me as a person. You *diminished* me as a person!"

Crawford looked about as though searching for an answer that wasn't there. He put his hands in his pockets and looked at the ground. "I'm sorry, CJ. I shouldn't have done that. At that point, I felt that you and your mother had slipped away from me. I guess I just thought you would still show me some loyalty and help me out. It was a mistake. I shouldn't have put you in that position."

"I don't get it. You're a wealthy man, a captain of industry. In the thoroughbred business, everyone knows who you are and respects you. You've got everything."

"I don't have a family."

CJ stepped a little closer to her father and looked him squarely in the eye. "The break between you and mom is irreparable, you have to accept that. What you should do regarding my mother is to try to be a considerate and respectful friend. On the other hand, you still have a daughter who would like to be a real daughter. Someone who will support and love you just as you have supported her and loved her in the past. That could happen."

"How do I make that happen?"

"You tell the truth."

"Tell the truth to whom?"

"To the Stewards."

Crawford shook his head and exhaled an exasperated breath. "If I do that, I'm out of racing for a year or two. They aren't going to be very forgiving."

"Nor should they be. I guess you've got to figure out what's most important to you: the truth and your daughter, or living a lie."

CJ and her Dad were quiet for a few moments while they each thought about the next step they would take. Crawford looked at his daughter and the hint of a smile came to his face. "I would have loved it if you had ridden one of my horses and won a race. That would have been really cool."

"It would have been cool. But you never asked me to ride, and I never asked for the opportunity. I guess we both have some ground to make up there, don't we?"

"Yeah, I guess we do."

Again, they were silent as they stood facing one another until CJ spoke up. "I have to get going. I need to change and attend an event with Backboard's owners. They're waiting for me."

CJ turned and started walking back towards the clubhouse. After taking ten steps in that direction, her father called out to her, causing her to stop and turn around. "Winning the Derby and the Preakness on two different horses is an extraordinary accomplishment. I'm very proud of you, CJ. You are an exceptional young woman."

CJ smiled. "Thank you, that means a lot to me." She turned and continued walking toward the main building, hoping that her father would do the right thing.

CHAPTER FORTY-ONE

Gallo and Jimmy walked through the main bar at the Washington Tavern toward the private room where a reception was being held by Backboard's owners. Both men wore suits. Gallo convinced Jimmy to substitute the purple shirt and yellow tie with a white oxford button-down and a conservative blue tie. Jimmy still insisted on wearing the fedora jauntily tipped over his right eye.

The left side of Jimmy's face was puffed up and he had a small bandage covering a cut on his forehead. Gallo had a black-eye and a fat lip. He could still taste some blood in his mouth.

As they approached the room, Mary Tierney, the reporter, intercepted them with a surprising question: "Mister Gallo, it's been reported that there was a brawl in the backstretch today after the Preakness and that you participated in the fight?"

Gallo gave his interrogator a confused look. "Brawl? Fight? I don't know what you're talking about."

That comment brought a smile to the reporter's face as she looked at two battered men who looked out of place, each dressed in a suit and tie. "It's also rumored that your jockey, CJ Jamieson, was in the middle of it."

"Well, I guess I don't have anything to say on that right now, Mary. I'll have to get back to you later."

The two men hustled into the private party to avoid any more questions, and Gallo immediately scanned the room looking for CJ.

"Did she seem different to you today, Jimmy? I mean . . . didn't she seem more *normal* than ever when she was speaking to people before the race? Then, after the race when she broke up the fight . . . Jeez, I've never seen such determination from her when she wasn't in the saddle."

"Well, boss, we have been training her for ten months. I just figured today that the filly finally figured out how to win off the track. Miss CJ ain't as weird as she used to be. She's not the strange little white girl anymore. Instead of me making fun of her, now she's making fun of me, and on top of that, she's ordering me around. It just don't seem right."

Figuring that Jimmy's insights weren't going to be particularly helpful, Gallo worked his way through the room shaking hands and receiving congratulations from members of the ownership group and their wives. Not far away, he could see CJ doing the same thing. She was personable, genuine, and charismatic, speaking with people she barely knew but making them feel as though they were old friends. Channing hovered behind her, beaming with pride.

He eventually met up with Elliot and his parents, who gave him a hug, and finally found himself in front of a happy and beautiful young woman named Cicely Jamieson. "Hey, Mister Gallo, you made it. Everyone's been waiting for you to arrive."

"Well, it took me a while to get Jimmy dressed appropriately. Say, let's step over here to the side for a second, I want to have a private talk with you."

As he took CJ by the arm, he traded smiles with her mother. They moved to an area in the corner of the room where they could be alone. "It took a lot of guts to jump into the middle of that mess today and defuse the situation. I've never seen you handle yourself like that before, unless you were on the back of a horse."

"Yeah, I'm not used to giving you or my father orders, but someone had to step in and bring some sanity to the situation."

Gallo laughed. "It wasn't my finest hour, that's for sure, and I really don't want to have your father as an enemy. I plan on a lifelong relationship with you and your mother. I hope I can have a civil relationship with Crawford."

"Well, rebuilding relations with my dad has become a bucket list item for me at this point, but he needs to get his priorities straight. The effort to cheat his way to a win today was disgraceful. I think a lightbulb started to illuminate in his head when we spoke in the stables."

CJ smiled and took Gallo's hand. "I owe you so much for what you have done for me in my life. All the advice you've given me, and the encouragement and faith you've placed in me, has made me a different person. My success in life isn't measured by blue ribbons, trophies, and prize money. It's measured by how I deal with other people. You've taught me that."

Before Gallo could respond, a member of the owner's group began clinking a glass with a fork to get everyone in the room to quiet down. "Ladies and gentlemen, if I could have your attention for a few moments, I think it's time to hear from the superstars that won this beautiful Preakness trophy sitting here before us. Since Backboard can't be here to speak for himself, I would ask Mister Ritchie Gallo to say a few words on behalf of the horse he has so ably trained. Ritchie, the floor is yours!"

Gallo quickly composed himself and faced the thirty smiling people in the room. "This has been an unbelievable year. The tragedy of losing Hit the Bid took so much out of my heart and soul, I wasn't sure how to move on. But I'm surrounded by amazing people and amazing horses. If you're going to find success in the racing business, you have to face the fact that tragedy often precedes triumph. It's how you handle those extreme highs and lows that determine your success or failure. I've been blessed to have the opportunity to train Hit the Bid, Tackle Tim Tom, and your great horse, Backboard. I'm also blessed to have the team I have at Stone Fence Farms and especially to have met and come to love this young woman to my left." Gallo turned and smiled at CJ. "I think it's time we heard from CJ and the plans she has for her future."

CJ stepped forward and smiled at everyone in the room. "Mister Gallo once told me that thoroughbreds and human beings really aren't so different from one another. Racehorses accomplish extraordinary things running on fragile legs. People accomplish extraordinary things running on fragile hearts. Fragile hearts can be broken, just like legs. But despite this frailty, we must find the strength in our hearts and our heads to move through life and make our lives worthwhile to others, as well as ourselves. For me, riding horses was about helping myself. It is now a time in my life to do things to help other people."

"I have this gift of communicating with horses, so I'll always want to be a jockey. But I've realized lately that I also have an interest in helping other people, especially children. I've reenrolled at Pomona College, where I will finish my degree in psychology, and I intend to spend a part of my life helping kids and being a spokeswoman for them. Whether I like it or not, I am a celebrity, which means that I can give disabled kids a voice. I mean, if I don't do it, who else will? I'm proud of what I've accomplished on the racetrack, but the greatest accomplishments of my life are still before me, and I'm going to pursue those goals with the heart of Hit the Bid, the strength of Tackle Tim Tom, and the determination of Backboard. Life is good, and I'm excited about the future."

CJ's words brought applause from everyone in the room, and another flow of tears from her mother. Before ending the party, CJ thought she would like to generate one more special moment.

"There's a song that I've heard Mister Jimmy sing to the horses at the end of the day. It's quiet in the stalls at sunset, and this wonderful tune leaves our thoroughbreds with a sense of peace and contentment after a rough training day. Would you sing it for us, Mister Jimmy?"

Jimmy stepped forward into the center of the room and removed his fedora. He began to sing, filling the space with the soft and gentle voice Gallo and CJ had heard so many times:

"Of all the money that e'er I had
I spent it in good company
And all the harm I've ever done
Alas it was to none but me
And all I've done for want of wit
To mem'ry now I can't recall
So fill to me the parting glass
Good night and joy be to you all

But since it fell unto my lot
That I should rise, and you should not
I'll gently rise and softly call
Good night and joy be to you all
Good night and joy be to you all."

After CJ's speech and Jimmy's heartfelt song, the room was filled with a feeling of joy and fellowship. Partygoers began to hug one another and say goodbye before again thanking Gallo, CJ, and Jimmy for the great job they did getting Backboard to the finish line at the Preakness. Eventually, Channing and CJ walked up to Ritchie for some final words before heading back to California.

Channing looked into the eyes of her first love through tears of joy. "I'm so excited about our future together. We have to take it slow, but we know where we're going, don't we?"

"I know exactly where we're going, Channing." He held her in his arms and kissed her, not caring who saw them. "Wow, that was really good!"

"Right," said Channing. "Something to think about tonight as you apply ice to your face."

Channing laughed and moved away, leaving CJ with Gallo. The jockey and the trainer embraced for several seconds until Gallo broke the silence. "I've got a gift for you." He pulled an envelope from his inside pocket and handed it to the young woman. "Do you remember that bone-head trainer at Churchill Downs last November?"

"Sure, that was the first time I saw you get punched in the face."

"Yeah, whatever. Anyway, I called him up a few weeks ago and made him an offer he couldn't refuse."

CJ opened the envelope and read the contents. She was delighted. "It's a title in my name conveying ownership of a horse named Breach Inlet. You bought him for me!"

"Yup, he's yours now, and you can find him a great home in one of those equine treatment centers. I'm sure he'll make a lot of kids happy."

The trainer and the lady jockey embraced again. "You know you will always be a part of my life, don't you, Mister Gallo?"

"Are you kidding? I'm there for you *any*where, *any*place, *any*time. You're my surrogate daughter."

"That's the way I want it—you're my second dad."

Gallo smiled at CJ. "And of course, Jimmy will always be there looking for a handout."

They both laughed as CJ and Channing gave Gallo one more hug before heading for the airport.

Ritchie Gallo, the winning trainer of the Kentucky Derby and the Preakness Stakes, stood alone in the middle of a room and watched two women he loved venture out the door. He was happy and excited about the future he would have with them, but in the short run, it was sad to see them leave.

As Gallo tried to sort through his thoughts and emotions, Jimmy approached with two crystal glasses filled with ice and Kentucky bourbon. "You look like you could use this, boss."

"Yeah, thanks, Jimmy." Gallo took a sip of the brown liquid and let out a sigh. "You know, as I watched them walk away, I realized that I won't see them again for a few weeks—and I don't know what the hell to do with myself."

"You don't know what to do with yourself?" asked Jimmy in a loud voice. "First of all, you gotta stop looking for the spot your snot hit the floor, and secondly, you gotta step up and fulfill your destiny. We are horsemen. We train and prepare the finest horses in the world to compete on the biggest stage. The third leg of the Triple Crown is three weeks away. I'll tell you what you're going to do with yourself—you're going to win the doggone Belmont Stakes. We got work to do, boss!"

Gallo smiled and then broke into a laugh. "Jimmy, you're right, as always. We do have work to do, and we will win the doggone Belmont Stakes. Let's go into the restaurant, have another drink, and order some big-time steaks."

"Sounds great—you buyin'?"

Made in the USA
Monee, IL
31 July 2021